FUNERAL SINGER

A Song of Betrayal

Lillian I. Wolfe

Published By

Pynhavyn Press

First Edition: September 2017

ISBN-13: 978-1-942622-14-7

Cover Design: SelfPubbookCovers/thrillerauthor

ACKNOWLEDGMENTS

Many thanks to everyone who contributed to this book, especially to my awesome beta readers, Jill Berticus, Peggy Hancock, Patricia Kelly, and Nancy Sorbets. I send my deepest gratitude for your honest observations, encouragement, and suggestions.

A huge thank you to my editors for your invaluable input to this book. Any mistakes left in this work are completely mine.

More thanks go out to the cover artist known as *thrillerauthor* at SelfPubBookCovers.com. I feel fortunate to have connected with a cover that sets the mood of my book so well.

Finally, my deepest thanks to the readers of this series. I appreciate you more than you may know.

Table of Contents

One

"Who the hell are you?"

Battered, bloodied, and angry, the petite woman glared up at me from a crouch on the ground. A clotted slash of blood tore across half of her throat and her light-blue silk nightgown bore a ragged, crimson hole where a bullet had ripped into her chest. Her walnut-colored eyes blazed with fury as her nostrils flared like an angry bull.

"What is this place?" she asked.

I wasn't her enemy, but that mattered little at this moment. Echoing at the edge of my awareness, I heard the melody and indistinct words that my physical self, back in the chapel, sang for her, but my full attention focused on this distraught victim of a horrible murder. Her appearance duplicated the way the Reno police had found her, not the pristine version of the body lying in the coffin for family, friends, and curious gawkers to view before they tucked her away forever.

Zoe Sarkis had been brutally murdered, presumably by her husband. He had disappeared soon after committing the crime, along with all of the money from their joint bank accounts, or so the story went. She certainly had a right to be pissed off. But my job as a spirit escort meant trying to calm her down and guide her to the gate leading to the next stop where she could, I hoped, find peace and come to terms with her death.

At the moment, she didn't seem amenable to a peaceful walk in the ethereal cemetery to reach the exit, but I had to give it a try.

"Zoe, my name is Gillian. I'm here to help you find the path to the next plane. It's time to let go of your anger and move on."

Her brows dropped as her eyes narrowed and she hissed, "Move on? Move on! I am dead. That bastard is not getting away with it. All I want to know is how the hell to haunt him for the rest of his sorry-ass life."

She clenched her hands into tight fists as she talked. I could see the tendons in her throat tighten as she flexed her shoulders in the desire to lash out at something.

An unwelcome dip hit the pit of my stomach. I knew this wasn't going to be a simple case. Damn...

Taking a deep breath, I said, "I can't help you with that. I'm only an escort."

She cocked her head to the right and frowned. "Escort? You're some sorry angel, aren't you?"

In spite of the words, I noticed that her fists relaxed and her fingers unwound.

"I'm not an angel," I answered. "In fact, I'm actually singing at your funeral right now. Only my spirit is here with you to help you cross over. So, if you follow me to that glowing path over there..." I paused to point to the silver path that flowed through the cemetery.

She turned her head slowly, taking in the details of the graveyard where we stood. Behind her, a stone topped with an etched circle of zigzags bore her name, but the ground surrounding the stone wasn't an open pit. It overflowed with an array of fall flowers–golden chrysanthemums, red gladiolas, and tiny white star lithodora–carpeting the space between.

Her mouth dropped open in surprise. "My favorite flowers." Eyes darting toward the hedges and the other tombstones, she frowned. "I'm not ready to go. I have unfinished business. Have you seen Saffi? Did you take her across?"

"Who?"

"Saffi. She was with me when I was murdered. Did that bastard kill her also? Or did she get away?"

"I don't know what you're talking about. Who is Saffi?"

She seemed to crumple all at once as she sank to the ground, folding her legs under her as if she'd been deflated.

"Saffi Alden... Nick's secretary." She stared at her left hand, her eyes focusing on the wedding ring there. "And my lover."

"What?" I blurted. I'd seen the reports on television and they'd said nothing about Saffi Alden or even an affair with two women.

"No, I don't know anything about her."

"What about Nick? Did the police get him? Is he going to prison?"

I shook my head, reluctant to deliver bad news. "'Fraid not. He disappeared after the crime. I think the police are still looking, but there was no mention of another victim."

"Maybe she's safe and he didn't kill her." Zoe's voice sounded weary, defeated. "He caught us together that night, in flagrante dilecto, as they say. He burst into my bedroom with a gun in his hand. I thought he was going to shoot her. I hoped I could reason with him. I didn't think of anything else as I stepped in front of her. The bullet took me down as I yelled at Saffi to run. I remember the room spinning in my vision as it hit me, then I stumbled and fell to the floor. I felt weak, but no pain at the time. Just the shock that he'd shot me. I heard him yelling at me and maybe at Saffi. I couldn't be sure. After that, nothing."

Her right hand went to her throat, touching the caked blood on it. "I don't remember him doing this. I might have already died before he–" Her voice broke as she thought about her husband slashing her throat.

A flash of insight struck and I knelt down to her level. "It's over, Zoe. He can't do anything more to you. He'd hurt you before, hadn't he?"

Nodding, tears welled in her eyes. "Several times, mostly knocking me around. He's a hot-tempered man, quick to ignite. Saffi knew about it and came to offer support, and we became close friends. Soon, it blossomed into more. Nick found out about us. As angry as he was, I don't believe he wouldn't have killed Saffi also. She should be here. Wouldn't she come this way?"

"Maybe she didn't die or maybe she went straight through to the light. Not everyone stops here. And I only see the spirits I was sent to see."

She cast another look around her. No doubt she was puzzled by the peaceful garden appearance. "What is this place?"

"I guess you could call it an interim cemetery on the way to the next place. Spirits who come here are confused or have unfinished business before moving on. At least, those are the only ones I've encountered."

Zoe's face scrunched into a frown as she tried to understand what I said. "If you're not an angel, what are you? I mean, are you a spirit or something?"

With a wry smile, I answered, "I told you. I'm a singer and a spirit guide. It's a long story, but the short version is I have a gift that allows me to help unsettled souls cross over. So come on, let me show you the way."

She shook her head, not moving, and set her mouth into a stubborn line. "I'm not ready. I won't be going anywhere until I find Saffi and that bastard is in prison."

There it was. I'd been afraid she'd take that stance and it would mean getting involved in something I'd prefer to avoid. "That could be a long time, Zoe. The police will keep looking for him, but you're just drawing out your own pain."

"So you can't force me?" Her lips tightened into a satisfied smirk.

"No, I can't."

"Then your job here is done, I guess."

The look of exasperation on my face must have clued her to the idea that I wouldn't be able to abandon her. After a couple of encounters with prior spirits, I'd learned that until they moved on, I would be like a case worker, bound to them until the issues were resolved, and they went into the light.

"Maybe not," she said. "Are you stuck with me?"

"Possibly I can help you," I replied, drawing my words out as I thought. "I have worked with a sheriff's office detective and he might help out. At least, I can point the authorities toward Saffi if they're not aware of her involvement."

"It's a start." She plucked a mum from the carpet of flowers, sniffed at it, and pinched a petal off. "I'll be waiting here until I know the whole story and that Nick will get what's due to him."

"Waiting?"

"It's not like I have anything pressing to do, is it? Unless you can *tell me how to go back and find him myself."*

Her eyes locked with mine as I gaped at her. "Sorry, I can't help with that. But I'll see what I can do." Taking a last look at her, I turned away and walked toward the silver path with the expectation I would zap back to my body before I reached it.

I'd gone a few steps when I glimpsed something out of the corner of my left eye. A dark shadow passed across the field, streaking toward Zoe. I spun around, my eyes searching for the shade I expected to find there. I only saw Zoe, sitting where I'd left her on the grass in front of her headstone. I shifted my gaze toward the hedges, searching for movement or something to indicate a shade hid in them.

Had the shadow been an illusion? Or was one of the dark creatures keeping an eye on me? I shuddered, turned back, took another step, and...

I returned to my body where I finished up the song I'd been performing for Zoe Sarkis in the little chapel at a Greek Orthodox Church. Once again, I'd been on autopilot and singing improvised lyrics that I had no conscious recollection of composing. In some ways, this seemed even weirder than my spirit conversing with the dead person.

Almost a year earlier, I'd had a little accident that resulted in an unwanted gift that allowed me to not only create and sing custom songs at funerals for the recently departed but to interact with them in this cosmic graveyard. Since I'd gained the new power, I'd been called to sing at funerals for close to twenty deceased people.

Most of them had gone to the next level with joy, a renewed soul, and little persuasion, but a few had asked for a small favor—or a big one—before they had closure with the world they were leaving. My first had been a young girl who had been the victim of a serial killer and I'd been drawn into helping her identify the murderer. Although I'd helped Marielle, that job had nearly ended my life. I still had nightmares about it.

While I'd wanted to walk away from this duty, I'd found it hard to turn my back on a force that wanted to prove that the Universe harbored more than stardust and black holes. My faith had never been that strong and maybe part of me wanted to believe the God I barely believed in truly existed. At any rate, something had conscripted me to the cause and this funeral singer, spirit escort, and problem solver gig had sucked me in without my consent.

As the funeral service wound up, I packed my music into my leather portfolio and prepared to slip away. Zoe's mother, the grieving parent who'd contacted me, managed a momentary glance of thanks at me as several of her family and friends gathered around her to follow the coffin to the cemetery. I watched them move into the aisle, arms wrapped around each other as they made their way toward the exit.

Another face popped into view once they'd cleared the front of the aisles and I caught my breath. A familiar woman leaned against one of the side pillars, arms folded across her chest as she watched me. Gayle Trumbull, ace reporter for one of our local independent news stations, and my recently acquired annoyance. She'd taken a little too much interest in me over the summer, wondering why I sang at funerals, and why my name seemed to crop up in a certain Washoe County Sheriff's Office detective's cases on occasion.

Seeing that I'd noticed her, Gayle lifted a hand and swirled it in a brief wave of acknowledgment before straightening her shoulders and starting toward me. I picked up my purse, slipping the strap over my shoulder, and tucked the portfolio under my left arm, ready to leave.

"Hello again, Gillian Foster," Gayle said as she drew closer. "Why am I not surprised to find you performing at the funeral of a high profile murder victim? Did you get any insights while singing that strangely intimate song about a woman murdered by her husband?"

"I don't have any idea what you're talking about. I simply sang what Mrs. Sarkis' mother requested."

"No, I doubt she asked for those lyrics. The music may have been a farewell love song, but the lyrics reeked of betrayal and abuse.

That's your unique style, isn't it? Somehow you learn secrets about the deceased and pull them into the song. But I think there's more than that going on."

She closed in on me, making this conversation seem like a threat. I backed up a couple of steps.

"That's absurd. What are you suggesting?" I glared at her, defying her to make an accusation.

She shook her head. "I just think it's odd that you seem to have so much information. I don't know. Maybe you have a special relationship with Egan Moss and he tells you things."

"That's really reaching. I've been involved in a couple of the cases that Moss has worked, but this one isn't his case. It's simply what it looks like. A mother contacted me to sing at her daughter's funeral. End of story." I took a deep breath and looked pointedly at my watch. "I have to go. So quit pestering me about this. I have nothing to say to you."

Gayle's face took on a sour expression, but she didn't say anything more. I pivoted away from her and set a quick pace to the parking lot and my Jeep. I listened for any footsteps behind me, wanting to be certain she wasn't following me. I refused to turn around to be check. I couldn't let her know that she got to me in any way.

The woman meant more trouble than my possible stalker, Roger. She'd appeared in my life during the trial for Marielle's murderer and seemed to think that my involvement in that case would make a good story. I worried she would tumble onto the truth about me, something I definitely didn't want splashed across the evening news. Only a few people knew about my gift–my best friend, Janna; the two detectives from the Sheriff's Department, Moss and Rodriguez; and the psychic, Madame Astrid, who was helping me learn more about it. I hadn't even told my two band mates in Spicy Jam.

I reached my Jeep and climbed in before glancing back toward the church entrance where people still straggled out after Zoe's service. Relieved that I didn't see Gayle Trumbull heading my way, I locked the door and started the engine just as my phone rang. I'd left it in my car so it wouldn't disturb me during the service.

I glanced at the screen and read Dr. M.K. Mercer, my sometimes boyfriend and a fourth-year resident at Reno City Hospital. Another person I hadn't told about the paranormal side of my life. I'd met Mark in the emergency room on the night of the accident that had bestowed my questionable gift. Between his schedule, my two jobs and the spooky sideline, our relationship teetered down the lane like a drunken sailor at the end of shore leave. Very unsteady.

"Hi, stranger," I said into the phone.

"Hey, gorgeous. How's your day?" His low voice sounded sexy but held a serious tone I had come to recognize.

"Probably better than yours. What's happening?" I could guess.

"The ER just exploded and that afternoon I thought I had vanished in the aftermath. I'm sorry, babe."

"Me, too. Maybe next time."

"Right. I have to go now. I'll call you later."

As I ended the call, I shifted into reverse and pulled out to head home or maybe stop for a late lunch at my favorite coffee shop. The canceled lunch date was nothing new and I'd come to expect it about three out of four times Mark and I had plans. It came with the territory of dating a doctor who still did residency, but I had doubts it would get better after he finished. The hard reality amounted to our romantic liaison checked in almost DOA and if he ever learned the truth about me, it would likely not survive.

A short time later, I sat in a booth at the Perc-o-later Coffee Shop sipping on an iced tea and tapping notes into my phone about the funeral. I wanted to write them down while they were fresh in my mind. After that, I'd figure out what I could do to help Zoe with the problem.

I wasn't an investigator but I did have unique abilities when it came to solving the problems that the spirits handed me. In one instance, my gift allowed me to see through the victim's eyes and another time an object the deceased had used yielded a full vision of a scene, so I knew I could tap into my client's memories to get information. I just didn't know how reliable I could expect the talent to be since I hadn't exactly controlled how it worked.

So far as Zoe Sarkis went, the more I had to tap into her energy, the less likely she was to attempt to haunt her husband, although it might speed up the search for him if she could locate him. To be honest, I didn't know exactly how it worked or if every spirit had the ability to vision project, as I'd come to call it. Nor did I know which objects might yield a valuable memory. I'd only done that a couple of times and if I understood Madame Astrid correctly, the object needed to be charged with a strong memory or emotion in order to get a vision from it.

My lunch arrived and I devoted my full attention to eating the hamburger salad. Afterward, I decided I'd give Egan Moss a call to see if he had time to chat with me.

Two

"**I** had an interesting encounter at a funeral yesterday," I said, getting ready to explain Zoe's situation to Egan Moss as we sat at an outside table at a coffee shop. With temperatures cool enough that most customers stayed inside, we had adequate privacy to talk openly.

The ruggedly handsome detective sipped at his coffee and arched an eyebrow at me. A rock solid man in his late forties, he tended to be critical of anything in the paranormal world but had come to accept that I might be gifted after I'd helped him with a few things that led to solving a couple of difficult cases. In spite of that, he didn't accept everything I said without questions.

"How so?" he asked. He reached for the muffin he'd bought for lunch and broke off a piece.

"It was for Zoe Sarkis, the woman who was murdered by her husband last week."

"Presumed murdered," he corrected. "Reno's case."

"Yes, I know. She was found in their jurisdiction. Nonetheless, I had a little chat with Zoe and her murderer may be presumed, but she confirmed it, and she looked a bloody mess."

I had his interest now and he leaned forward, listening. "Go on."

Grabbing a sip of my vanilla latte, I began telling him about the encounter, taking the time to describe how Zoe looked and what she said. "Here's the thing, Moss. She says that Saffi Alden had been with her when Nick Sarkis burst into the room."

"Who?"

I couldn't see his eyes through his sunglasses, but his eyebrows dipped toward each other.

"Nick's secretary. She and Zoe were having an affair. They'd been in bed together when he arrived."

Moss held a hand, "Wait a second. Zoe was gay? And the secretary? None of this was in the report I saw. But it's not my case."

"I get that. I'm just telling you what Zoe told me. She tried to stop Nick from shooting but got hit by the bullet. She doesn't know if Saffi got away or not. She's refusing to go to the other side until she knows about Saffi and Nick is caught."

Moss nodded, ate more of the muffin, and thought a bit. "All right. I can understand that view. What do you want me to do?"

"Well, I thought you could look into the case and find out more information about it. Maybe clue in the Reno detectives that the Alden woman was at the scene, find out if they found her body, or if they know about her."

He chuckled at that. "Yeah, how's that going to happen? I just call up and say Zoe Sarkis' ghost told a physic friend that she got caught in bed with her husband's secretary when he showed up and shot them both? Not even an option, Gillian. I need to keep my credibility and that would not do it."

"Right. I get it." I chewed at my lip and tried to think of alternatives. "I would think that additional information might be worth a little bit of a risk."

"That's more than a little. And I repeat, it's not Washoe's case. I can't interfere in their investigation."

"I get it." As I thought, I tapped the edge of the table with my strumming fingernails. They were longer on the right hand than the left and shaped to double for guitar picks. While the left ones were longer than usual for a guitarist, they were still shorter and more rounded than the right.

"Okay. How about this idea? Can you get an object or two from the crime scene that might have belonged to Zoe? I can try to do a reading to see if I get anything from it."

His eyes narrowed and he hunched forward. "Are you kidding? No, I can't do that. I don't have access to RPD's evidence and even if I did, I sure couldn't hand it over to you. That would seriously breach the chain of evidence."

"But you handed me the one for your dead homeless guy," I objected.

"First off, that was my case. Second, it was a cold case. The evidence had been thoroughly examined and yielded nothing. Furthermore, I gave you the man's personal effects and not part of the evidence trail. And... I stayed with you the whole time you were holding it. A whole different situation." Moss' cheeks had reddened with his emotions as he spoke.

"All right. Don't blow a gasket. It was only an idea."

He shook his head as he took a couple of deep breaths. "Look, I know you mean well, but there are laws and rules that we follow and I can't do it. Maybe you could call RPD directly or even Secret Witness and tell them what you know. Let them decide what to do with the information. Just keep my name out of it."

I bit my lip. "Yeah, I'm sure they're going to pay attention to the kook on the line who claims to have talked to a ghost. I barely have any credibility with you and they don't know me at all. Besides, I want to keep my name out of it as well. Bad enough I have that reporter still trying to get an interview."

"Trumbull's still after you?"

I nodded. "She went to the funeral and approached me afterward."

"Well, that's not good. If she thinks she's got a story, she isn't going to back down."

"I noticed." I turned my gaze toward the street, fearful of seeing the reporter lingering on at a corner, waiting to question me. "I don't need to have her trying to connect the dots."

Moss finished his muffin and downed the rest of the coffee. "I have two suggestions. Stop singing at funerals and quit meeting with me."

He rose to his feet, ready to leave, then leaned toward me, both hands on the table. "And don't try to find out more about the Sarkis case. You don't need to be linked to it in any way. Got that?"

"Yeah. I got it," I muttered and, chastised, I gazed down at the table. As he left, I finished off my latte and contemplated my next move.

Well, that didn't go the way I'd hoped it would. He'd basically told me to keep my nose out of it. The problem was I couldn't walk away from the ghost's request that easily. I had to find answers for Zoe in order to get her to move on and if I didn't do anything, she'd find a way to haunt me. I needed to talk to Janna to see if we could come up with a different plan.

As I pulled out my phone to call my friend, I noticed a text message on it that I'd missed from Gavin. Brief, it simply said he'd returned to town and to call him when I had a chance. I'd been trying to get in touch since last spring and he'd been on leave from the University of Nevada Reno with no apparent return date indicated. One of his assistants told me he'd seized the opportunity to go on a dig. While it seemed a little odd that he'd take off at almost the end of the semester, he *was* an archaeology professor, and he still liked to participate in his chosen field.

I had a Civil War button for him that I'd gotten from a young man I'd helped after his father died. I thought my old professor would really appreciate it. I'd give him a call after I talked to Janna, although it might be better to wait until later. He might be teaching an afternoon class on this fine Saturday.

Janna, on the other hand, was at work when I called and sounded a bit harried, which probably meant a busload of people to check into the hotel where she worked.

"I'll be brief," I said as soon as I heard the tight tone of her voice. "Call me when you get off and maybe we can meet for pizza and beer. I need to talk to you."

"Right. Got it," she answered and hung up.

Definitely a busload of tourists in the lobby... maybe two, I decided. I returned to my Jeep and pointed it toward the river to do some thinking about my current problem. While the park downtown wasn't too crowded, I had to park about three blocks away from it. Seeing the trees in their variegated shades of gold and burnt orange made it worth it. I loved the fall colors and the sweet smell of the moist earth by the river. Being close to the mountains meant the area enjoyed the beauty of the four seasons. Although sometimes spring could be really short, fall always made me happy.

I sat on a bench along the river walk where I could watch and listen as the Truckee tumbled along its course and pulled out my phone to do a little investigating. I put in Zoe's name and death in the search box and waited for any articles about it to come up. Four popped up immediately, two from local television stations and one from the newspaper. I opened the newspaper first, expecting it would give more information.

The article did cover the murder, although not in too much detail, but made no mention of the third person at the scene. Nothing at all about Saffi Alden. The reporter talked about Nick Sarkis' work and that he owned a business as a financial consultant. However, nothing more than that police were investigating the murder and if it tied in with his business. Nick had disappeared and police considered him a suspect in the murder. While the report was interesting, it didn't tell me anything I didn't already know except that Sarkis owned the company where he worked.

I played the newscast at the first television station's site and heard pretty much the same report. The only thing a little different came in the report on Zoe, noting she had been active in a couple of charities in the city and had graduated from UNR. In fact, I realized with surprise, she'd graduated the same year I had. I didn't know her back in those days, but we could have run into each other on campus. And now she was dead. A little shock ran through me at the realization that someone I'd gone to school with had been murdered.

I shook it off and called Gavin, expecting to get his voicemail. Instead, his warm, deep voice surprised me by being live.

"Hello, Gillian. How's life treating you?"

"You're there. I mean, I thought you'd be busy. I'm good. How 'bout you?" Well, that sounded like a lame start.

"I'm doing great. Had a busy few months. I saw you've been trying to reach me. What's up?"

"Actually, I have something for you, a little artifact that you might be interested in."

"Really? Well, I do love artifacts, so what have you got?"

His voice sounded amused and a bit playful. I recalled his half smile that often went with that tone.

"I'm not going to tell you 'cause I want to see your face when you see it. So, can I meet you or bring it by your office next week?"

"Sure. How about we meet tomorrow for lunch? There's a little Chinese place near Old Town Mall–"

"The Bamboo Palace," I interrupted. A group of us from the school had gone there a few times based on Gavin's recommendation.

"That's the one. Say at twelve-thirty?"

That settled, he signed off, saying he had some work to do.

While it felt awkward, my spirit surged with excitement. I'd never dated Gavin while I took his classes, but I had been attracted to him from the get-go and had a fantasy or two. Something about the Indiana Jones mystique with the man, although he absolutely never made a move toward any of the co-eds. A brilliant man and a top-notch archaeology professor, he'd garnered quite a few field assignments over the years. I hoped he would tell me some about his most recent trip and what, if anything, he might have found.

My phone tone went off again and I answered Janna's call as I noted the time at nearly five o'clock.

"I'm off in another ten minutes. Where do you want to meet?"

"I'm at the River Walk, so how about going to the Truckee Pizza Stop? Is beer strong enough?"

"Yep, it will do. Or we'll move on to something else. See you soon."

Almost twenty minutes later, Janna came through the door of the pizza place and spotted me at a corner booth toward the back. I'd already ordered a pitcher of beer and a plate of garlic knots so she didn't have to wait. She slid into the booth, tossed her blond hair away from her face, and flashed a brief smile before replacing it with a scowl.

"What a bitch of an afternoon," she said, the complaint rolling out before anything else. "Poor timing, three buses arriving at one time and one of them loaded with Japanese tourists. Right at the time that I'm down two people at registration. And of course, there were computer problems."

I produced a sympathetic grunt and shoved a mug of beer her direction. "Sorry, sweetie. This will help."

"I am so glad we got the last one taken care of and everyone is settled in their rooms. It's days like this that make me think about taking an executive secretary job." She hugged the mug and took several large sips.

"Are you considering it?" I pulled at a garlic knot as I tried to recall if she actually had any secretarial skills.

"Thinking, but not really. I just need a break from the craziness. Winter's coming soon and things will slow down, so it will get back to normal."

Taking a deep calming breath, she asked, "How did the funeral yesterday go? Anything strange?"

"Strange? They're all strange, you know. But yeah, this one is one of those that is more complicated."

Her hand paused on the way to a garlic knot. "Uh oh, unwilling spirit?"

"To say the least. You remember the woman whose husband murdered her last Tuesday, don't you?"

She nodded, giving me her full attention even as she stuffed the bread in her mouth.

"She looked brutally attacked and she says her husband did it. There's more..." I leaned in so I could speak softer and told her the whole story, even about the affair with the unmentioned-in-the-news secretary.

"That is juicy gossip, girlfriend, and she says it was definitely the husband who killed her?"

"Yes. Now, she wants my help to prove it and get him arrested. She also wants to know what happened to Saffi. So, that's where that story is." I waved over the waitress to order our pizza.

After the waitress walked away, I went on. "Now I just have to figure out where I can find more information. The newspaper doesn't seem to have a lot. Neither do the TV stations."

"What about Moss?" she asked.

"I already talked to him. Not his case, he says and he really can't help with any extra information on it. I know where the house is—the one in the news reports. The story is the husband has fled with no trace left behind."

"I recall the news saying that she'd been dead two or three days before anyone discovered her body." Jana's forehead wrinkled in a frown as she thought. "Have you thought about object reading? You've done that before, haven't you?"

"A couple of times. And yes, I've thought about it. However, I don't have anything connected to Sarkis to read and Moss can't get me one. I need other options. Maybe the internet will have more reports and rumors to give me clues." I chuckled, finding the thought of chasing after rumors amusing.

"Can't you learn more from the victim? Her name was Zoe, right?"

"Yeah, I can. Except what I can find out is limited to what she saw, and once he shot her, she didn't have anything else." I paused and thought about that for a few moments. "Or does she? I wonder how quickly a spirit can become aware after she dies? She's worried about Saffi and didn't know what happened to her, but maybe she knows more than she told me. It might be worth another visit to the cemetery."

Janna shook her head as I spoke. "This is totally a weird conversation, Gilly. You're talking about dropping by the cemetery like it's someone's house."

I could tell this was freaking her out, which was ironic since she had believed in supernatural stuff since she'd been twelve or so, and I was the skeptic. It seemed that having a friend who talked with spirits pushed her belief further than she wanted.

"I know. But that's not a bad analogy. I tend to think of the ethereal cemetery as a motel room for spirits. Once I can help them resolve the issues, they're on to the next stop." I paused as I saw the waitress returning with our sausage and bell pepper pizza.

"It's too bad you can't charge the spirits for the help they need to complete their departure," she quipped. She motioned to the almost-empty beer pitcher to indicate we wanted another one. When had we gone through that much beer?

"Let's move on to something else," I said. "Gavin is back in town."

"Gavin Haines, our professor?"

I felt a bit of a blush rise on my cheeks as I realized what she was thinking. "The same. Didn't I tell you that I contacted him last spring about a dream that I had? In it, I saw an ancient-looking inscription on the wall that I wanted his help to translate. Turned out that the internet had done an admirable job and I had it pretty much correct. Anyway, the meet-up led to a little chat and I saw him again when I got involved in the Civil War stuff."

By now, her mouth had dropped open. "You must have missed telling me that, so make up for it now."

"After we eat," I said, making it clear that food came first.

About twenty minutes later, we pushed the pizza away and I asked for a box to take the rest. I poured another beer and shifted closer to Janna. "Okay, I had a strange dream that I was being held captive in a dark basement or something like that. It was after I was kidnapped, so I thought that might have triggered it. Anyway, I saw a glowing inscription on the wall and when I woke I wrote it down. Later, I looked it up and it translated to something along the lines of a light will illuminate the darkness, which sounded totally stupid. So much so that I thought Gavin might see more meaning in the Aramaic symbols. Sadly, he didn't, so it still ended up a puzzle."

"Okay, that seems kind of strange," Janna agreed.

"I know. You'd think your subconscious would send a better message, wouldn't you? The upshot was that I connected with Gavin again. I really enjoyed seeing him. He still looks uber-sexy even though he's in his forties now."

Her smile grew as she recalled how he'd looked.

I went on. "Later on, when I did some research in the cemetery near the University, he joined me and filled in some information on the place and how the school had once owned it."

"UNR owned a cemetery?"

"Yeah, the man who had it left it to them in his will. I guess he thought they could use the land or something like that or maybe he thought it belonged with their history department. At any rate, they couldn't do anything with it and sold it."

"Whoa. I didn't know that."

"Did you hear about the uproar when the company that now owns it announced they were going to move all the bodies and sell it for housing?" The Old Hillside Cemetery housed many of the founding people of the city of Reno, as well as some from Sparks, so it became a big deal that the cemetery had gotten run down and the owners wanted to relocate the bones.

"I heard a little about it, but I didn't know it had been connected to the school."

"Bottom line to this whole thing is I know Gavin likes artifacts, and he has an interest in the Civil War. I just happen to have a brass button from a Union uniform that Thomas Willits gave to me after I helped him out last spring."

"The one you got a reading on while we were at Shiloh?" Janna's eyes brightened as she connected it.

"The same," I answered. "So I want to give it to Gavin. He'll appreciate it more than I do. Besides, I'd like to build a friendship with him."

"Romantic?"

"No, I don't think so. However, he has a lot of knowledge about things I might run across in this strange adventure I'm on. I have a feeling I might need his expertise. And it would be fun if it developed into something closer." I dropped my eyes to my hand on the beer mug and cast a sheepish glance at her.

She cleared her throat pointedly. "Ahem, and what about Mark?"

"Well, what about him? I haven't seen him in about a month now. He's canceled the last two lunches we'd planned because of work. I don't know if there's anything there or if he's just so busy he can't spare any time." I'd shot that back at her in one hurried breath and I realized that I'd expressed my fears about my relationship with the doctor. I kept thinking he'd come to his senses and decide I couldn't be anything more than a brief fling. After all, his career mattered more to him than anything else.

"I'm sorry, honey. I thought you were really into him and he seemed pretty hot for you," she said, her eyes looking a little sad as her mouth turned down at the corners.

"The truth is I don't know how I feel about him. We haven't had an intimate night since the one where I freaked out on him. Maybe that scared him off, although he seemed really understanding about it."

Since that creepy murderer had attempted to rape me, I had been reluctant to get intimate with anyone, even though I really wanted to with Mark. Instead, I'd panicked and turned into a puddle of nerves when he tried to touch me. Even though I had improved quite a bit, we hadn't had another occasion to try again.

"Maybe things will turn around soon." Janna finished her beer and pulled a couple of bills out of her wallet.

"No, my treat," I said.

"Nope, mine," she answered. "You bought last time."

I rolled my eyes at her, knowing that my treat of breakfast at a coffee shop had been much cheaper. We left the pizza joint, hugged, and reminded each other to drive home safely.

Three

On Sunday, I decided to visit Zoe's grave before I met Gavin for lunch, so I hurried to the Park Memorial Cemetery on the east side of the city to get there by ten. I'd overslept and had only awakened when Nygard, my Himalayan cat, slapped me in the face and meowed in my ear. Thank goodness for that cat, protector and alarm clock.

When I arrived, I noted quite a few people visiting departed loved ones as I made my way to Zoe's grave. Here, the raw earth of her recent interment looked forlorn even though a funeral wreath covered it. Although grass would grow back over the dirt in a few weeks, it looked unfinished at this time. Maybe that was appropriate because her funeral and departure from this earthly plane were certainly incomplete.

I approached the grave, focused on it, and began singing "Ain't No Sunshine", one of her favorite songs, or so I had been told. It took a full verse before I detected the slightest tingle to indicate she heard and was responding. She didn't rush, and she didn't seem overjoyed to see me.

"Why are you singing that?" she asked as she fully materialized in my vision.

"Your mother said you loved it."

"Ha! Not a chance. Maybe, when I was thirteen." Her dark eyes looked sadder today. "I prefer something more heartbreaking now, like 'Torn'. It suits the situation more. Do you have news for me?"

"Not yet, but I hope you can help me a bit." Facing her in the ethereal cemetery, I glanced around before I perched on a boulder near her headstone. Bearing no resemblance to the flat slab with nothing engraved in the real graveyard, this pillar stone stood about four feet from the grass to the round circle on top. Her name and the date of her death were engraved on it. Another line caught my eye and I blinked as I read it. Where the word birth appeared,

the date didn't show. Odd. Perhaps it was something to do with the Greek Orthodox Church.

"In what way?" Zoe asked and sat on the grass, her blood-covered legs tucked under her flimsy nightgown. Her image hadn't improved any and I guessed it wouldn't until I resolved her situation.

"When you, pardon my bluntness... When you died, did you immediately move to spirit form? Do you recall anything at the point of death?" Boy, that really lacked tact. I just didn't know any other way to say it.

If it bothered her, she didn't show it. She frowned as she thought about it. "I think I might have blacked out for a bit. I don't remember much past falling to the floor, the feeling of panic, and nothing more until I became aware that I floated above my body, and I saw the bloody mess on the floor. Panicked, I looked around for Saffi, not seeing her in the room. Not her body, not her. Nick crouched over me, looking afraid. Maybe he thought someone might have heard..." She paused to think. When she resumed, her words flowed faster. "Maybe he realized that Saffi got away and she could notify the police. That was probably it. He grabbed a couple of things off the dresser and rushed out of the room. I tried to follow him, but I couldn't push through the walls yet."

Surprised that she had remembered that much, I tried to guide her back a little. "You said he grabbed a couple of things. Do you remember what they were? Can you see them in your memory?"

Her eyes shifted up to mine as she tilted her head, then she closed them, focusing on her memory. "I'm not too sure. I think a set of keys and the other looked like a credit card. I can't be positive. I was still stunned by what happened."

"That's all right. You're doing fine. Could you tell what the keys were for? Did they fit a car or his office or what?"

Her head rocked from side to side, and she spoke softly. "I think they belonged to Saffi. Her car keys, apartment, and maybe her office key." As her voice drifted off, she began to fade.

"I'm sorry. I can't hold here any longer. I don't have enough strength. Please help me." She turned transparent now. I knew the *spirits had limited strength until they recharged. She was just learning it.*

"It's okay," I said. "I'll see if I can find out more. Thank you."

In a blink, she disappeared and I stood in front of her grave gazing at the blank headstone. I shook myself out of the almost trance and turned away.

I arrived at the busy Chinese restaurant in time to see Gavin getting seated at a table near the back. A smile tugged at my lips as I strolled across to join him.

He looked up, a grin breaking across his face and his hazel eyes seemed to twinkle a bit although it could have been the candle on the table. Even at lunchtime, the place was on the dark side and a small glass votive provided extra light.

"Hi, there," he said and motioned for me to sit.

No pulling out the chair for a lady with this man, but that was all right. I slid it out and slipped into it, setting my purse on the chair next to me. "Hello, world traveler. Glad I finally caught up with you. How's the glam life of an archeologist?"

"Not so glamorous," he answered. "Only a couple of countries and you're digging in old dirt with a spoon. How exotic is that?"

I laughed. "And you love it. It makes for great stories, though."

"Some," he agreed.

"Where was it this time? Or is it a secret?"

"Not so much. Just a little on the dangerous side. I was in Syria."

"Are you kidding? The Middle East? Yeah, a little dangerous. What took you there?"

"A colleague of mine found an indication of an old building from around 100 B.C. and asked me if I'd like to help him uncover it. Of course, I said yes once the University cleared my leave to do it. It's not that often that I actually get to practice my profession, you know."

He flashed a charming grin at me and my heart jumped back to those days in his classroom when I thought he was the dreamiest professor ever. Of course, I'd had a huge crush on Indiana Jones and Gavin seemed like my real-life version. I never totally got over him and right now, he still looked damned attractive.

In fact, he looked slimmer and more fit than when I'd seen him in the spring. Working a dig had to be harder physical work than teaching a class, so I figured it must have been good for him to get out in the field again.

Lunch arrived and as we stopped to eat, our conversation dropped to brief anecdotes of classroom moments.

"What happened with that phrase you wanted me to translate? Did it pan out?" Gavin asked as he shoved his plate aside.

"No. It didn't seem to be important."

"What was the book? You never told me." His eyes reflected his curiosity.

"Book?" What book?

"You said you saw it in an old book."

Oops. I tried to cover my faux pas by saying, "Oh, that. It was online and I stumbled onto it by accident. I don't recall what it was. "

Silence. "An online book that happened to have an inscription in the margin? Or the front piece?"

I said nothing. I didn't remember what I'd told him, so I gazed at the table and looked sheepish.

Finally, he said, "Uh huh."

I shrugged. "Anyway, it turned out to have no significance."

"What's going on with you, Gillian? A book on the internet? Really?" His look changed to one of concern.

"It's nothing, Gavin. I just had a few bad months and as I was researching a dream, this came up and it struck me as odd. I thought it might be something important. Nothing to worry about since nothing came of it."

"Right." He drawled the word out, then changed the subject. "What is it you have that you wanted to show me?"

Relieved that he didn't pursue my little lie any further, I reached into my right jean pocket and pulled out the Civil War button I'd been saving to give him. As I passed it to him, his fingers brushed the edge of my hand. A spidery tingle shimmied its way up my arm and across my shoulders. Yep, he could still give me a thrill with a touch. His eyes grew wider as he saw the object and realized what I'd given him.

With a sheepish smile, I waited as he turned the shiny disk around in his fingers, examining it in detail. His eyes barely contained the excitement he felt.

"Tell me about this," he demanded.

"Well, I got it from a college kid that I helped with a problem. You remember the grave issue last year? I was searching for a Civil War soldier buried at Old Hillside, who was an ancestor of the kid. He had this button in some of the things from his family and gave it to me in thanks. I figured you might be interested in it."

"It's from a Union uniform," Gavin said. "Early in the conflict. Which battle, do you know?"

"Shiloh."

"This is terrific and beautifully kept. It's a real treasure."

"It's yours," I said. "I figured you'd appreciate it much more than I do, so please take it."

A pleased grin blossomed on his face as a sparkle of joy filled his eyes. "Thank you. I have just the place for it. I'll give it a safe home." He held it up to the candle's light to see it better.

A different glint caught my eye as I noticed a ring on his left pinky finger, a silver band with a dark blue stone. I could barely make out the scratches on the side of the stone setting that could have been an engraving or etching into the metal. Curiosity compelled me to ask, "That's an interesting-looking ring. Might I have a look at it?"

Caught off guard, his expression looked blank a moment, then he realized what I'd said. "Oh, the ring. Yeah, sure." He slid it off and handed it to me before turning his eyes back to the button. So he missed seeing my reaction.

As soon as I touched the ring, flashes of past events began to fill my mind so quickly I couldn't comprehend anything. After a dozen or so, the images settled on one.

I saw a lush-looking land, filled with growing vegetation, then

I centered on a garden of green vines and flowers climbing on wooden trellises and exotic-looking trees against a sandstone wall. As the image turned, I saw a whitewashed building in the background, something simple in a Middle Eastern style with a portico and arches covered in a scrollwork facade. Marble tiles formed a patio and walkway from the garden.

Abruptly, the vision shifted to a war, close fighting and heavy swords, a glimpse of leather armor, and Roman-style helmets. Ancient battles, I deduced as the blur of motion whirled in my vision. Another sudden shift and more modern-looking buildings, still in the Middle East, surrounded me. They bore the block-like look of businesses rather than houses. In spite of that, they looked like older buildings and the area wasn't very clean.

Again, the view bounced and shifted. Now, I had the sense I was running. I came around a corner and entered a marketplace with stalls and people in tunics or gowns, women wearing hijabs, and milling around as they shopped. I had the impression of racing through the market at an urgent pace and sensed a feeling of alarm in the ring's wearer. When he glanced back, I saw the market behind me for a moment before the view spun back to the front. The alarm seemed to grow and another glance back revealed a pair of pursuers, figures dressed in black. The pace increased and the vision whipped back again to show the figures coming closer. With shock, I saw they weren't people; they were shades! They hurried toward me, or rather the ring-wearer. Bigger than any I had encountered, this pair appeared more dangerous and aggressive.

I gasped, fumbled the ring, and it clanged to the table, rattling as it spun around. For a moment, my vision seemed clouded and I had trouble grabbing for it.

"Are you all right?" Gavin asked, his voice tight with concern.

As I pressed my right hand over the ring, his left hand landed on top of it. I shook my head as I tried to clear my thoughts, then focused on him. Worry lines creased his forehead and his eyes had shifted down to our hands covering the ring.

"I'm okay," I managed to say. "I just dropped your ring and

thought I'd lost it for a moment. Sorry."

"It's fine," he answered as he lifted his hand away. I did the same, leaving the ring resting benignly near the edge of the table. He picked it up and slipped it back onto his finger.

I reached for a glass of water and swallowed a gulp down while I waited for my heart rate to return to normal. I hadn't expected a vision from the jewelry and certainly not the situation I'd seen. Had Gavin been wearing the ring or was it someone prior to him? Did he see the shades or what? The questions popped into my mind as he continued to watch me like a specimen from an ancient tomb.

"You sure you're okay? You look flustered and a little pale."

"No, no. I'm fine, I just–" Just what? What was I going to say to him? I just had a vision and I was being chased by dark spirits?

"I'm sorry," I managed, reaching for my water glass. "I had a moment of dizziness is all. Maybe there's MSG in the food and I had a reaction to it. I'm fine now."

"You're sure?"

I smiled and nodded. "I am curious about that ring though. What are the markings on the side?"

"They're Aramaic symbols, although they're pretty worn. It's a very old ring." He relaxed, more at ease now.

"Have you translated them? Did you find it on your last dig?" Even to myself, I sounded so nosy. Of course, I was.

He laughed. "Still the curious one, aren't you? I've partially translated them. The ring is supposed to offer protection to the wearer."

"What kind of protection?"

"Well, that's the question, isn't it? Regrettably, it's not specific or it's in the part I haven't translated."

"I see," I said, putting a coy smile on my face. "Still keeping secrets, aren't you?"

He laughed and a giggle tumbled out of my mouth. Could I sound any more like a silly co-ed? I pulled myself together and asked, "So, spill a little bit. Did anything exciting happen in Syria?"

"What can I say about a dig? It got exciting when we uncovered something and boring when we struck only dirt. Fortunately, we did find relics that made it all worthwhile although there's a lot more to be discovered on the site. Of course, all I really have from it are photographs and my journals. The rest is with the authorities in Syria."

Except for the ring, I thought. I didn't push him on it though. "Did you go to any bazaars there? They always look so interesting."

"You know, people always think that every Middle Eastern city has bazaars like they see in the movies. They've moved on a bit and the marketplaces are pretty nice. They still have the stalls with food and goods, but it's cleaner and more organized, so they're not so different from any farmers' market here." His expression reflected the smugness in his words.

"So no monkeys running around?"

"No, definitely not." He swallowed the rest of his tea and smiled. "I'm sorry. I have an appointment I need to get to this afternoon..."

I glanced at my watch, surprised that two hours had passed. "Oops, I need to get going also. I have a rehearsal this afternoon."

"Still singing?"

I nodded.

We walked out the door together, then Gavin turned to me, catching my hand. "I enjoyed this. I'd like to see you again, Gillian. Would you have dinner with me next Saturday?"

"Oh, I'd love to. Except I have a gig at eight. Can we make it early?" I could barely believe he'd asked me.

"Sure. Let's say four. Will that work?"

"Perfect," I said. "Where?"

"I'll call you on Wednesday with the details." He leaned toward me, his face moved closer and my mouth opened a little in anticipation.

Then, he kissed me on the cheek. Not what I was expecting, so maybe the professor and student barrier still stood between us. Nonetheless, I floated back to my Jeep.

Four

I decided I needed to have a chat with Madame Astrid, the medium and my paranormal consultant, about the vision I'd experienced with Gavin, so after work on Monday, I headed to her place. Janna had steered me to her psychic last spring and she turned out to be the real deal, although not as helpful in regards to my specific gift as I would have liked. Still, she offered good advice and interpretation, which I could use right now.

She had just finished up with a client when I walked in and was tidying up her room a little. As she removed a tea cup, I wondered if she read leaves also. She always seemed to have a cup of brew handy. She motioned me to one of the comfortable chairs by the window.

"Would you like a cup of tea or a water?" she asked, pausing before she went through the curtains to the back of the house.

"No, thank you. I'm good." I sat in the chair on the left to wait. There you go, offering tea again.

A couple of minutes later, she returned, taking the other chair to face me. "You're looking well, Gillian. But I sense you're troubled by something, so how can I help you?"

Standard mumbo-jumbo, I thought, since people, especially me, didn't come to her unless something bothered them. "I had an interesting experience yesterday. I was with a friend and noticed he was wearing a unique and old-looking ring, so I asked to see it. When I touched it, I got a series of visions from it."

She nodded. "Psychometry, of course. We know you can do that."

"Yes. Only this was a little different. When it's happened before, I saw just one scene from the object, something strongly imprinted. This one started in a garden of a building back a long time ago, possibly before Christ. I had the sense it was in the Middle East, maybe when the ring was created. In the next vision, I saw a battle with warriors wearing early Roman armor. I recognized the style and the area of the battle seemed to be a semi-arid desert with scant vegetation, some trees, and water in the background. I'm guessing the Mediterranean Sea."

Her eyes reflected the increased interest in my descriptions as they grew wider and the pupil seemed to expand more as if she was peering into my mind. "If this is true, and I believe it is, then the ring is quite an ancient artifact. What happened next?"

"That's where it made a big jump to more modern times and I seemed to be wearing the ring as I ran through the town's buildings and into a marketplace where stalls of merchandise lined the walks. I felt a sense of urgency as I ran and glanced behind me several times. At that point, I spotted a pair of very big shades pursuing me."

Astrid's eyes popped even more. "Shades? You're certain?"

"Yes."

"What happened next?" Her voice sounded tense.

"I dropped the ring. I was so startled by this that I let go of it and it fell onto the table. My friend took it back although he was curious about my reaction to it."

Her shoulders slumped and I could see she was disappointed I didn't have the ending of the tale. She blinked as her eyes returned to normal.

I shifted uncomfortably. "Maybe I could use a glass of water."

"Of course," she replied, rose, and disappeared through the curtain to the back of the house.

She soon returned with a bottle of water and two glasses, setting them on the table between us and pouring as she spoke.

"Tell me about the shades."

"I pretty much told you all I know. They were larger than any I'd seen before, probably about seven feet and dense. Not wispy in any way. They were pursuing me, not just watching as they have in the past. Or rather, they chased whoever wore the ring."

From previous encounters and readings, I knew the shades were unsettled, disaffected souls that had failed to move on and had chosen a darker path. Some were considered evil spirits from another plane, a lower one than ours. If there's a Hell, that's where these creatures existed.

Astrid thought about what I'd said as she sipped at her water. She leaned forward, catching my left hand in hers and holding it firmly. "Think about them again. Show me."

Taking a deep breath, I closed my eyes and pictured the vision I'd seen of the shades. I had seen them for only a few seconds, maybe three or four, before I'd let go of the ring. I'd felt the anxiety and fear from the person wearing the ring. With a certainty, I knew it had been recent and the ring was on Gavin's finger.

"Slower," Astrid said. "Slow the images down."

How? How did she expect me to do that? As I began the vision again in my mind, I realized it had slowed to almost a frame-by-frame image as if I watched a slow-motion film. The shades were clearer, more detailed, and I could make out eyes and mouths, defining features I'd never seen before on them. They didn't look like people exactly, and they had shifting features. What the heck?

I shuddered as I watched the images and realized they were devoured souls. All the anxiety I'd felt about them since I first encountered them in the ethereal cemetery intensified as I realized how frightening they really were and that they were dangerous.

Astrid released my hand and sat back in her chair, sighing heavily. Her expression grew serious as her mouth formed a tight line. "Was your friend the one wearing the ring?"

"I don't know. I suspect as much though."

"But you didn't say anything?"

I glanced down, avoiding her eyes. "I asked him if he'd been in the bazaar there and he side-stepped the answer. But I couldn't outright ask him about the shades or the incident."

"Why not?" Astrid tapped the edge of the table.

I lifted my eyes to meet hers. "How could I ask him without revealing that I'd gotten a vision from the ring? He'd think I was insane."

She stared, studying me for what seemed like minutes. "You remember that I told you that someone would be a mentor to help you with your gift? I saw that would happen and I said you already knew the person. Did it occur to you that this man might be the one?"

"What?" I gaped at her, jerking forward in surprise.

Madame Astrid lifted an eyebrow, letting her expression speak for her.

No, it hadn't even crossed my mind. Gavin was an archaeologist, a scientist. He wouldn't believe in the occult or paranormal abilities... Or would he? He studied the past and history. Maybe he even sensed the power in some of the relics. If he was running from the shades, did he know what they were? Or did he see them differently?

"You think I should confront him? Tell him what I saw and ask him what was happening?" My mouth felt a little dry, and I reached for my water. I didn't want to risk my potential friendship with Gavin.

She nodded. "How else will you learn if he can help you? If you present it in the right way, he won't think you all that odd. If he is to guide you, you need to trust him with your secrets."

As her words sank in, I thought about them and how I wasn't trusting any of my friends, except Janna, with the knowledge of this gift. Fear of damaging or changing our status quo kept me from sharing it. Fear that they wouldn't understand or think that the head bump had done more than endow a strange compulsion on me. They already thought singing for funerals was peculiar; what would they think about the rest of it?

"Maybe I should," I answered, drawing the words out a bit as I considered how I might tell Gavin without sounding insane.

"As to the shades, I can tell you I have never seen any that big or powerful-looking. In truth, I have only encountered them a few times. I fear that you may be more involved with them as you continue to travel in the ethereal plane." Astrid paused and looked off into the distance as if she might be seeing something, before she continued. "More alarming, I didn't know they could come to this plane, to our world. If your friend truly saw them, they are more powerful than I realized. Guard yourself and use the protection spells every time you cross over. In fact, put a spell around your house."

She rose and went to a shelf where she had several books and herbs for sale and searched through them. She found a couple of items, came back, and set them on the table in front of me. I picked up the packet of dried herbs—star anise used for repelling evil spirits among other things. I turned the booklet in my hands and read the title, *Herbs and Instructions for Casting a Protection Spell Around a Dwelling*.

"You're serious?" I said. Yes, I used the protection spells when I sang for funerals or when I went to graveyards to seek information, but a spell around my house... Really? This was more of a stretch for my barely-there belief in the supernatural than appealing to my guardian spirit to protect me.

"Very much so, my dear. Trust me on this. You are dealing with some very dark spirits here. I will try to learn more about them through my contacts."

Astrid's eyes had gone very wide and unfocused as she said this and I shivered as I sensed the danger she perceived. She shooed me away saying, "Go now. Be cautious. I'll call you."

Murmuring a quick thank you, I tucked the booklet and herbs into my purse and hurried out the door.

I barely had time to get home to change clothes and feed Nygard before I needed to get over to the recording studio. My band and I had two last songs to record for the album we had been working on for the past three months and we would wrap it tonight.

Nygard greeted me at the door with a meow of complaint delivered in his cello-like voice. My Himalayan cat had a Siamese voice rather than a softer Persian one and he definitely had the 'mese attitude. He dashed for the kitchen, expecting me to follow.

As I crossed the living room, I noticed a light blinking on my answering machine. Since this was the number on my business cards, most of the calls on it were for band work or a solo singer. Although my agent used it sometimes, she called my smartphone most often. I stopped and pressed the play button, frowning when the message started.

"Hello, Ms. Foster. This is Gayle Trumbull. I know you aren't enthused about me doing a story about you. In spite of that, I do think it would be an interesting interview to chat with a woman who sings at funerals and happened to get caught up in a murder investigation. I believe people would be fascinated and it could do wonders for your career. Can we at least talk about it? Give me a call..."

Annoyed, I cut the recording off while Nygard returned to jump on the chair next to the machine, put his front paws on the phone table, and howled insistently at me.

"All right," I told him as I pointed to the kitchen. Once I got there, I saw that he was completely out of food. I must have forgotten to put any down when I left the house for work. I quickly remedied that by filling his bowl with dry food, giving him a plate of moist cat food, and a scratch behind his ears.

Ten minutes later, I came downstairs in clean jeans and a light sweater, ready to head to the studio. I cast an unhappy look at the answering machine along with a mental curse toward the annoying reporter. What would it take to get her off my back? I couldn't tell her what she wanted to know and I couldn't take a chance it would go public. I knew for sure it wouldn't help my career in any way, but would only complicate my life more.

Another twenty minutes to the northwest of town and I headed into the small studio set up in an older house in a renovated neighborhood. Ferris and Digby were already getting instruments into place as I walked in. Ferris looked up, smiled, and nodded toward the stand he'd placed for my keyboard.

While I got my Yamaha board plugged in and ready, Izzy, our sound technician adjusted the microphone and tested the equipment. I'd just finished when our friends and fellow musicians walked in carrying their instrument cases. Dana, a fiddle player extraordinaire, and Rob, who played bouzouki and guitar like a madman, had agreed to help us with the album, filling out the sound. In exchange, we would play with them when they were ready to record. I waved Dana over and gave her a friendly hug, thanking her for her help, while Ferris chatted with Rob and helped him set up his amps.

With everything in place, we ran through a few bars of our first song to make sure we were in tune. Izzy ran a sound check and made a few adjustments on the board. Satisfied, he gave us a thumbs-up to indicate we were recording, and we started again for real.

A little over two hours later, the five of us sat on the floor and listened to the playback while munching on pizza. Izzy worked the soundboard, adjusting it in places to balance the sound to perfection. As the music filled the room, we nodded our heads in enthusiasm. Ferris flashed a huge grin at me and I felt exuberant. One dream completed. Mark our first album done. Now, we could begin pressing discs to sell wherever we performed.

"It's really ace, don't ya think?" Digby said, his eyes sparkling with pride.

"Pretty damn good, if you ask me," Rob said. "I love how Gillian's voice soars on that break. Gives me chills. And your mandolin work is awesome, man."

"Everyone is awesome," I said, and I meant it. I felt incredibly lucky to have these talented friends in my life. Having Dana and Rob add their musical talent into the album added such depth to sound. "Dana, Rob—thank you both so much for helping out. You've made this so special, and we owe you big time."

"She's right," Ferris chimed in. "Anytime we can reciprocate just say the word."

Digby nodded his agreement and grabbed another piece of pizza with a beer to chase it down. He glanced at me and winked an eye, his gorgeous face glowing with pleasure and possibly too much alcohol.

As the recording ended, our friends packed up their instruments and said good night. Like the rest of us, they had jobs to do in the morning, so they had to be on their way. I promised them copies of the album as soon as we had them pressed. Once they were out, we began to tear down and pack up our instruments and other equipment.

Ferris was going on about how great the album sounded and how we'd sell a lot of copies at gigs. "I can't believe we finally got it done. Remember when we first formed and we swore we'd make an album one day? That day is now. We did it!"

"That we did, mate. You know, I'm thinking we could put the album out on one of the music sites to sell," Digby said.

"You may be jumping the gun a little, Dig," I said. "Let's see how it does at events before we try to reach people who've never heard of us."

"I dunno. We have nothing to lose, babe."

"Gillian may be right, Dig," Ferris said. "Let's get the album pressed and see how it does. If it sells well, we can think about expanding. For now, we can do a little research before we go that route. Find out what it takes and how to promote it. In fact, we might be able to score a shot on the PBS station to perform for a fundraiser or something. Let me look into that as a promotional possibility."

"Not a bad idea, Ferry," he answered, as he started outside with his instruments to load them up.

Following behind him, Ferris lugged part of his drum set out to his van. Grateful I only had a keyboard and a tambourine, I picked up my things, took them to my Jeep, and noticed Digby leaning against his car as he talked on his phone. Probably calling Steve, his partner, to tell him he'd be heading home soon.

I returned to pack up the pizza leftovers and waved at Izzy, who was turning off the lights in the sound booth.

"Just shut the door behind you when you leave and it'll lock the place up," he said as he popped his head into the studio. "Great session tonight."

Ready to grab the next load, the boys came back in as he went out. Pulling me into a bear hug, Ferris spun me around the room, his excitement infectious. Digby opened the last can of beer and we passed it, toasting each other in celebration. I swallowed the last of it and gazed fondly at my two pals.

I opened my mouth to say something, to tell them about the cemetery and what was happening to me, but I stopped. I couldn't do it.

Digby and Ferris– I could count on them for just about anything. We'd been friends pretty much from when we first met in theater arts on the UNR campus. They'd been with me through all my ups and downs, good times and bad. So, why couldn't I tell them about this darn paranormal ability I'd been saddled with? In spite of my confidence that they'd understand and support me, I still doubted.

The moment slipped away as they grabbed the last of their gear and headed out to load it into the vehicles. Feeling a bit let down with myself, I followed them out and locked up.

Five

"**W**ake up, woman. You need to find my lover and my sucking lousy husband."

Startled, I jerked and opened my eyes to look around. Zoe's voice had been so clear in my mind that I almost believed she had materialized in my bedroom. The only company I had was Nygard, who opened a sleepy eye to peer at me in curiosity. He stood, stretched, and came up for a morning ear scratch.

I knew she would haunt me, I thought as I sat up and rubbed the cat's ears. This so-called psychic gift amounted to more of a burden than anything I ever wanted. Why did the Creator choose to endow me with it? I wasn't particularly religious, more agnostic than an actual believer, so why had this unwanted task plagued me?

However, the only way to stop Zoe from hounding me meant solving her unfinished business, which came down to finding out what happened to Saffi Alden and helping to find her murdering husband. I swung my legs out of bed, pulled the covers up to straighten it, and made my way to the bathroom at the other end of the loft.

As I showered, I thought about what I could do to learn more about Zoe's case. I hadn't checked for any more news on the internet. Maybe my earlier search didn't turn up everything. Apart from that, I needed to get my hands on something that might have registered what happened that night and give me a clue to where they were. According to Madame Astrid, objects picked up impressions when great emotions or violence occurred around them. Items that are worn or are on the person at the time would be more likely to record the event than something not directly used or touched. Most of those items were now in the Reno Police Department evidence locker and out of my reach. Being frank with myself, even if they were in the Sheriff's Office, Moss would not be able to hand them to me either, so dead end there.

I dressed, went downstairs, and fed Nygard, grabbed a berry yogurt for myself, and headed out. On the way to the pet grooming shop where I worked, I decided to swing by the address for Zoe's house.

Located in an older and richer neighborhood of Reno, the two-story colonial-style house sat on a large lot, at least half an acre, and reflected the wealth of its owners. A hedge border of neatly trimmed japonicas separated the property from its neighbors on each side, big bushes cornered the front, and garden beds edged the house with an assortment of flowering bushes, including a variety of chrysanthemums that bloomed now. Made of various shades of tan bricks, the house sat three steps above the ground and boasted a spacious front porch with a swing on it. The upper floor had three dormers across the front and likely the bedrooms were there. A yellow crime scene tape still covered the front door. Bet the neighbors loved that.

Still, all those bushes and the border hedges provided a certain amount of privacy and cover. I began to formulate a plan.

After work, I spent some quality time with my computer to do some research on the case. I did turn up another four articles, none of which revealed anything I didn't already know, and three speculative blogs that voiced opinions on what happened, all variations of the same theme. The popular theory was that Nick and Zoe argued that night and neighbors said they had often heard them fighting. Angry, and possibly drunk, he murdered his wife, took everything of value, emptied the bank account, and fled the country to parts unknown. No mention of Saffi Alden in any of those reports.

On a hunch, I entered Saffi's name and got over a dozen hits, but only one response that related to the Reno person. Opening that, it turned out to be a blog post by a friend. Lamenting that she hadn't seen or heard from Saffi in over a week, the pal noted she hadn't been able to make contact with Saffi at home or at her work. Phrased as a plea to her friend to get in touch, she said she wanted to know if she was okay. She mentioned that Saffi had been dating someone from the office where she worked and thought they had gone off for a holiday together. She made it clear she was concerned and if anyone had information about it to please email her. She had included a photo of Saffi, a beautiful, Swedish-looking blond girl with a friendly smile.

Dating someone from the office? Zoe didn't work at the office, so had Saffi been stepping out on her? If this was the correct Saffi, it could indicate she was missing, either dead or she fled with Nick.

Leaning back in my chair, I thought about this for a few minutes before calling Janna. "Hey, girlfriend, how about I bring dinner to your house for a change? I have something to run by you."

A long stretch of silence made me wonder if I'd lost the connection. Finally, she said, "Yeah. Okay. I guess that's fine. You know my house."

I chuckled. I did, indeed, and loved her anyway, cluttered mess and all. "Mexican or fish and chips?"

"Fish sounds good. We haven't done that in a long time."

"All right. See you in about thirty minutes."

Janna had bought a one-bedroom fixer-upper in the area just east of downtown Reno. It was a cute little place with the emphasis on little. The exterior looked decent with fresh paint on the gray siding and recently repainted dark blue trim around the windows and the woodwork. Inside, it was a work in progress as she remodeled the kitchen and upgraded the fixtures in the living room. Since she spent a lot of time at work, improvement on the place was slow, even with hiring people to do it for her. She hoped to turn it for a nice profit in order to upgrade to a bigger fixer-upper.

I walked into a reasonably picked up living room given that Janna tended to toss sweaters and coats over the backs of chairs and leave her mail scattered across the coffee table. A neat pile of papers sat at one end of the table and the sitting space had been cleared. Magazines and books were piled on the floor next to an armchair and a shopping bag from a department store leaned against the wall behind it.

I set the takeout food on the coffee table and gave my bestie a hug. Smiling, Janna disappeared into the kitchen and came back with a bottle of white wine and two glasses, which she placed next to the takeout bag. At that signal, we proceeded to get comfortable and chow down on the food.

By unspoken agreement, we talked about very little and nothing important while we ate. We aimed for fun and giggles rather than any serious conversation over food.

After we'd eaten and refilled our glasses, we settled back and I brought her up to date on the case. Then, I told her my not-so-elegant plan.

"No! Absolutely not. Have you lost your mind?"

Janna's response lacked the enthusiasm I'd hoped to hear.

"I don't have many options. The only thing I can think to do is try to get a reading on one of the objects in the house. That means going into it to get it."

"That is breaking and entering. It's a *felony*." Janna shook her head back and forth a couple of times and repeated, "Nope, nope, nope."

"What if Zoe gives me permission to go in?"

"She's dead."

"Well, aren't you picky?" I pouted at her. "Honestly, Janna. We've done worse."

"When?"

"Well, is it much worse than breaking into people's lockers in high school?" We'd gone through a spell in the eleventh grade when we'd picked the locks on certain people's lockers just to annoy them because they'd been such jerks to us. Yeah, the B&E carried more severe penalties if I got caught, but it would be my risk, not hers. Nonetheless, I needed her help.

"Technically, I'll be doing the B&E; you'll be in the getaway car and if everything goes smoothly, we can drive away with no one the wiser."

"And if it doesn't?" she asked.

"Then I won't incriminate you. I'll tell the police I was working alone."

"Oh, sure. And they'll believe you. You do realize this place is likely to have an alarm system, don't you?"

I nodded. Janna was talking practicalities now, which meant she was edging toward the plan. "I have a plan for that also."

"When do you want to do this?" She rolled her eyes toward the sky as if she couldn't believe she was even considering it.

"Thursday night. Late at night after everyone's tucked in. Less chance of anyone so much as walking by the place."

"Oh, all right. But you owe me big time."

"Deal," I said and raised my glass for a toast.

She clinked it and after we sipped, she asked, "What's happening with Mark? Has he called?"

I shook my head. "Pretty much nothing. I knew he would have very little time when I started seeing him, but it's practically non-existent. He hinted at getting a long weekend off and we could go to the coast. That was over two months ago and nothing's come of it. I'm not sure I would be ready for that anyway."

"Still edgy?"

"Some. And now there's the added layer of how poorly it went last time we tried..." Attempted rape and murder threats can screw you up pretty badly in relationships. Emotionally, I had improved a lot, and while my therapist said I had it handled, I wasn't so sure.

Janna gave me an odd look, as if I had food clinging to my teeth and she didn't want to say it. She shook her head and her expression cleared. She went to a coat closet just off the living room and pulled out a white box, about ten inches on all sides. She handed it to me. "I bought this as a Christmas gift for you, but I think you may need it sooner. So happy early Christmas."

I raised an eyebrow in surprise. "It's something I need?"

"You'll see. Open it."

Curious, I broke the tape on the sides and lifted the lid. Tissue paper covered the object inside and I lifted it off carefully, uncertain if the gift was fragile. A thin glass basin appeared and underneath it, more tissue paper and three protrusions of some sort held up the dish. As I lifted it out of the box and the paper fell away, I caught my breath in delight.

"It's an oil scent diffuser," I gushed. The little nubs turned out to be the tips of dragon wings and horns on its head. Below, on the back of the dragon, between the wings, nestled a mini-sized votive candleholder. "It's awesome, Janna. Thank you."

As I packed it back in the box, she smiled and leaned across to hug me. "I figure since you're using oils for protection, you might as well have a proper oil warmer and a fierce symbol for what you're facing."

"I really appreciate it." An explosion of affection warmed me at her thoughtfulness. She'd always been there for me, ever since we were kids. I hoped I was being as good a friend for her. Here lately, I seemed to be dragging her into my schemes more than anything else.

I cleared my throat and said, "On a different note, I'm seeing Gavin on Saturday for an early dinner. The band is playing at the Rainbow at eight. You're coming to our show, aren't you?"

"Still not sure," Janna answered. "I may have to work. The swing shift manager leaves on vacation Friday and his backup is out with pneumonia. If the doctor doesn't release her, I'm on the hook for the shift."

"Dang, that's a royal bust. I hope she makes it back or you can tag someone else for the shift." I glanced at the wall clock. "Whoops. I need to get going. I'll call you later with the details of the plan, where, and when, okay?"

She nodded as I scooped up my gift and we said goodnight with a sisterly hug.

Before I went to bed, I decided to take a look at photos of Palmyra where Gavin said he had been digging. I found several images of the obvious Roman ruins in the old city. He was likely in the new city. Even though the surrounding area looked like a place where old buried cities might be found, I didn't see any showing clear evidence of a recent dig. I switched over to mapping software and the actual image of the land around the city. If the images for the area were current, I might get a glimpse of the place where the dig had occurred. Without a clear idea of which direction it was situated from the town, I fumbled around running the mouse over various hills, gullies, and spotting very little that looked promising.

Going back to request photos of the Tadmur marketplace, I found five that claimed to be from there. When I linked to them, I found photo after photo of the old ruins and nothing of the new city.

Worse, I saw references to it being a war zone and visitors not allowed in.

How on earth did Gavin get into the country? As an archeologist, he might have some privilege, but I seriously doubted he could get into a restricted place. Why would he? What was so important he had to drop everything and go into a dangerous place? Was he not telling me the truth? Why had he been so evasive about talking about it? Stupid question for me to ask when I hadn't told him about my experiences either. If he had encountered shades, he would hardly be likely to tell me unless he had a reason, would he?

With that, I came back to having to make a decision whether to tell him what I knew and saw from the ring or keep it a secret. If he was to be my mentor, I would need to trust him. Darn, I finally scored a dinner with him that didn't include a group of students and I feared I would ruin it with my weird psychic trick.

Six

After work on Wednesday, I paid another visit to Zoe's grave and found it had improved a little. The headstone was now engraved with her full name, Zoe Athena Panagakos, the dates of her birth and death, and only the words Much Loved Daughter and Sister; no mention of her murdering husband or even his name on the stone. Above her name in the curved rise of the granite, a recessed circle displayed an etched cross. Even as the wreaths on the grave were beginning to look faded and worn, the ground under it looked smoother. I thought that someone had been out to level it more and maybe prepare it for seeding. There might be time before winter for the grass to get a foothold.

Clearing my mind and focusing on Zoe's image, I started to sing. I'd learned "Torn" just for her, although it was a great song and I didn't mind adding it to my repertoire. As the words flowed and I let myself slide into the music, the graveyard shifted to the ethereal cemetery.

Zoe waited for me, a cynical leer on her face. "You got my message. Did you bring news?"

"Yes, I got it," I said, noting that she wasn't quite as bloody as the last time I'd seen her. "I don't have anything new yet. But I do need your help."

Her eyebrows lowered as she frowned. "How so?"

"If I am to get any clues as to what happened and where your ..." I stopped, hesitant to call him her husband. "...where Nick might be, I need to get into your house and search for something that might point me in the right direction."

"You mean papers or travel brochures or what?" I could see the confusion in her eyes.

"I mean objects that might have events or emotions attached. I can sometimes touch objects and see what happened when something intense, like murder, has occurred to whoever was wearing or holding it. So I'm hoping to find an object or two that

might show me more of what happened and where Nick might have gone."

She almost laughed. "That sounds pretty weird. Then again, being dead and in this in-between graveyard talking to someone who isn't dead, but isn't physically here is also weird, so why not? What do you need?"

"First, I need to know about the alarm system and how it's set up. Do you have an override code for it?"

"Sure, the code is eight-zero-four-nine-one. If it's been changed, you can bypass it with the master code, which they probably didn't change. But the easier way would be to disconnect the phone line into the house from the outside so even if you did set it off, it wouldn't send the alert to the alarm company." As she talked, she picked up a piece of broken bush and used the twig to write the code into the dirt around the base of the bushes.

"You're serious? It's that easy to circumvent the alarm system."

"When we moved in, the system came with the house and communications weren't as advanced as they are now. Nick planned to upgrade to a wireless system but never seemed to get to it. Maybe his procrastinating will bite him in the ass now." As she gazed up at me, her face displayed a positively wicked grin.

I returned the smile and said, "Let's hope. Now, can you give me a layout of the house so I'm not wasting too much time hunting?"

"Sure, it's pretty easy." With that, she starting scratching the layout of the house, both floors into the dirt and showing me where to find her bedroom.

"You and Nick didn't sleep in the same room," I said, noting he had one on the opposite side of the stairs to the upstairs hall.

"No. We did at first, but I moved out. We..." She hesitated, her eyes reflecting pain and sadness in the brown depths. "...fought a lot."

She sat on the ground and I knelt next to her. "What happened?"

She shrugged. "When we married, it was the happiest day of my life. Nick and I had fallen in love in college. He'd gone on to graduate school to get his masters at Berkley, and we waited until he graduated to have the wedding. For the first couple of years, our marriage seemed to be everything I wanted it to be. We bought the house, then Nick started his own firm. Probably a little too soon to make that move, but he worked hard.

"Our marriage started to crumble. He worked late, we argued. We fought about money because the income fluctuated and he worried. When he wanted me to ask my parents for a large loan, I refused. He drank heavily, unleashing an abusive streak." She dropped her head toward her knees, staring at the ground.

"He hit you," I concluded.

"Yeah. Not all the time. Enough that I moved to a separate bedroom. Saffi knew we had problems. She came by the house to talk to Nick about a contract that was due. I answered the door and she saw the black eye and bruises. She literally walked into my life at that moment, becoming my support system. We fell into the relationship. Shortly after, I moved into a separate bedroom."

She lifted her head and gazed at me. "Neither of us thought we were lesbians, just two people who found mutual comfort and love together. Although things got better with Nick, I refused to go back to bed with him. I asked for a divorce and he refused. I never thought he'd –" Her voice broke as tears welled in her eyes.

"I'm sorry, Zoe," I said. "I'll do everything I can to find justice for you."

As she nodded, she began to fade, her energy exhausted.

I stopped singing, ready to return to my body, when a shade appeared from the edge of the shrubs. Pausing for a moment, it shifted and sped toward me. I felt certain it wanted to intercept me before I vanished. I thought about the one at Shiloh that tried to interfere with my guiding a young soldier's spirit to the gate. That one had claimed the soul belonged to it. Did this one come to make a demand for Zoe's life?

"Go away," I shouted. "Zoe is not yours!"

A blaze of red flared in what passed for the creature's eyes and I felt malevolence at its core. I sensed thoughts in my mind, not exactly words, feeling creepy and alien, as it responded. "She is not yours either, guide. Be careful for your own soul. Do not meddle with what you do not understand."

The roughly human-shaped blob made a leap toward me as I willed myself back to the real graveyard.

I found myself kneeling at the foot of Zoe's grave. I felt drained while my heart raced with the exertion and fear. That threat had felt very real and I had questions and concerns about that warning it had issued. Drawing a deep breath, I pulled myself to my feet and walked to my Jeep. I cast several nervous glances back over my shoulder the whole way.

My thoughts plagued me all the way home as I tried to make sense of what I'd seen and heard. The shade represented the despair, torture, anger, and fear of Hell that people envisioned. From what Madame Astrid hinted about them, they were more than souls that couldn't reconcile the sins and misdeeds of their mortal lives. Shades were denizens of another plane of existence. Ones like I'd seen in my vision chasing Gavin were not lost souls, but creatures of the lower plane. Even though I wanted to talk to Madame Astrid, I feared she didn't have the answers about this. Did Gavin? I needed to find out more from him and if he actually saw the shades.

My other option amounted to pleading for Zac, my so-called guardian angel, to explain this. Come to think of it, I never heard Zac exactly say he was an angel. He looked like one and seemed to be guiding me; however, he'd been surprised by the shades appearing to me when I'd told him about the ones at Shiloh. Add in that I could only contact him in a dream state and it made for a poor communication highway.

Pulling the Beast, also known as my Jeep, into the long driveway of my little house, I hurried in, locked the door behind me, and checked to make sure the whole place was empty except for Nygard. I breathed out in relief to find nothing amiss and no dark spirits lying in wait.

Not that I thought for a moment I could keep an unwanted spirit out of the house, I looked up the protection prayer for places and grabbed the necessary herbs to say it.

Pulling out my gift from Janna, I set the dragon up the middle of the coffee table and placed the dish into place. I added a little water, sprinkled in a pinch of sage and a bit of star anise. Opening a vial of almond oil, I added two drops on top of the anise. I touched a match to the candle in the base and waited for the herbs to warm and release their protective scents.

Sitting crossed-legged on the floor in front of the table, I repeated the protection spell three times before dropping a bit of melted wax into the water. For a moment, the wax appeared to flare with light. There, that was done. From where he'd sat silently by my side, Nygard nudged my arm with his head and purred his approval.

"Let's hope it works, Nygard. This whole deal is getting worrisome. It's grown beyond just guiding confused souls to the next plane. The dark side is raising its ugly head. Where's the Force when I need it?" I hugged my cat, rewarding his devotion with a can of tuna. Not the cat variety, either, but good white albacore.

That done, I went to surfing on the 'net for information on the various planes that philosophers have theorized. While most seemed to count the physical plane where we exist as the lowest one, at least one alluded to a lower level, and my recent experience felt this one might be closer to it. However, the information about it was pretty much non-existent. Only a theory, the author admitted he built the opinion on speculation.

So, I was back to my two best options. I resolved I would give Gavin a partial insight into my peculiar gift in the hope he would level with me. Tonight, I would plead for an audience with Zac before I went to sleep and hope he came through.

Next, I turned my attention to researching the alarm system installed at the Sarkis house. With the information Zoe had shared, I thought I had everything I needed to bypass the alarm. The more I read, the more I thought her second suggestion might be better. I could disable the phone line from outside the house, assuming I could locate where it came into the house in the dark. Otherwise, I'd have to disconnect it once I was inside. While I wasn't crazy about breaking in, I wanted to help her. I hoped I'd find what I needed and that I wouldn't have any unwanted company in my escapade.

Seven

On Thursday night, Janna pulled her car up to the curb on the opposite side of the street and almost a whole block from the Sarkis' house. She peered around anxiously, alert to anyone on the street who might notice a darkly clad person making her way down the street.

For the break-in, I'd dressed in a black jogging suit and pulled a black knit cap over my hair that hid it well. I'd even put dark makeup on my face to make it harder for any light to reflect off my fair skin. I'd brought a small bag of tools attached to a waist belt that held cutters, a couple of screwdrivers, and a few other things I might need. I had hairpins in my hair holding the cap down. Taking a deep breath, I pronounced myself as ready as I would ever get to do this. Like my friend, I gazed around the neighborhood to see if anyone lingered in a yard or walked along for a late night stroll. It was after eleven and most people should be indoors.

Satisfied, I set my phone to vibrate, pulled on my new black leather gloves purchased just for this, and said, "Keep watch and text me if anyone approaches the house. Once I've found what I need, I'll text you."

She nodded. "Be careful, Gilly. Don't take any chances."

"The police tape is down now, so it's not as big a risk as it was." When I'd driven by after work, I had been pleased to see the yellow tape gone. Now, it would be a straight B&E without the tampering with a crime scene charge added to it. I slipped out of the car, crossed the road, and made my way quickly, without running, down the street. Although cool out, the suit kept me warm enough. Nonetheless, I felt conspicuous and hoped none of the neighbors happened to look out a window as I passed.

I reached the edge of the property and scurried in along the bushes, bending down as I went to stay below the tops. A wooden fence separated the front yard from the back and a simple gate with an ordinary padlock barred the way. I pulled a thin pick out of my bag and proceeded to pick the lock.

I still got it, I thought, pleased that my high school skill hadn't diminished.

As I stepped into the backyard, I scoped out the area. Spreading out in a vast lawn with few trees and shrubs, it left the center open for entertaining. The hedge continued all around the property providing a border and privacy screen. The end of the property was above a ravine, so no back side neighbor could see into the yard, a fact that relieved another worry.

I searched for the phone line connection into the house and, after a few minutes, found it behind a rose bush in the bed along the back entrance. Holding the flashlight between my head and neck with my chin, I pulled out a screwdriver and attempted to remove the screw holding the line in place under a clamp, not an easy task with the bush so close to it. Rusted and stubborn, the screw wouldn't budge and I soon figured I'd wasted enough time on it. I pulled out the clippers and cut through the line. They didn't need a phone anyway.

With that done, I moved to the sliding glass door from the back patio. Like most of this type, the lock was pretty simple to pick. A few quick bounces of the panel, which didn't have a security lock on it, and I could slide it. While I'd hoped a bar didn't block it on the inside, I wasn't surprised one did. As I started to slide the door, it moved three inches and stopped. Gripping a small screwdriver with the tips of my fingers, I slipped it through, manipulated it to grab the end of the bar, and lifted it enough to slide it a bit further so I could get my whole hand inside. From there, I kept lifting the bar as I pushed the door with my arm until I could get through. Piece of cake. Now, I needed to get inside and check that the alarm couldn't send a message.

I spotted the panel as soon as I stepped into the house; the glowing lights on it provided a clear beacon. A quick check indicated a flashing alarm light and showed the communication down. Following Zoe's instructions, I entered the code and breathed a sigh of relief as it disabled the unit.

I turned my attention to the rest of the house. The sliding doors opened into the kitchen with the dining room to the left of it. I went into the main part of the house, a long rectangular living room with the staircase at the far end and a hallway running behind it. The garage entrance came in from the other side of the hallway. As I progressed through, I kept my flashlight held low, so the light wouldn't show through any windows. I went up the stairs carefully, not as secure in this venture as I thought I would be. Although confident no one else was in the house, I still felt nervous about breaking in. Something about being in another person's house, especially one where a murder had been committed, made the hairs on the back of my neck rise up in wariness. At times like this, I asked myself what the hell I was doing. A year ago, I wouldn't have ever pictured myself creeping around someone's house illegally.

At the top of the stairs, I turned my light onto the hallway. It branched both directions with one room at the end above the garage to the right and another four doors opening off it on the left side. The master bedroom was to the right and Zoe had told me she used the bedroom at the end on the left. Immediately off the stairs, I spotted another bedroom and an office situated between it and a bathroom that also connected with the end bedroom. If I wanted to find something of Zoe's from the night of the murder, her space seemed the obvious place.

As I went down the hallway, I swept the flashlight across the floor and up the sidewalls. I noted that only a couple of paintings and a mirror adorned the beige-colored walls. Zoe and Nick hadn't done much to decorate the house. I stopped at the door to the last bedroom and hesitated a moment before reaching for the knob. No resistance as I opened it and stepped into the room, pulling it shut behind me.

My flashlight illuminated a few feet ahead of me, enough to show the end of the double bed and the edge of a vanity. I kept the light pointed downward and well below the windows in the room. As my eyes adjusted, I realized the blinds were closed and the curtains covered those most of the way. I moved toward the vanity and the light reflected back partially from a mirror above it. It showed me something else; a dark, dried-blood stain on the beige carpet between the bed and the dresser. I caught my breath, somehow surprised it still remained. Well, no need to guess where the murder had occurred.

I started checking the vanity for any items that I thought Zoe might have endowed with an emotional charge. I couldn't detect any feelings or vibes through my gloves, so I'd have to apply my best instincts on this. I picked up a tube of lipstick, considering and dismissing it, as I doubted any memorable event happened while she applied makeup. Hairbrush, comb, makeup tray—all the usual beauty items a woman would normally need—sat on top. Opening a side drawer on the left, I held the flashlight over it and pawed through the contents. Hair clips, ribbons, a box of bobby pins—nope, none of those would do it.

As I got a glimpse of the next drawer, I shut it as quickly as I'd opened it. Sex toys and yeah, they might have some emotional memories attached, but none I would want to explore. I turned to the right side and pulled on the first handle there. My eyes locked onto a packet of letters secured by a ribbon. Love letters? Possibly and they might trigger something; however, I reflected with belated insight, anything in the drawers wouldn't be likely to hold an image from the events that happened that night.

I turned away and ran the flashlight over the floor in slow sweeps looking for anything the police might have missed that could have been on Zoe's body when she was killed. The floor around the vanity and the left side of the bed was clear of any objects. Going the other way, I passed the blood stain again, and bent to examine the carpet on the right side. Nothing. Getting down on my hands and knees, I crawled under the bed, picking up a little lint, but not much else. If there had been anything, it appeared the forensic team got it all.

Discouraged, I started to back out and my flashlight caught the edge of something blue caught at the end of the bed. I wiggled down to it, shining the light directly on it. About an inch and a half long, it looked like a piece of frilly lace from a nightgown. A piece of splintered wood held it to the bed. As I reached for it, I recalled Zoe's hand going for the neckline of her grown as we talked. She had rubbed nervously at the lace where a section of it had been torn loose. I could almost envision Zoe falling against the bed and the lace catching on the frame as she went down. Or maybe Nick grabbed her and it tore as they struggled. Whoever checked under the bed missed it. I worked it off the splinter and stuck it in my jeans pocket. I thought it might be a long shot that it could have any images. Still, if a button carried them, why not?

As I turned to slide out, I spotted the glint of a bit of metal in the light's beam at the edge of the rug, barely visible. I crawled there and ran a finger along the edge, flipping a ruby stud earring onto the carpet. I closed my eyes and pictured Zoe in the cemetery. Had she been wearing ruby studs? Even though I couldn't recall the details or if one was missing, I thought she did have something in her ear. I picked it up and tucked it away.

Heading back toward the door, I paused to stare at the stain, noting how large it was and how much blood seemed to have penetrated the fibers. Zoe's blood...

On an impulse, I hurried back to the vanity, grabbed the nail clippers, and returned to the stain. Using the clippers, I cut a chunk of the saturated fibers and put them into one of the little baggies I'd brought with me.

Going to the nightstand by the bed, I looked it over. Clock radio, lamp, a box of tissues... the usual stuff. I opened the drawer and found a necklace inside with a gold Z charm dangling from the chain. I was surprised this was still in the room and hadn't been confiscated by the police. A gold-plated cigarette lighter caught the light and I pulled it out. Nice quality, it could have been Nick's as easily as Zoe's and the etched bird on the case gave no indication of the owner. I pocketed both items, not sure if either would give me something useful if anything at all.

Next, I turned to the connected bathroom and pushed the door open. For not being the master bathroom, it was huge with a large Jacuzzi tub and a separate shower. I didn't expect to find anything helpful in here, but I still went through the drawers and the cupboard finding toothbrushes, contact lenses solution, toothpaste, and towels. All the usual items that would be likely to carry no emotions. A little black velvet ring box sat on the counter and I flipped it open. Empty. Had it held Zoe's wedding ring? I pocketed it. Now I began to feel like a thief except I was stealing worthless items.

As I stepped back into the bedroom, I felt a vibration in my back pocket and pulled out my phone. Janna's text message was a brief warning: *Man hedng ur way. @ frnt walk.*

Damn! I sent ok back to her and put the phone away, scurried out of Zoe's bedroom, and darted into the one across the hall. The windows facing the street also had blinds and I slipped beside them to peer out the edge. Sure enough, a man dressed in dark clothing with a cap over his head came up the walkway and turned toward the house.

Where could I hide? The closets in any of the bedrooms seemed too obvious if someone happened to know I was there. Maybe the alarm worked after all or a neighbor called in it. If he suspected a burglar, the closets would be a place to check.

Frantic, I hurried out and went into the next room, which Zoe had said was Nick's office. I slipped inside and looked around for any place I could get out of sight. The office also happened to be in the dormer, which meant there were storage areas beneath the lowered edges of the eaves. I found the sliding panel to the nearest dormer hidden by a short rolling file cabinet to my right and crawled into the cramped space, pulling the file back into place, and sliding the door shut behind me.

As I turned on my flashlight to look around, I saw several storage boxes shoved into the nearest corner and a few more on the other side. On my knees, I slid over behind the smaller stack and tucked myself into the very tight corner behind them. For once I was glad I wasn't taller. Any bigger, I wouldn't have been able to slide in. If the intruder happened to look in the storage, I hoped he would do no more than see it was only boxes and not investigate any further.

Wouldn't you know? Of all the things I'd packed for this caper, I hadn't brought my gun. As I heard the door open, I squeezed my body tighter, pulling my knees almost to my chin, and said a quick prayer hoping Zac would hear. I really needed my guardian angel right now.

Eight

A muffled squeak alerted me as someone entered the office. I tried to take shallow breaths and from a slim crack between boxes, riveted my eyes on the sliding panel to the storage area. A narrow slit of light appeared from the bottom of it. Whoever it was had no qualms about turning on the lights in the house. Maybe it was security. Even though Janna didn't mention a uniform, his clothing could be more subdued if he'd come to investigate a potential break-in.

Whoever he was, the important thing now was that he not spot me. I heard noises from the desk area, drawers being tugged on, and a rattle that indicated he touched the blinds, probably to look at the street. Thank goodness Janna's car was out of sight. The footsteps on the hardwood floor came nearer as he circled the room. I held my breath and scrunched down as much as I could as the steps paused and I heard the door start to slide.

I tried to recall any calming techniques I knew and held my breath as the beam from his flashlight bounced around the enclosed space, lingered on the boxes, and moved on. When the light flashed in the corner where I attempted to make myself invisible, it illuminated a spider web above my head where a plump-looking spider scurried to the top. I hated spiders! In spite of my first reaction to squeal, I stifled the noise that wanted to escape my lips.

A sudden thought hit me. Was there dust on the floor? Did I leave a trail leading to my hidey-hole? Crap! I didn't have room in here to use any of my defensive moves. I sure didn't want to explain to the police why I was here. Go away, I repeated over and over in my mind, hoping I could will it to be so.

The light flashed over the boxes in front of me and lingered a moment before shifting away as it returned to the opening. Tensing, I waited until I heard the door scrape shut. As I peered toward the slider again, the light under it winked out and I heard it click as it shut. I let out my breath and relaxed my muscles. Thank goodness. I shifted my body forward, straightening my legs. Now to get out from the vicinity of that spider.

I crawled out, pulled out my phone, and sent a message to Janna asking if the man had left the house yet. While I waited, I turned my flashlight on the room, looking for any place that might allow light to show on the outside of the house. Completely enclosed, the only light leak came from the panel. I did notice a hanging light in the ceiling and a wall switch not too far from it. Luckily, the guy didn't find that and turn it on.

Janna's return message said she hadn't seen the intruder yet and to wait. She would send a text when he left the grounds. I agreed. No need to take unnecessary chances. In the meantime, I planned to take a look at the contents of these boxes. Maybe one might yield a hint to where Zoe's husband had fled.

I pulled one of the boxes from my fortress toward me and lifted the lid. Folders and manila envelopes filled the box. The only labels on the folders were dates, successive ones over the past seven years, it seemed. I pulled out one of the older ones and opened the envelope, shining my light on the contents. Dozens of photos, from small ones to 8x10's were in it. I grasped one to look at and saw a younger version of Zoe and the dark-haired, handsome Nick Sarkis on a beach somewhere. The vibrant blue sea formed an endless background and they cuddled under a green and yellow beach umbrella. I flipped it over to see a hand-scribbled note on the back that said Tortuga, December 2012.

The Caribbean, nice. It wasn't their honeymoon since they hadn't married yet, so maybe an engagement trip or just a nice Christmas holiday. They looked like happy young lovers, not a care in the world. The next picture appeared to be from the same trip, the two of them dressed up to go to dinner. Zoe looked beautiful and elegant in a spaghetti-strap floral dress and her smile could have lit up the island. I could see why she fell for Nick. Even in casual attire, he had movie star clout. Too handsome, the kind of man who could get anything he wanted with a charming smile.

I thumbed through a few more photos and returned them to the envelope. I reached for a date in 2014 when my phone vibrated and Janna gave me an all clear text. Relieved, I crawled over to the wall switch and turned on the overhead light. While a low-watt bulb, it provided enough light to see the pictures without straining. This box had their wedding photos in it. They had married at Lake Tahoe, an outdoor wedding in the fall that appeared breathtaking. More images taken from the Eiffel Tower, the Louvre, and other spots on their French honeymoon. Other pictures showed them in Italy, Greece, and on a cruise. Man, they had lived the dream of most people. What the heck went wrong? How could their love have ended so horribly?

I closed the box back up and pulled another toward me. More photos, some of them going back to high school where Zoe and Nick had first met each other. I felt like I was intruding on their lives as I flipped through the photos. More like a peeping tom than a detective, I thought, and none of this helped to tell me where Nick might have gone or where Saffi was. As I replaced the pictures, another envelope caught my eye. This was dated more recently, within the past seven months. I pulled that one out and my mouth fell open.

Clearly surveillance photos, these were a series of shots of Zoe with a stunning blonde woman at a winery having an intimate lunch. This had to be Saffi. They were leaning together, foreheads almost touching and Saffi had her fingers on Zoe's left hand. Even in the photo, I could see the hot connection between them.

I shifted another photo from the envelope to reveal a close-up photo of the two women in bed, naked and locked in each other's arms. No doubts about their relationship from this photo. The investigator must have either shot it through a hotel room window or had set up a surveillance camera in their room. Otherwise, he had to have been hidden in the room with them. I shuddered. It was downright creepy.

So Nick had an investigator gathering evidence that Zoe was cheating on him. Why? Was he looking to divorce her? Why not just do it? Maybe there was a prenuptial agreement that he wanted to invalidate. How much was he worth and what would Zoe have gotten in a divorce? That might be a key to her murder, although I was certain the police were pursuing that aspect of the case.

In addition to the photos, I found a report from the private eye Nick had hired with all the details of Zoe's liaisons with Saffi Alden. He'd followed them for three weeks to get the photos and information in the report. And he'd included his bill. Using my phone, I took pictures of them, although I wasn't sure it would be helpful to me.

A smaller envelope with the big one peeked out and I pulled it out. As I opened it, I got a strange vibe from it and pulled out the top photo. I sucked in my breath as I stared at the photo of Zoe. Bruised and nearly swollen shut, her left eye looked like she'd run into a punching bag. A cut at the left edge of her lip showed dried blood and more swelling. I swallowed and slid the next photo out, studying the marks on her face and bruising at her throat. Two more photos showed her bruised arms where fingers had left their imprints on her flesh.

Bastard! He'd beat her. She'd said as much when I asked her. I'd failed to realize how much. *Not all the time*, she'd said, although the photos showed the severity. Who'd taken these photos? Nick? Did he want to keep a record of his handiwork? The background looked like the house, possibly the master bedroom or even downstairs. Nothing on the walls showed the location.

I put two photos side by side on the floor and snapped an image. I wanted to have these even though part of me wanted to take the packet with me to see if the vibe led to any visions. Did I really want to see anything that I might pick up from this? Would it provide any clues to helping Zoe? Although my hand hesitated with my indecision, I replaced the envelope in the bigger one and closed the box.

Were all these boxes photos? I moved to the ones closer to the sliding door and opened the first box. No, they were not. This one contained printed files of financial information. As I pulled out a folder and thumbed through it, I began to get an idea of how Nick's consulting business was doing. The numbers looked good, as near as I could tell, with solid six-figure monthly incomes for the past two years. That seemed pretty good. I could see a couple of places where it took a downturn, but never dropping that low. However, the next folder, labeled B, showed the same time frame and a different set of numbers, much lower than the first set. Was he reporting false information? Other folders contained similar information from three and four years earlier, although not so lucrative and only one accounting sheet. The rest of the box contained copies of invoices and payments from clients of the firm. Why were these here and not at Nick's office?

Going back to the first folders, I pulled out the most recently dated ledgers of each set and took photos of them before returning them. That the boxes were here in this little storage area at all meant that the police had not found them. Whoever had searched the house failed to spot the sliding panel, which meant that it had probably had a piece of furniture in front of it. It also meant that someone, maybe Nick, had moved it after the police investigation. However, he had been missing since the murder, hadn't he? Did that mean he was still in Reno or had he come back and not been spotted by the authorities? Or did he have an accomplice?

As I replaced the box and slid the lid off the next one, I glanced at my watch to see how long I'd been here and realized it had been nearly an hour. I needed to get out. A quick look at the box revealed more files, more folders, and several travel pamphlets to various island locations. Maybe they were part of his escape plan? Whatever. The police needed to see all this, and I wasn't about to call them in. No way could I tell them I broke into the house.

Moving the boxes back to their original places, I turned off the light, slid the door open, and crawled out into the office. I paused to listen; just to be sure I was alone in the room and, by extension, in the house. Satisfied, I turned on my flashlight and replaced the filing cabinet that had been in front of it.

Still concerned about a possible intruder, I turned off my light as I left the office and let my eyes adjust to the scant available light in the house. When I could make out the staircase, I made my way across to it while moving as quietly as I could. With my right hand on the railing, I took each step carefully as I continued to listen for any other sounds in the house. Maybe too cautious, but better than being caught off guard. Cat burglar definitely didn't hold a position in my skill set.

Near the bottom of the steps, my right toe caught against something on the carpeted step.

Clink!

The sound of it hitting the tile floor sounded loud in the still house. I stopped, held my breath, and waited a few moments to see if any other noises indicated anyone was there to hear it. Reassured, I continued down the steps, swung around the banister, and switched my flashlight on to look for whatever had fallen. A glint of metal flashed in the light. I reached down to pick up the object, a metal key. Not very large, I thought it could fit a padlock or something like that. I added it to the collection in my pockets to be examined later.

I picked up my pace as I hurried across the living room moving into the kitchen again. The alarm still showed a no transmit indicator on it, so the intruder had not reset it or repaired the phone wire. Nonetheless, I figured he knew that someone had broken into the house. If he was from the security company, they would be back to investigate further and repair the box. If he was a thief, he'd be back to take advantage of it. Either way, I needed to get out before someone else showed up.

Once outside, I clung to the side of the house, working my way through the garden, so that I had a little cover. I was almost to the corner when I heard a rustling at the other side of the house. I dropped to my knees to take advantage of the roses and crawled toward the taller bushes at the end of the bed. I settled in behind a large, leafy photinia that provided sufficient cover to keep me hidden. As I reached the end, I glanced back toward the patio where I spotted a figure dressed in dark clothes. Was this the same person or someone new?

He—or she—shifted the flashlight from side to side, checking for any activity. At the glass door, the person paused to check the lock. Thank goodness, it had an automatic lock on it and tested as secure. Satisfied, the person continued forward, barely glancing at the garden and passing by my hiding place without a second look.

I let my breath out and leaned back against the edge of the house. I waited ten minutes or so before I pulled out my phone, bent low over it to cover any light from the screen, and sent a text to Janna asking if she'd seen the person come out of the yard.

What person? She sent back. *Didn't see anyone. Wait.*

A minute or so later, she wrote back. The security person had just come out the front and turned to head up the street away from the side I was on. Relieved, I pulled in a deep lungful of air, slipped out of hiding, crouched low and scurried through the gate at the back fence. From there, I sprinted across to the line of bushes at the edge of the property. Ducking down again, I moved as fast as I could toward the street.

Without warning, I heard a dog barking in the adjacent house. Crap, had it heard me?

I hustled faster, hoping to make it to the end of the fence and down the street to the car before the dog convinced the owner to let it out. The howls and barks continued and I heard a man's voice saying, "Brutus, shut up."

Between the deep bark and the dog's name, I pictured something the size of a Doberman and did not relish the possibility of being chased by the canine. I'd just reached the sidewalk when I heard the bark growing louder accompanied by the click and crack of the door opening.

That was it. I rose up and sprinted into the street as fast as I could run. Behind me, the barks grew frantic. I did my bat-out-of-Hell imitation and saw the headlights flash as Janna started the car. Flinging myself into the seat, I looked back to see the monster dog that chased me. I choked back a laugh as I saw a chubby Dachshund dog trundling down the street, his short legs churning as fast as they could. Further back, his owner, dressed in a heavy robe, arrived at the curb and started into the street.

"Shit!" I slunk down into the seat, barely able to see above the dashboard.

"I see him. Hang on." Janna whipped the car around in a u-turn and headed back the opposite direction as I slid further down in the seat in case anyone might be watching.

"That was close." I slid the hat off my head, caught my breath, and inched my way back up the seat.

"You can bet that man is going to call the police on this," Janna said. "Hope you didn't leave any clues behind."

"I didn't. I never took my gloves off and the only evidence left is the cut phone wire. Whoever the first guy–the one who came into the house–was, he had to know someone had broken in. The alarm system showed offline and he could see the sliding door had been opened. Yet he didn't call for backup and investigated on his own. That doesn't sound like a security guy to me."

She cast a frown face at me and turned toward my house. "Oh, man. I know this is gonna come back to bite us."

Nine

I handed Janna a glass of wine and raised mine toward hers in a toast to our successful adventure. She waved hers back at me and gulped about half of it down.

"I don't know if we should be celebrating yet." She set the glass down on the coffee table and dropped to the sofa like a sack of potatoes. The spray of dust from the fabric as she hit added to the impression. Obviously, I needed to take a vacuum to it.

"We'll be lucky if we aren't arrested, charged, and convicted. How did you talk me into this?" In spite of the annoyed glare she shot toward me, I knew it stemmed from worry rather than anger.

"Unless the guy got your license plate, all he had was a glimpse of a running figure that could have been anyone and the car pulling a u-ey down the street. He probably couldn't even tell the color or make of your car." Slipping a glove back on my right hand, I knelt on the floor in front of the table and began digging in my pockets and pouch for the objects I'd obtained.

I set them down, one by one, taking a few moments to study what I'd grabbed and wonder if any of them would give me any information. Here I was, nearly a year into this psychic gig, and I acted as if I had a clue of what I was doing.

As I bagged each item and lined them up, Janna leaned forward and gazed at them. She frowned and pointed to the plastic baggie with what looked like a dark red caterpillar in it. "What's this?"

"A piece of bloodied carpet from Zoe's room."

"Ew. Gross." She pulled her hand away as if it might contaminate her or something.

"Well, it's definitely personal and maybe it can tell me something." Although saying that now seemed a little far-fetched, even to me. I touched one of the objects with my ungloved hand to see if the plastic would act as a barrier to any readings I might get from it. Nothing tingled or gave me an impression as I applied more pressure.

"Interesting assortment. Do you really think you'll get anything from any of these objects?" Jana asked.

I shrugged. "Maybe. I don't know if it will help me any though. Will any of them hold a memory of the murder or what happened to Saffi? It's a long shot."

Janna sat back and reached for her wine glass again. I pulled myself off the floor and sat down beside her, removing the glove again. We both sipped and stared at the items on the coffee table.

"It's a really long shot," I mumbled. Now that the deed was done, I felt the let down that came with the realization of exactly what we'd done tonight. She was right; we'd be lucky if we weren't arrested.

"Are you going to try to read them now?" Her voice came across hushed and raspy, a bit strained. Maybe she felt as if ghosts lurked in the house, although I didn't sense anything. If Zoe had managed to project, I knew I would sense her presence. So far, she seemed to have remained firmly in the ethereal graveyard except for the one dream visit.

Nygard chose that moment to hop in her lap and she jerked and almost shrieked at the unexpected move.

"It's just Nygard," I said quickly, reaching for my cat before she flung him across the room.

"Well, damn! I didn't see him. I'm sorry, little guy." She reached over to pet him as I settled him on my lap. Her hand still shook.

"It's all right. Look, this whole evening has been a strain. I'm sorry I put you in this position. Thanks for helping me, Janna. I couldn't have pulled it off without you. If it all blows up and the police do track back to me, I'll do everything I can to keep you out of it."

She nodded, her eyes looking a little watery. "I know, hunny. I'm just stressed by all this, I guess. You know I'm always there for you and vice versa."

"I love you, girlfriend." I squeezed her hand and would have hugged her if Nygard hadn't settled in my lap. "So far as reading the objects, not tonight. I need to wind down some myself and I'm not ready to tackle even one of them."

I ran my eyes across the items again, not certain where to begin with them. Exhaling deeply, I pushed them out of my mind for now. In a perkier voice, I said, "Let me tell you about what else I found though."

Filling her in about the files I'd discovered with the photos and what looked like a second set of books. I concluded, "I think Sarkis may have been swindling his clients, skimming money off of their earnings. I also found travel brochures of places where he might have fled to after the murder."

"That definitely sounds like something the police need to see." Janna leaned forward, her shoulders hunching up a bit. "How can you get the information to them? Moss?"

I shook my head. "It's not his jurisdiction, as he's told me more than once. I could try Secret Witness, although I wouldn't want to give them any information about me. I don't need to explain how I learned about that hidden nook."

"Absolutely not," she agreed. "Couldn't you tell Moss that Zoe told you about it and he could pass the information on to RPD?"

I bit at my lip, uncertain if it would be a good idea. "It could also lead him to believe I was in the house."

"Which you were."

"And if the neighbor did report it to the police, he could put two and two together. In fact, he might do that anyway." I sighed as I realized I could end up in that situation. "I'll figure something out."

She rose and went to the kitchen, coming back a few minutes later with the wine bottle. She sat, refilled our glasses, and as she swirled the wine, asked, "Did you meet with Gavin?"

Nice subject change. "Yeah, I did. I gave him the button I had for him. It was an interesting exchange."

"How so?"

"He wore a ring that caught my eye, so I asked to see it. When I held it, I got a reading on it that was unusual and I think was from his view. I believe there is more to the professor than we thought. I'll be seeing him again this weekend and we'll see what happens." I lifted my eyebrow as my lips curved upward in a smug smile.

Janna frowned a bit, "Is this turning into something more than casual friends?"

"No. Not yet, anyway. You know I've always been attracted to him, so who knows?" I brushed it off as easily as I could. While I didn't know if it was heading that way, I did know I needed to find out if Gavin knew anything about the shades and the next dimension.

"Be careful, Gilly. What about Mark?" The disapproval came through clearly.

I pursed my lips and pondered that question for a few moments as I turned my glass in my fingers. "Well, that's a good question. You know, I've only seen him a few times in the past three months. His life is so busy. When we do get together, it's mostly to catch up on what's been happening and have a quick meal. He doesn't feel like a boyfriend anymore."

Her eyes dropped to the coffee table and her mouth drooped a little. "I'm sorry. I didn't think – I mean, I hadn't realized that your relationship had cooled that much."

"It's okay. We haven't broken up, but I can't really say we're together that much, can I? It's an hour here; an hour there. To be honest, it hasn't been the same since the thing." I didn't need to say abduction. She knew what I meant.

"So you guys haven't—?" Her voice trailed off as she saw the pained expression on my face. "Never mind. None of my business."

I looked away from her, letting my mind replay the last time I'd attempted intimacy with Mark. I'd panicked and he hadn't even come close enough to do more than plant an affectionate kiss since that night.

Janna cleared her throat. "So, getting back to these objects... Maybe you should see Astrid before you try to read them. She might be able to give you some tips or even enhance the attempt."

"You know, that's not a bad idea. I'll see if I can get a session with her next week." Depending on what I learned during lunch with Gavin, I might have more to discuss with the psychic about how to proceed with my potential mentor.

"Good. So, do you still have your gun?" Janna spoke the words with hesitation, an indication of her feelings about it.

She referred to the Luger handgun I'd bought last spring after the abduction. I thought it would give me a little more peace of mind. Instead, I worried about having the thing in my house and loaded. I'd accidentally pulled it on Janna while I practiced taking it out of my purse and into firing position. That had scared her. Fortunately, I hadn't loaded it. Besides, I didn't pull the trigger. Since she didn't know I had bought it, she thought I'd lost my mind and was aiming at her.

"Yes, I keep it upstairs in my bedroom. At one point there at the house, I wished I'd brought it with me."

She jerked forward and gaped at me. "To do what? Shoot someone? How would that help when you were the one breaking in?"

"You're probably right. Although, at the time and not knowing who was on the other side of that door, it seemed like a better defense plan than trying to kick him from behind the boxes." Shrugging, I urged Nygard out of my lap, sprang to my feet, and picked up the empty wine bottle. I took it and my glass back to the kitchen, depositing the latter in my dishwasher and putting the bottle by the back door.

"It's getting late and I have that lunch date tomorrow." I leaned against the archway door and cast a fond smile at my best friend. "Thanks for all your help tonight, Janna. I do appreciate it, you know, and I realize it made you an accomplice. I swear I'll do my best to keep you out of it if it explodes."

"I know. Let's not do it again, okay?" She swallowed the rest of her wine, got up, and picked up her purse.

Crossing to her, I yanked her into a heartfelt hug. "What would I do without you? I love you, girlfriend."

"Me, too." She squeezed me back. Before heading out the door, she paused to add, "Call me on Sunday if I don't make it to the gig tomorrow night."

I nodded, watching her as she walked out to her car, got in, and pulled out of the driveway. I closed the door and locked it, making sure the deadbolt clicked in. Once upon a time, I hadn't worried about how secure the door was and often left it unlocked. That had changed.

I gazed at the articles on the coffee table again, wondering if they would reveal anything. Not tonight, I thought as weariness and wine tugged at my eyelids. I scooped the smaller bags into a large baggie to take upstairs for safekeeping until I could do the readings.

As I glanced over at the landline, I noticed the message light blinking. Two calls, I noted and thought I'd wait until morning on them until curiosity got the better of me and I played them.

"Hello, Gillian Foster," the first one started. Gayle Trumbull's voice... Didn't that woman ever give up? "I think we got off to a bad start and I really would like to talk to you about your unusual skill and what happened to you. Please give me a callback."

She rattled off her cell phone number and repeated it twice more along with a final request to please call. I shook my head and growled a little under my breath.

The second call was from Roger, my stalker. Or, at least, over-zealous fan. He said he was having an engagement party in a couple of weeks and wanted to hire the band to play for it. Engaged? Good for him. Guess I'd have to quit calling him my stalker. I made a note of his phone number and would call him back in the morning.

At an urgent, rumbling meow from the kitchen, I checked in and refilled Nygard's dry food. Pleased, he circled around and between my legs before he ran over to sample the crunchy morsels.

Time for bed. I turned off the lights and headed upstairs with my baggie of spoils. After I tucked them into a drawer in my desk, I changed into my shortie PJs and climbed into bed.

As I tried to fall asleep, my mind kept cycling back through the photos and the books I'd found at the Sarkis' home. Somehow, without implicating myself, I needed to get the police to find those books before they disappeared. They might be the key to finding Nick and Saffi.

Ten

I jerked awake in the morning, the images of the dream still vivid in my mind. I fell back against the pillows and let it play through again as I sought details within the dark images.

Like the one I'd had a few months earlier, I was trapped in a dark place, like a narrow dungeon cell without any windows or lighting to illuminate any of it. While my eyes in the dream had adjusted to the dark as much as they could, the black extended all around me, not allowing me to see any detail. I stared straight ahead to see glowing letters form on the wall, appearing one by one as if someone inscribed them as I watched. The characters were familiar even if I couldn't read them. I felt sure it was Aramaic lettering.

I reached for the notepad by my bedside and began drawing the symbols onto it. I tried to make sure I got them as close as possible to what I saw in my mind. As I strained to pull more detail, the letters began to fade. I could see the surface was a block wall of some kind, maybe granite slabs, or some similar substance. In the lingering glow of the vanishing images, I glimpsed a deeper darkness, if that were possible, in the area to the left of where the inscription had appeared. I thought it might be my imagination, until the image fluctuated, moving slightly as if breathing. After several minutes, the afterglow had gone and the blackness returned.

The image faded from my mind leaving me puzzling over the whole thing. Why was I seeing this and why in a cell-like room? I suspected the wavering black form might be a shade. Was it watching me? Was this a warning? I sat up, exasperated, and muttered, "Dammit, Zac, I need some answers here. Why don't you help me out?"

My guide, or whatever he was, never seemed to be around when I really needed some guidance. You'd think there would be an easy way to contact him. Studying the symbols I'd written down for a few moments, I climbed out of bed and headed to the bathroom. I'd try to find them on the computer after a shower and breakfast.

Putting down a saucer of leftover eggs for Nygard, I went back upstairs to my computer and began searching the Aramaic pages for the symbols I'd written down. Stymied by several versions of the letters to choose from, I studied those with the closest resemblance to the scratch marks I'd drawn. They didn't look quite enough like them and the meanings varied. I needed expert help with it so that would be Gavin. I'd take the paper with me when I met him later and plead for his help again.

The issue of the possible shade in the dream was something I needed to discuss with Madame Astrid. Speaking of which, I glanced at the clock and decided it was a good time to call her. She answered on the second ring.

"Hello, Gillian," she said at once, not surprised to hear from me. "How can I help you?"

"Were you expecting me to call?"

Her laugh boomed across the phone line. "That's for me to know..."

"Yeah, I get it. I want to set up an appointment to talk about a situation with one of my clients and get some input from you. Do you have some time free?"

"Not today, my dear. I have a little time late Monday, around four-thirty. Will that work?"

I'd have to hustle with the dogs, but I could swing it. Heeni was pretty mellow about me cutting out early on occasion. "Yes, that should do. I'll see you then."

"Good. And Gillian, be cautious. I think you're taking some risks."

I blinked, set the phone back on the cradle, and puzzled over that. Did she mean with what I was doing or did she somehow pick up on what I had done? While I'd reluctantly accepted that Madame Astrid was the real deal, it still spooked me when she made remarks like that one.

My next call went to Roger and I offered congratulations right off the bat. He sounded happy as he explained that he and his lady wanted to make a formal announcement at a party. They both had quite a few friends, so they decided to have a big BBQ in a park before the weather turned and they thought a live band would be fun. Besides that way, he could invite Spicy Jam to the party as well.

I checked the band's schedule and the date he wanted two weekends hence worked out fine for us. It would be a Saturday afternoon and we could still schedule an evening gig if it came up. I gave him our price, a little lower than our usual since he was such a fan, and he had no problem with it. I wrote down the details and the address. "I'm looking forward to meeting your fiancée, Roger. I'm really happy for you."

As he thanked me, I realized I meant it. Even though he'd asked me out a couple of times and I'd never accepted, he was always at our shows. This gave me the idea he might be a stalker, albeit a harmless one. Now, I figured he just really liked our band. As I entered the party date near the end of October into my calendar, I realized we would be getting into the holiday bookings soon. From Halloween on until after Valentine's Day, the band generally got quite a few bookings, so I hoped for a lucrative season. Even more so now that we had an album to sell at all those concerts. I made a note to check if it would be available by Roger's shindig.

My cell phone rang and, seeing Gavin's name, I picked up. "Hi, I was just thinking about you."

"Obviously, the same," he replied. "I've decided to cook this afternoon, so wanted to tell you to come to my place around two o'clock. Is that okay with you?"

"You're cooking? I feel privileged. Absolutely fine with me. What can I bring?"

"Just your charming self. I've got everything else covered. I hope you like exotic food."

"That sounds intriguing. I'm looking forward to it."

Exotic food? Wow, I didn't even know Gavin could cook, let alone do fancy food. Now I was really intrigued. I couldn't even claim to be a cook. Scrambled eggs and hamburgers I could manage, but nothing too complex. In fact, I hadn't really tried. My life was so busy with work and the band, and now the spirit escort thing, that it proved easier to just eat out or grab a pizza.

I sat down and made notes about my dream, going through the few discernible details, particularly that shadow that was so black it stood out within the other darkness, so I could ask Astrid about it. I made a couple of other notes about the various items I'd found at Zoe's.

Should I take them with me when I went to my appointment? Or would it be better to talk to her first? While I itched to try reading at least one of them right now, I fought the urge. I didn't feel quite ready to connect with whatever energy the object might hold. To be honest, I didn't know if I could do it or if it had been chance that I'd gotten anything off the few items I had read so far. I could pick up lots of things and not get anything from them, so why did I get the images from certain items? Did I need to be in a proper state of mind or was it a need-to-know matter?

Too bad this spirit guide thing and my emerging psychic abilities didn't come with an instruction manual. Or at least a decent supervisor, if I could call Zac that.

I still had a little time before I needed to leave for Gavin's so I headed for my music room, which was the downstairs bedroom where I'd put my piano, guitar, and sound equipment to make it into a creative space. Inspired by completing our first album, I'd started working on a new song called "Treasured Lady" for the next one.

As I sat down at the piano, turned on the recorder, and started to play the melody for it, humming along and throwing out a few words, my mind went to Zoe and how she'd looked when I first saw her. I stopped playing, lifting my hands from the keys as a different sound formed in my mind. When I started to play again, the notes were more somber and bluesy. The words began to flow from me... *she's a broken lady, discarded and unwanted... she'd been adored, a princess in her childhood... she gave her heart to a lover until he wanted her no more. A broken lady, destroyed by the man she loved...*

Tears formed and trickled down my cheeks as I sang and the lyrics continued to flow to the heartbreaking melody. When I finished, I sat back with anger flowing through my blood. How dare Nick treat her the way he did, then kill her? I had to find a way to help her find justice and learn what happened to Saffi.

Song captured, I turned the recorder off. While I didn't know if I would use it at any point, I realized I had one powerful ballad preserved on that machine.

I went upstairs to wash my face and get ready to go out. I would be going on to the evening's gig from Gavin's so I dressed for the performance. Along with two other bands, we were doing a folk rock concert at Bartley Ranch in conjunction with the Italian Festival. Since it was an outdoor amphitheater, I dressed in a long blue jean skirt and a country-looking blouse that I could easily add a cardigan to if it got too cold. I pulled on my fringed boots, checked on Nygard's food and water, and headed for the door just as the phone rang.

I paused to hear the message rather than pick up. "This is Gayle Trumbull again. I see your band is playing the concert at Bartley. Perhaps we can chat after your set. I just want to clear the air."

Exasperated, I slammed the door shut as I went out. Just what I didn't need. Now, I'd be dodging that reporter all evening. While I drove to Gavin's home on the northwest side of town in an older, yet nice neighborhood, I considered whether it would be better to talk to the woman and try to put an end to her nosiness or continue to evade her. Part of me felt, it might make matters worse to talk to her.

I pulled up in front of the address for Gavin's house and did a double take. No way could he afford this place on his teacher's salary. Sitting on a large lot, the two-story red brick house looked like it had been there for at least fifty years, maybe longer. A gabled entry extended forward to the steps at least eight feet and was about ten feet wide making a nice porch. Beautiful bushes and fall flowers enhanced the landscape around the house and the lawn was still a deep green even if it needed to be cut.

I had assumed he would live in one of the smaller tract houses a few lots away, never thinking he would have a place this upscale. Even if it was a rental, how did he afford it? Maybe he hawked artifacts he purloined from his expedition. Naw, that would be illegal and he wouldn't do that. Another mystery to solve.

Or maybe I had the wrong address. I hesitated a moment before I rang the doorbell.

Eleven

After a few moments, while my stomach twitched with uncertainty, the door opened and Gavin grinned at me. I sighed in relief and managed a return smile.

"I've never even been by your home before, so I wasn't expecting this." I waved my right hand to encompass the porch and the whole house.

He laughed, motioning me to come in. "It belonged to my grandmother. She left it to me when she passed on."

"Oh, I'm sorry." Then I caught what I'd said and amended it. "I mean about your grandmother, not about the house."

I stepped inside and looked around the spacious living room, noting the elegant touches in the ornate molding, art deco lighting, and lace doilies on the tables. Gavin didn't seem like the doily type although he was an archeologist and they liked old things. I just didn't think it extended to frilly table dressings.

I must have been staring at them because he pointed to one and said, "My great grandmother made those. They're almost a century old. Would you like a drink? Wine or a cooler?"

"Cooler, please. Long on the soda and only a little wine. I don't want to drink anything with too much alcohol before the show tonight." I made a mental note not to set the drink on any of those table decorations. Shouldn't they be in a museum or something? I eased down on the big velveteen-covered sofa and set my purse under the end table by it. Nice furniture, sturdy with real wood finishing pieces on the ends.

He came back holding a tall drink, topped with a cherry, no less, and handed it to me. "I'm in the kitchen for now, if you want to come in. I'm making Thai food and have a curry going. I hope you like it."

"Sounds wonderful." I rose, took the drink, and followed him to the kitchen where the most delightful fragrances in the world assaulted my olfactory sense.

Though the house might be old, the kitchen had been remodeled in recent years. Spacious with lots of cabinets I envied, it featured modern appliances and a built-in grill. More than that, Gavin seemed perfectly at ease in the room, moving from the stove to the grill where he had some kabobs going, and crossing to add ingredients to a salad bowl on the counter.

When had I entered the Twilight Zone? This seemed surreal and not at all what I imagined when I thought of Gavin. I mean, he was my Indiana Jones avatar, an adventurer, and rugged archeologist, not the Galloping Gourmet. Maybe that stretched the image too much and he was more Bobby Flay.

He stirred the curry and grinned at me as he pointed to the dishes at the end of the counter. "Would you mind taking those to the table?"

That grin... Wow! All those memories from his classes when he'd flashed that grin and every woman in the class had imagined it was directed at her came back in a rush. Obviously, he could still tweak my heart after all these years. Get a grip, I told myself. This would not do at all and if he did turn out to be my mentor, I sure couldn't be getting all gaga over him.

What about Mark? I heard Janna's voice ask in my mind. Yeah, what about him? We hadn't broken up, but we weren't exactly together either. How could we be when he didn't have time?

As I kept looking at my former professor and thinking how handsome he still was, that old crush I'd had on him resurfaced. Doing a mental shake, I picked up the plates, took them to the modest table in the adjoining dining room, and placed them in front of the two chairs nearest the kitchen. I found napkins on the sideboard in the room, rearranged the silverware on top of them, and hoped I got the order right.

A minute or so later, Gavin brought out two bowls of soup, Tom Yum he called it, and we sat down to eat. Although spicy, the flavor burst in my mouth with chili and something tangy.

"Lemon grass," Gavin said when I commented on it. He watched me, an anxious furrow above his brows.

"It's good. I like the spice." I smiled at him and began to worry that the flavors might not mesh well with my digestion. I had visions of stomach cramps while I tried to sing. I only ate half and pushed it away, which brought another frown. "It tastes great, but I can't eat a lot. I've got a show tonight and I don't do well if I overeat before it."

He relaxed a little, nodding his head. "I didn't think of that. You'll eat some of the rest, won't you?"

"Of course. Just make the servings small for me, okay?"

"Got it." He stood up, picked up the soup bowls, and took them to the kitchen. When he returned he had a platter with the ka-bobs and little fried bread pockets of some kind on it.

He set it on the table. "Help yourself and try some of the sauce with the pakoras." At my look, he added, "Those are the bread pockets."

I tentatively took one of each item and tasted them. Oh, delicious. Now I wanted to eat the whole platter of them. Somehow, I restrained myself. I didn't want to over-do it and the curry was yet to come.

"So, I wanted to talk to you about a couple of things. More or less on a professional level."

His left eyebrow shot up a little emphasizing the questioning look on his face. "Professional? As a professor or as an archeologist?"

"A little of both, I guess. And maybe something more." I finished the second little pocket and grinned. "These are really good, by the way."

His head dipped in acknowledgment and he continued to gaze at me.

The ball was still in my court, so I bounced it. "The thing is I had a strange dream with another of those inscriptions like the one I brought to you last spring. I need help translating it."

"A dream? Didn't you find the other in a book?"

He would remember that little fib. "Not exactly, no. It was a dream also."

Now his eyebrows pulled together and a valley formed between them. "I think you need to explain this a little more. Hold on while I get the next course and grab another beer. You want another cooler?"

I shook my head. "No, thanks. I'm fine. A glass of water

though?"

He turned back to the kitchen with those plates and I stared at the tablecloth. I felt stupid and I needed to explain the whole thing to him. I should have waited.

I looked up as he came back in and set down two more bowls of food. "You know what? Let's talk about this after we eat. Okay?"

"Sounds like a plan to me." He dropped into his chair and motioned to me to help myself. He waited until I picked up the spoon in the curry bowl nearest to me before he helped himself to a big serving of steamed rice. He pushed it my way as I edged the other toward him.

"So, tell me more about the trip to Syria. You said it was a really old city?" I said, diverting the conversation to him.

"Yes, dates back to long before Christ. A friend of mine was working on it. He called and asked me to join him. Said it was right up my alley."

"And was it?" I ladled a small amount of curry onto my plate and mixed it with the rice as we talked.

He spoke generally about the dig without going into much detail, avoiding it for the most part. Maybe he couldn't reveal much, I thought, finding it amusing how he sidestepped any of my specific questions.

"You know, I looked up Palmyra on the 'net. The information on it said it was a restricted travel zone. How did you get in?"

"That's my secret," he said with a short laugh. "It's all about who you know."

"Isn't it dangerous?"

He shrugged. "Maybe a little, but there wasn't any fighting where we were. Our dig was about five kilometers away from the ruins. No one came around."

When he'd had enough of my questions, he said, "So what are you doing now besides music? Which, by the way, I think is terrific. I remember you in the university productions and you really had on-stage presence."

"Why, thank you, sir. My band and I just cut an album, so that will be releasing soon. It's our first and we're really happy with it."

He lifted his beer toward me as if in salute. "On a label?"

"Just a local one. They produce quite a few area musicians." I set my fork down and got up to pick up my dinnerware to take to the kitchen. I felt that admission made me seem like less. Lots of artists self-produced their albums and it didn't make it a bad album.

He stood and took the dishes from me. "It's a start, Gillian. No harm in that. Go on in the living room and I'll bring coffee or tea if you'd like."

"Coffee would be great. Thanks." A tingle ran up my arm as his hand brushed against mine when he took the dishes and I gazed into his eyes for a moment, seeing a sparkle of something there. Desire? Interest? Or just amusement. Oh, lordy me, I needed to get a handle on this attraction.

After he brought the coffee, he settled in the chair next to the sofa where he could face me. "Now tell me about the dream and the inscription."

So I did, starting at the beginning with the first one that I'd been reluctant to divulge was a dream. Eyes focused on me, he listened intently, nodding his head in encouragement. To wrap it up, I described the latest one from this morning and pulled out the paper with the symbols on it.

"I tried to look it up on my computer, but I couldn't find characters that matched exactly. Some were close, but they didn't seem to make sense."

A smirk formed on his lips. "Well, if computer translation programs for ancient languages were reliable, there wouldn't be jobs for us scientific types who studied archaic language, would there?"

"You're right, absolutely. That's why I came to you." I winked at him, sitting back and relieved he would help me.

He studied them for several minutes, went to a bookcase, picked up his tablet, and brought it back to the chair. He tapped something in and looked at it for several more minutes, then began typing in more information.

"Are you using a program to do it?" I asked. If he'd found one I didn't know about, I wanted to have access to it.

"No, I'm calling up some of my documents to check the symbols.

Like people now, writing, even in symbols, varied from person to person even though they may be copying the same thing. Some took shortcuts and the letters don't look like what they're supposed to be. Now, if I have this right, it's a similar message to the last time and it says –" He paused. "Are you ready for it?"

Pulling out my little notebook and pen, I nodded.

"Okay, it loosely translates to 'Dark is conquered by pure light.'" He leaned forward and looked directly into my eyes. "Do you have any idea what that references?"

I shook my head as I thought about. "I dunno. I might. Jeez, it's such a... vague phrase."

"A bit like the first one, isn't it? What's it talking about?"

I shrugged as I wrote it down. "Darkness... it's dark in the room from the dream. At first, I thought it was because I'd been through a traumatic incident and the dream represented my fear. I don't think so now. It's a message of some sort, but I can't piece it together."

Gavin rubbed at his jaw as he thought. "Both of these messages appeared as glowing symbols on a wall in a completely black room. Are you certain it was a room? You could see the wall?"

"I could see it when the symbols glowed, enough to tell it was brick or granite blocks, and it was small." I hesitated, chewing at my lower lip. How much should I tell him? If I was going to trust him, it had to start now. "There's more to it, Gavin."

He raised an eyebrow and waited.

"I saw an even blacker shape within the wall that was moving, shifting like a blob of ink trying to get through the wall." I jerked when a cold chill ran up my spine as I said it. I hadn't connected that it was trying to get through the wall.

Gavin's eyes turned stormy-looking. "What aren't you telling me?"

I took a deep breath and glanced away for a few moments. Where should I start? "When I asked to see your ring the other day, I got impressions. I saw flashes of past images from it. I saw someone, from the ring holder's view, running through a marketplace. He was being pursued by two huge dark shapes."

A look of shock, brought under control in moments, crossed his face. His voice sounded a little rough as he repeated, "Dark shapes?"

I nodded. "You were the one running, weren't you? The ring recorded your attempt to flee."

"That's... interesting." He gazed out the window and sipped his beer as he thought about it. "You saw dark shapes? Not very big men chasing someone through the market?"

"Dark shapes. Shades. Bigger than any I've seen before."

Incredulous, he said, "You've seen shades before?"

I noticed he didn't question shades, just that I'd seen them. So, that meant he knew about them.

"I can sometimes pick up images from objects. The Civil War button I gave you showed me some images as well. I saw shades at Shiloh, on the battlefields."

"Criminy. You do psychometry readings?"

"Sometimes. It's hit and miss."

He flashed a smile at me. "Most psychic stuff usually is. How long have you been able to do this?"

"Not long. It's only developed in the past year. Back to my question. You're not telling me if those were shades chasing you."

More seriously, he said, "Yeah. Truth is, I only glimpsed their dark form for a few moments before they took on a human appearance and pursued me through the market. That's why I'm surprised you saw their true form in your vision."

My mouth felt dry. "But they were in this world, this dimension. I thought they were only in the spirit realm."

Gavin jumped out of his chair and sat down next to me, catching my left hand and peering into my eyes as if he might see something in them. "What do you know about the spirit dimension and shades?"

I wanted to look away from him, but I couldn't. He was so intense in that moment that I could only focus on him. I managed to croak an answer. "Not much, it appears. I know they exist, and I've seen them in visions. I've been told they're evil spirits." I swallowed hard, getting the nerve to question him. "You seem to know more about them and what they can do. So, you tell me."

"I dunno. I think you should stay away from this. You are way out of your league, Gillian."

Pulling my hand free, I crossed my arms and glared at him. "Well, I'd like to stay out of it, but it seems to be pulling me in. I didn't ask for these dreams or seeing these things. It's happening and I can't stop it."

"Well, have you seen someone about it?" His jaw tightened as he spoke, worry or anger driving it.

"Yes!" I didn't need to tell him she was a psychic. So far as the physical aspect of my situation, I'd seen doctors, who had pronounced me fit and sound.

He took a deep breath. "I don't like this. You better tell me everything from the beginning and don't leave anything out."

I glanced at my watch and realized I needed to get going if I was going to make it to Bartley Ranch on time. "I can't right now. There's too much to tell and I need to go."

"Gilli —"

"Seriously. I have to leave, Gavin. I want to tell you the whole story if you'll level with me also. Can we meet later in the week?" I got to my feet, reaching for my purse under the end table.

Chagrined, he rose along with me. "Next Wednesday afternoon. Five-thirty. Can you make it?"

I agreed and turned to leave when he caught my arm and pulled me into an embrace. I went stiff. He'd never done that before and it shocked me, but he didn't seem to notice.

"Be careful, chica. Call me if anything else comes up before we talk."

Chica? Where did that come from?

I mumbled something in agreement as I hurried out the door to my Jeep. That had turned a bit weird.

Twelve

I arrived at Bartley Ranch about fifteen minutes after I should have been there. If I was lucky, the concert would have started a little bit late and the group that opened would still be on stage. If not, I was going to be playing catch up again. Either way, I'd hear about it from Ferris and Digby.

I pulled my Jeep into the first place I could find, grabbed my keyboard, and ran for the amphitheater that was about a half mile from the parking area. By the time I got there, the Rum Bear Ramblers, a group from Lake Tahoe named after a bear incident, were just finishing up. I gasped my relief and looked for a bottle of water in the backstage area.

Ferris wore a disgruntled frown that made him look especially angry as he came over. "That's their third encore number while we've been waiting for you. Dammit, Gillian, are you ever not going to be late?"

"I'm sorry." I opened my keyboard and pulled it out. The guys carried the stand with the rest of the band equipment so I only had to get the instrument and myself to the gigs, thank goodness. "I had an appointment on the other side of town and traffic was heavier than I thought it would be." I'd actually been doing much better at getting to gigs and rehearsals on time in the past few months. Ferris soon forgot that when I slipped up.

"Allow extra time," he snarled. He walked to the edge of the curtain and gave the band a sign that we were ready.

I took deep breaths to calm myself after the sprint and the chewing out, then hustled on stage when we were announced. It only took a few seconds to plug in and flip the microphone on and we launched into our first song.

The crowd roared and we were in the zone for the next forty-five minutes. Ferris plugged our album and introduced the band, a task he'd taken over from me when he'd relieved me of the leadership because he thought I was too distracted. His opinion, although he may have been right. I'd had a bit of upset in my life over the last year even if he didn't know anything about it.

We played an encore number, promised to be back later, and vacated the stage to the third group. We would be the final band of the day, pulling two sets instead of only one. More money and more sales opportunity. I'd negotiated that deal.

As we headed to the merchandise table just outside the theatre entrance, I excused myself to go to the drink bar a short distance away. "Can I get you guys something? A beer or a soda?"

"Not just yet," Ferris said. "Just hurry so we're all here to sign these albums if people want it."

"Right. Be back in a few."

Even though I hurried, I still had to wait in line to buy a cold soda. As I grabbed it and started away, Roger spotted me and stepped out of line to greet me.

"Hey, great set, Gillian Foster. You guys are so hot. Thanks for accepting my party."

"Oh, glad to do it. Thanks for asking us to play. Is your fiancée here?" I glanced around him, hoping to get a glimpse of the woman. I wondered if it was the blonde I'd seen him with at New Year's.

"Uh, no. She couldn't make it tonight. Had to work." He glanced away from me and seemed a little nervous.

"That's too bad. I'm looking forward to meeting her." A brief hint of a smile tugged his lips up and he nodded.

That was odd. I changed the subject. "Did you hear the announcement about our CD? Just released. This is the first gig we've had it with us."

"That is..." He paused and thought a moment. "...truly awesome. You're selling them here? I'll be over in a little bit to buy a couple."

"Great! See you later." I waved bye and hurried back toward the table. Partway there, I decided I needed to make a side trip to the ladies' room as my stomach spasmed. Maybe that Thai food wasn't such a good idea. Or maybe it was the chat with Gavin that left me feeling queasy.

Ten minutes later, I stepped to the washbasin and splashed water on my face and deemed myself ready to return to our fans. At least, I hoped we had a few buying albums.

I rounded the corner of the theater heading toward the table where Ferris and Digby talked to a small group of people and signed albums. A short distance away, I noticed a familiar figure slouching against a tree. Egan Moss. What was he doing here?

He spotted me and knew I saw him so he jerked his head to the side, indicating he wanted me to come over. This couldn't be good. I glanced back at the busy table. The guys were going to hate me. I marched over to Moss with the hope that this would only take a moment.

When I reached him, he said two words. "Follow me." He pivoted and moved further up the hillside into the trees to a more private area.

"Hey, Moss. What's up?" I flashed a smile and hoped this wasn't what I was afraid it might be.

His face wore that "I just ate a sour lemon drop" expression. "I saw a report today, not in my jurisdiction, mind you, but it came as a matter of amusement to some in the office. It seems someone broke into the Sarkis residence and a neighbor reported a black clad person, short—maybe a teenager—running from the house. You wouldn't happen to know anything about that, would you?"

I put on my puzzled look. "Huh? What do you mean?"

"Foster, I am sure hoping you didn't break in, but that description could fit someone your size and build. As I was thinking about possible motive and suspects, I recalled a conversation with you where you wanted me to try to get an object or two from evidence to do a reading on. So, I don't think it's too much of a leap to think you might try to procure your own objects. Is that an unreasonable theory?"

I tried to maintain my not-guilty face, but I felt it slipping under his steely-eyed gaze. "No, not unreasonable." My voice squeaked a little.

He straightened his shoulders, his mouth formed a straight line. "Foster, did you break into that house? Or even attempt to do it?"

Busted, I shifted my gaze to the ground and tried to figure how I could weasel out of this without getting myself into more trouble. I looked up, my mouth twisting as I tried to form words to explain my position. "In a way, I had permission to do it."

His right eyebrow shot skyward in a skeptical response that clearly said explain.

"Okay, so she's dead. In spite of that, Zoe not only told me I could do it, but how to do it. She even gave me the code for the alarm. And I was careful, Moss. I wore gloves and didn't leave any fingerprints anywhere. I didn't move anything around."

His mouth dropped open, his left arm went over his head, and he turned around in a half-crouch as he, no doubt, fought the urge to hit me. A palpable wave of energy, his anger washed over me. Completing the turn, he glared at me and spoke with tight, clipped words.

"Son of a bitch! Of all the dumb things... Foster, I should arrest you here and now."

"I didn't hurt anything and I would have gotten in and out without any trouble if that darn doxie hadn't started barking so much the owner let him out. Moss, I'm trying to help Zoe Sarkis and I can't do that if I can't get any leads to where her husband and her friend are." I shouted it in a loud whisper so I didn't draw anyone's attention.

"You are not the police! Just leave this to the people who are trained to do it. The only reason I am not arresting you is because I don't want to explain anything about you and your extrasensory crap. Stay away from the house and any possible evidence in it."

"The police tape was off. I thought they had already gotten all the evidence."

His eyes grew wider and I realized I'd said the wrong thing. "It's still breaking and entering and that is a felony. Dammit, I like you, Gillian, and I'm trying to give you a break here. Stay away from the house and the case."

Even though I nodded my seeming agreement, I didn't know that I could stay away from the case itself as long as Zoe counted on me, and by extension, haunted me until I helped her. "I won't go near the house again, not even a drive by."

He calmed down, his shoulders dropping as he relaxed. I knew I might push his buttons again, but I took a chance anyway. "If the police have all the evidence, I think they might have missed a couple of things that could prove useful."

Moss' brows pulled together again as he listened. "Go on."

So I explained about the secret room in Nick's office and what I'd found in it. I didn't mention the dark clad, presumably security, guy who'd also entered the house. "There are books that might explain what happened with Nick's business. Double ledgers that looked like he might be skimming money. The little storage area was missed or they would have pulled all of it, wouldn't they?"

His expression shifted as his eyes focused on the distance and he thought about what I'd said. "Yeah, they should have taken all of that, so you're right that they missed it. Damn, I am not going to get involved in their case."

"How can I let them know without implicating myself? I thought maybe Secret Witness, but I can't risk them finding out who called. What's the best way?"

He ran a hand through his hair, shook his head and said, "Here's the best way I know. Write it on a computer; print it out on a laser printer at a store. Put it in an envelope and mail it to RPD, attention to Detective Wagner. Take it to the post office drive through late at night so no one notices you. Don't touch anything, the paper, the envelope or the stamps with your bare hands. Use gloves. You got that?"

I nodded.

"Do not mention my name. Do not involve me in this case in any way. Don't make me come after you again. I cannot believe I'm doing this."

"I'm sorry, Moss. I didn't intend to cause you trouble. I had to do something to help her."

"Did you find some— Never mind. I don't want to know. Just steer clear of it. Unless you want to try to explain your paranormal kink to Detective Wagner and put him in the same position I'm in."

"Understood." I shrugged my shoulders and tried to give him a sincere apologetic look.

He stepped past me and went down the hill toward the exit path. I sighed, turned, and hurried back to the table where about a dozen people stood to one side while five or six others talked to Digby and seemed to be buying the album.

Deflated, I hurried behind the table, apology ready to spout from my lips.

"There you are," Digby said, barely glancing at me. "Those folks at the end are queued up for your Betsy Ross, so get to it."

Betsy Ross—my signature. He used that instead of John Henry for a woman's signature. "Where's Ferris?"

"Off to get a couple of beers."

Right. He'd be upset with me. I smiled at the lined up customers, picked up a marker, and began signing the CDs they had in hand while apologizing for being late. Most understood, which is more than I could say for Ferris when he returned and glared at me every chance he got.

As I got down to the last couple of waiting people, someone handed me a CD to sign and I looked up into Gayle Trumbull's face. Of course. I knew she would be here, and did I really think I could avoid her? I forced a little smile. "Personalized?"

"Yes, please. When can we talk?"

I signed as I talked. "I don't have any time right now. I have a few more of these to sign, then back to the stage. You know how I feel about this whole interview thing."

"I do. Still, I would like to try to convince you otherwise and get across that I'm not your enemy. I'm just a reporter doing her job."

Her voice sounded so sincere. Why didn't I believe her?

"Here's the problem. After the last set, we'll be back out here for at least thirty or forty minutes selling and signing until the people leave. After that, I can give you about ten minutes before we all have to leave so they can close the park."

"Deal. I'll be back here thirty minutes after the concert wraps." She flashed a satisfied smirk and took her CD. At least, we made a sale off her.

We only had a few minutes left before we needed to get back on stage when we left the table in the capable hands of the Bear group. I didn't know all their names. Digby had checked them out and felt comfortable with it, although he did grab the money pouch.

Ferris latched onto my arm and pulled me aside for a minute. "What the hell happened to you? Thirty minutes to get a drink and go to the bathroom?"

"I ran into a couple of people I couldn't avoid talking with." I yanked my arm away and surged away from him.

Digby overheard, caught up to me, and asked, "Who was that woman talking to you at the table? She looked familiar."

"Gayle Trumbull, a reporter. She wants to get an interview with me."

"Ace! That could do magic for our album," he enthused. "Only you? Not Ferry and me?"

I sighed. "It's not about our band. It's about my gigs at funerals."

His chin dropped two inches as his mouth fell open. "You're kidding." He turned back to Ferris. "Hey, did you hear that? News lady wants to interview Gillian about funeral stuff, not about our amazing album."

Ferris shot a peculiar look my way before he climbed behind the drums. Shrugging, I continued on to my keyboard. The emcee announced us again and we fired up the sound, putting our all into the last set.

Forty minutes later, we wrapped up after Ferris pushed the album again. As we packed up the gear quickly, except the drums—Ferris would pull his van up later to speed that up—he came over to me and asked about the interview thing.

"What's so special about singing at a funeral that she wants to interview you?"

"Beats me. I think it ties into the abduction last February and it being connected with a funeral I played. While I don't see anything worth reporting in that, she seems to think there's a story, so she's been bugging me about it."

Wrinkles formed across his forehead and his eyes took on a concerned look. "Something is going on with you, babe. I think you're holding back on Dig and me. When are you going to read us in?"

I bit my lip. He was right. I needed to trust my bandmates with the whole truth. I just had a hard time telling them about something I was having trouble accepting myself. "I'll tell you all about it soon. I promise. Hey, at least we know my stalker isn't one. He wants us to play for his engagement party. Isn't that great?"

A momentary puzzled look until he connected. "Roger? So, he's engaged. That's a relief."

I picked up my keyboard and purse and we headed for the merchandise table. Digby had gone on ahead and was already selling copies of the CD. After about twenty minutes, the sales dwindled down to the last two people. We signed those and began packing up the remaining copies.

Ferris said he'd take them and ran off to bring his van down closer to the theater. I spotted Gayle standing by a lamppost and turned to Digby. "I'm going to go talk to her for a few minutes. If you guys get packed up before I'm done, go on and leave. I'll be all right."

"You sure? I don't know if we can trust her not to murder you on the spot."

"Silly, there's still four or five park rangers here to herd people out and lock up. I don't think she's likely to pull a knife on me. Besides I can handle myself." I punched his strumming arm lightly before I flung arms around him in a tight hug. "I'll see you guys at practice on Thursday."

I headed uphill to meet Gayle and she pointed to one of the tables under a canopy not far from us. "We might as well sit."

Once we settled, she said, "I know we got off to an awkward start. I can be pushy. When you're following up on crime stories and the like, it's the only way you can get any information."

I nodded my head, acknowledging that she was pretty aggressive.

"Anyway, I'm sorry for the rocky start. I'm not out to cause you problems."

"I'm glad to hear that because I don't need any more. So end of story?" I raised my eyebrow and smiled pleasantly.

"Maybe not. I still think your funeral-singing gig is unusual and would make a great human-interest story. People I talk to who have been at one of them tell me that your music is quite unusual, that you write personalized lyrics that are a remarkable reflection of the deceased person's qualities. That alone makes it fascinating." She almost bubbled with enthusiasm.

"That's also exaggerated. I change a few lyrics and try to personalize the song to make it special for the family. I seem to have a knack for it." I did my best to downplay this.

"How did you get started doing this?" Gayle moved into reporter mode and I knew she wanted to do the interview.

"I'm a musician. I have flyers up around town with information about contacting me for special events. Someone called me to sing at a funeral. A little odd, but still a paying job. It grew from there."

Gayle grinned. "That wasn't so bad, was it? Just a few questions on camera and we could have a nice little story."

I tightened my lips as I tried to frame my response. "Except the questions will be more detailed and leading to places I don't want to discuss. Tell me they won't circle back to Marielle Sanders' murder and my whole involvement in that and some associated rumors. You already have misleading information and trying to set the record straight puts the suspicion out there, doesn't it?"

"No, not at all." She waved a hand as if sweeping it all away. "Why are you so determined to keep this private? It could be a boost to your career, drawing more interest to your music. I could even do a part of it on your band and your first CD release. It could mean more work for you."

Oh, damn, there was the carrot. It could help the album and the guys would love that, but I didn't trust her not to dig where I couldn't have her go. "All that's true, I guess. My problem is, some of it is very personal, and I don't want everyone in town knowing about my freakish ability to compose unique songs on demand. In fact, I don't do it for anything except the funerals. While I write original material, it's not like that."

A flash of exasperation crossed her face as she leaned forward a little, trying to make a more personal connection. "I think you're worried about nothing. How about if I promise you that my station and I won't air anything that you don't approve? Would you at least consider this offer?"

"Full approval? Anything I dislike removed from the interview? My choice not to answer anything that I feel is too personal?" I had to think about this with a clear head and maybe some additional counseling from Janna or the guys.

"That's the offer." Her face took on a perky look and she sat back, confident she'd convinced me.

"I'd like to take a few days to think about it. This is a big step that could impact my life."

"Of course." She whipped out her business card and handed it to me. "Give me a call or email when you decide."

I nodded and sat watching as she rose and walked up the hill to the parking area. Was I really going to consider this? I tucked the card into my purse.

Time to trudge out to my Jeep in the north forty and head home. I saw Ferris almost had the van packed up and was emptying the last load from his cart. I strolled over to him and he pulled me into an embrace. He always forgave me quickly.

"Tough night, babe? Did the mean news lady give you a hard time?"

"Actually, she was pretty nice and made an interesting offer that could benefit us all, but it still leaves me with an uneasy feeling. I'll tell you and Dig all about it on Thursday."

"Check. Want a lift to your Jeep?"

I shook my head. The walk would clear my mind. He kissed me on the forehead, and I pointed my tired body toward the distant field.

Thirteen

Coming out of a deep sleep, I rolled over and stretched my arms, the lingering drowsiness still making my eyes half-slits. Something rustled in the room and I looked toward the end of the bed expecting to see Nygard pawing at something. I caught my breath.

The most beautiful being I'd ever seen stood at the end of my bed. Clad entirely in white, blond hair framing his face with loose curls, Zac waved a hand at me and raised his eyebrows. What he really was I couldn't say and he never had told me, so I had assumed he was my guide, be he an angel or an incredibly gorgeous spirit. To find him in my bedroom, in the flesh so to speak, was a shock.

I pulled my blanket up under my arms and sat up. "Zac, what are you doing here?"

"Good morning to you also, Gillian," he said. His voice matched the beauty of the vision, velvety smooth and perfectly pitched to be soothing and dreamy. "You are troubled, therefore, I felt it prudent to pay you a visit."

"I appreciate that. But in my bedroom?" My voice shot up the scale at the end of that.

"Why not? Did you not request I come?"

"That's true. I did. I need your help. The shades are showing up more often and I don't know how to fight them or repel them or whatever it is I need to do. Heck, I don't even know what they are for sure." If he sensed my frustration, he would be correct.

"I believe you know part of it. Madame Astrid explained that the shades are souls who are not satisfied or feel unworthy to cross through the gate to the next level. At least, those are the weaker shades. Those spirits are claimed by the original denizens of the dimension, the True Shades."

I didn't like the sound of that. "Are they lost souls then?"

"No, they were never souls." His mouth shifted to a thin, grim line as he spoke.

"Never?" I felt a shudder of dread when I considered it. "What are they?"

"Not every living creature has a soul. But they live, nonetheless. For these dark spirits, the lower dimension is their home and they lure lost souls to them to try to claim them. If one can claim a soul, they can be born on the next level."

This level, I realized as he said it. They could be born as an animal or a human on this plane. "If they are born here, are they still evil? Could they be born with the desire to take souls?"

"It is one scenario." Zac turned and walked to the side of the bed, gazing down the walkway past my computer toward the bathroom. Nygard sat in the middle, watching us with an intense interest. Could he see Zac as well?

Zac pivoted around to face me. "It depends on the strength of the soul the True Shade has devoured. If the soul is strong enough, it can still fight for its humanity and good. If not, the darkness can take over and a degree of evil exists on this plane."

I heard the word "devoured" and I whispered, "Soul eaters. They're soul eaters."

He nodded. "They have been much more active in the past fifty years, growing stronger and more aggressive in the past decade. There is a lot of unrest in the world."

I dreaded asking the next question, fearing the answer. "How do I fit in?"

"You are a pure spirit. Did you not know this? That is why you were selected for your task." He made it sound so natural and ordinary.

"I didn't want to be! I don't want to have this ability or whatever it is." I shuddered, horrified by the implications.

"You were selected," he repeated. "You have allies in this fight. You have Madame Astrid, who is gifted in her own way, and the aid of her spirit guide. You have also found your own mentor and you need to connect with him fully."

"Gavin?"

"Yes. He is a paladin."

"A what?"

"A paladin, although the term is human, it applies. He is a

leader and a warrior. He can train you. Trust him."

My mouth gaped open. "Train me? For what? No—no, I want out!"

"Sleep well, Gillian." He raised his hands at elbow level, palms up as if invoking something, then disappeared.

I gasped, grabbing at my throat as I sprang up in bed. Confused, I swiveled my head as I looked around the room. Nygard stretched out at the end of my bed and raised his head to stare at me, a questioning look in his eyes.

Wait! What had just happened? I caught my breath and leaned back against the headboard to think about it.

My previous visits from Zac had been during my dreams. Suddenly, it occurred to me that this had been a dream also. One of those ones where you dreamed you woke up, while, in reality, you were still asleep. It had seemed so real, full color and all. Thinking about it, I realized all the dreams relating to the spirit gift had been in color.

My cat ambled up the bed covers, coming up the right side to get his morning love. I scratched his ears and my fingers dropped to rub under his chin. His rumble of a purr started as he dipped his head and shoved his chin against my knuckles demanding more.

"That was a very strange dream, Nygard. You were in it. Only you weren't, were you?"

He peered up at me and made a *merrow* of sound that could have been a yes before he ducked his head under my fingers again. Or it could have been a negative response.

"Time to get up." He perked up his ears and hopped off the bed, ready to bound down the stairs to breakfast.

Once breakfast was done, I latched onto my coffee and went back upstairs to compose a letter on my computer. Not really a letter, more like a note, I thought as I started writing my account of the secret room and the filing boxes in it that might be pertinent evidence in the Sarkis murder case. I tried to not inject any of my personality into the account, keeping it very basic and minus an explanation of how I knew about it. If it was to be anonymous, I didn't want even a hint of my expedition entering into it. Finished, I read it a couple of times, made an adjustment or two, and copied it to a thumb drive, not even saving it on my computer.

Once that was done, I printed a label addressed to the detective Moss had named. Careful not to touch anything with my bare fingers, I pulled on a pair of plastic gloves, picked up the box of envelopes I had in a drawer, and pulled out one. Next, I carefully removed the label that tried to latch onto the plastic and managed to manipulate it to the envelope. It went on a little crooked, but that was all right. It didn't need to be perfect.

That accomplished, I looked for a copy place that had self-copying options. I only needed one printout and it needed to be private. Slipping the gloves into my sweater pocket, I headed down to the little shopping plaza where the small shop was located.

Luckily, it was open and not crowded on a mid-morning Sunday. Three other customers waited for the attention of the sole employee, a middle-aged scrawny guy who pushed his glasses up his nose as he talked to the first one in line. That made it easy for me to go to the self-copy station set up at the end of the counter, pop in the thumb drive, and call up the file.

I had a bad moment when the clerk noticed me and asked if I needed anything. In spite of the lined-up customers, I thought he might come down to see what I was doing.

"No," I called back. "I just have one page to print. Easy enough to do. Thanks."

He nodded and turned his attention to the customer he'd been helping. I pressed the print button, slipped a glove on my right hand, and extracted the completed paper from the laser printer. Sliding it into a plastic folder I'd brought with me, I removed the glove and returned it to my pocket. No fingerprints, just as Moss instructed. I took my place at the end of the line to pay for it.

Act normal, I told myself, fearful that against all odds someone might recognize me. I kept my head down, not looking around or at the others as I moved up the line.

"That's seventy-five cents for the one print," the clerk told me in a twangy voice.

As I handed him a dollar, I thought it expensive for one page; however, I wasn't about to argue. Nothing to draw attention to myself. I took my change and left without running out the door. Back at the Beast, I took a deep breath, climbed in, and headed to the post office. I went to one of the stamp machines and bought a book of stamps, not opening them so that I didn't touch the stamps until I had a glove on again.

That done, I headed back home. I'd actually mail the letter after dark when no one was likely to be at the post office. I wasn't at all paranoid about this, much. I just didn't want anyone to even see me put it in the mailbox.

Once I arrived at my place, I put on the gloves again, folded the letter, and put it into the envelope, and used a moist wipe to wet the seal. The only thing printed on my inkjet was the address label and I didn't think they would be able to trace that to me. At least, I hoped not. I pulled a stamp out of the book, applied it to the envelope, then put the latter back in the folder so I had it ready to mail.

What a production! I celebrated getting that much done by making a sandwich for lunch and having a glass of wine. Settling on the sofa with my lunch, I put my feet up on the coffee table, took a bite of the ham and cheese, and reflected on my latest dream and the additional, possibly questionable—after all, it was delivered in a dream— information Zac had provided.

I needed to talk to Gavin about everything that had happened to me and find out how much he knew about the lower plane and True Shades. From talking to him, it seemed he didn't always see them in their real form. So many questions niggled at my brain and the whole situation made me anxious. This was definitely not something I had expected to be involved with and it landed way out of my experience.

At least, if I got the letter mailed to RPD, I could feel like I was making progress on the Zoe problem. No wonder my love life was at a stall. Mark wasn't the only one who didn't have time for a relationship.

I wanted to call Janna and tell her about the dream, yet at the same time, I didn't want to do it. Not yet. I needed more information before I could use her as a sounding board. Even if I managed to fill Ferris and Digby in on the whole seeing-dead-people thing, I didn't think I could level with them on the shades. They would think I'd gone off the trolley on a hill in San Francisco.

My thoughts circled around to the objects I'd found. While I had planned to wait until I'd consulted with Madame Astrid, another little voice in my brain urged me to read one now. Just one. What would it hurt to try? If I failed, I could always try again. It's not like any attached emotions vanished.

Decision made, I refilled my wine glass, put the plate in the dishwasher, and went upstairs. Pulling out the big plastic bag with all objects, I reached in and withdrew the small brush from Zoe's nightstand. To be honest, I didn't expect a revelation, but maybe some emotion had attached to it.

I sat on the bed, stretched out my legs, and wrapped my fingers around the handle. Closing my eyes, I opened my mind to any images I might get. Even though I sensed movement through hair and smelled a fragrance that reminded me of lilacs, no visions passed into my mind. I frowned and rubbed my hand on the bristles, hoping to trigger something. Failure again. Maybe I was trying too hard to get something or the brush didn't have any events attached.

Damn. I set it down and took several deep breaths. Should I try another object or wait until I could talk to Astrid? The feeling had been so strong that I was sure there was something. One more, I decided, closed my eyes, dipped my hand into the bag again, and let my senses guide me. I pulled out the little pouch with the ruby earring in it.

I took a deep breath as I settled on the bed again and dropped the object out of the bag into my hand. I felt warmth as soon as it hit...

A dark-haired man, whom I recognized as Nick Sarkis, held a gun in his left hand pointed toward me and yelled, "You slut! Did you think I didn't know what you were doing? I trusted you!" His face screwed into an angry frown as he waved the weapon.

"Nick! Stop! Are you crazy?" Zoe's voice yelled.

From the right, Zoe ran in, dashing between my point of view and Nick just as he fired the weapon. Someone screamed as Zoe lurched forward and froze for a moment or two until her eyes widened in shock. Her knees folded and she slumped to the floor as blood pooled out from under her.

Face grim, Nick stepped over her as he rushed toward the earring wearer and grabbed for her. I could see his face, a scowl distorting his mouth, as if he was right in front of me. Fear shot through me.

Abruptly, the vision shifted and blurred as the room seemed to tumble upside down.

I dropped the earring on the bed. Shit! That was the moment Nick had killed his wife and the earring must have been Saffi's. That was from her point of view. Was Nick going to kill her rather than Zoe? Or did he intend to kill both of them? He'd grabbed Saffi as she started to back up, I was sure.

If he hit her and she fell, maybe they struggled and the ruby popped out of her ear to fall to the floor where I found it.

My hands trembled as I slid the stud into the pouch without touching it again. With Astrid's help, I might learn more from it. For now, I didn't want to revisit that scene. I'd felt the fear and the wave of Nick's anger in the room. I'd also heard him talking and the screams. Previously, I hadn't had any audio with object visions.

Returning the object to the larger bag in the drawer, I sat on the bed with my knees pulled up to my chin to think. I needed to talk to Zoe about the files I had found. I wanted to know what she knew about them. The key to this whole mystery had to be in those boxes.

Going downstairs, I popped open a cold soda and headed for my music room. If nothing else, writing or even practicing would take my mind off the two events that had disturbed my day.

Much later, I grabbed the folder with the letter and drove to the post office in the south of Reno to mail it. As I drove up to the mailboxes on the curb, I realized I hadn't brought my gloves.

Annoyed with myself, I opened the folder and half-shoved it into the slot while shaking it to get the envelope to slide out.

Nerves on edge, I looked around the area to make sure no one saw this strange display. It could have been interpreted as a terrorist act if it looked like I was dumping something into the box. The area was quiet. No one in sight and no cars moving on the side street. Relief washed over me. At least, that was one thing I had accomplished today.

Fourteen

I'd just finished up with my last dog when my phone rang. I pulled it out to see Gayle's name on the screen. What did she want now? I pushed answer and propped it between my shoulder and chin, not as easy to do with a mobile phone as with the old desk models, and talked to her as I put the newly groomed Shih Tzu in his cage.

"What's up?" I asked as she identified herself as if I didn't know.

"I'm following up on our conversation from Saturday night. Have you thought –"

The phone slid from under my chin as I secured the cage door, and I didn't hear the rest. I grabbed for it, missed, and winced as it tumbled to the floor. That probably gave her an earful. I picked it up and said, "Sorry, the phone slipped. What'd you say?"

After a long pause, she replied, "I..uh... just asked if you'd made a decision about doing the interview."

"Oh, that. No, I haven't had time to really think about it. I'd like to take my time to consider the pros and cons, you know. I'll call you by Friday, okay?"

"I had hoped for sooner, but I guess it will have to do." Her voice reflected her annoyance with my lack of commitment.

Too bad. I wanted to talk to Janna and the guys about this before I made a decision. After the conversation, if you could call it that, with Zac, I wasn't sure it was a good idea at all.

As I ended the call, I noted the time on my phone and called out to my boss. "Heeni, I need to leave now. I have an appointment in twenty minutes. Ming is done and waiting for pick up."

"Gotcha." Across the room, she clipped a shaggy-looking poodle mix and raised her head for a moment. She waved her free hand to indicate go and I didn't hesitate.

I arrived at Madame Astrid's with two minutes to spare. I grabbed the small bag I'd put the items in from my excursion to Zoe's, and trotted up the sidewalk to the house. Stepping inside, I saw that she was waiting for me.

She shuffled a deck of Tarot cards. Not the way you'd shuffle playing cards, but with the process of splitting the deck, then gradually working the cards into the opposite stack with gentle persuasion. She claimed it picked up the vibes from the person better although how she could shuffle the cards for me and still get an accurate reading eluded me.

I hurried to the chair on her right and sat down, watching as she finished the shuffle. She held the deck out to me and I cut it. She put it together again, and we repeated the split and assemble process two more times before she told me to draw a card from anywhere in the deck. I dug for the middle and pulled out a card.

"Put the card face-down in front of you," she ordered.

I did and waited as she put a card on top of it, one above, and another below. As she placed the cards, she told me the positions.

"This is called the Celtic Cross layout and it's been used for many years. This card covers yours; this one is above it and this one below. This card is the past and this is the future."

She placed another four cards in a line alongside the cross she'd made. Then, she studied the various cards, holding her hands just above them as if they might emanate impressions. I had to believe that she did it more for show than to gain any insight that wouldn't come to her by looking at them.

While she communed with the cards, I peered at them, trying to see if I could get any clues. Only two faced me while the rest faced Astrid. One upright to me was a crumbling tower in a storm. It didn't look promising, yet I knew from Janna that the cards could be interpreted several ways.

At last, Astrid seemed ready as she reached to the middle cards, shifting the one that covered my card out of the way, and flipped it over to reveal the one I'd chosen—the Ace of Cups. She bobbed her head in agreement. "This is good. It represents you, a creative person with talent who is still growing. Covering you is what challenges you now."

That card was the eight of swords. "This means you feel inadequate to the task before you. You fear you don't have skills or the talent to do it." Astrid tapped the card below that one. "This has what has just passed, the four of wands, which represents your home and safety. Something has threatened your home. Above you is what you hope for in the outcome."

The Sun was in that position and I knew it meant a good ending. "Success and happiness," I said. "The resolution of all this chaos."

"Good. Now this one..." she pointed to the card on my right, "...is the immediate future and the moon upside down means you might have difficulties in accepting or distinguishing what is real. If you stray from the path set before you, the images you see may not be as you perceive them."

What the heck did that mean? I wanted to ask, but I hesitated to interrupt Astrid at this point. The card on the opposite side was my distant past, and that was a three of swords.

Astrid made a tic-tic noise with her tongue and frowned.

"What?"

"This card shows heartbreak and betrayal. You've been disappointed and hurt by someone you trusted, someone who was very close to you. Family..."

My emotions must have shown on my face as I thought about my parents. My father had betrayed me by leaving when I was still young. My mother waited until I started college before she took off. Lives to live, they said. I had been a block in their respective roads. Yes, heartbreak and betrayal.

She moved her finger to the bottom card of the line of four, an eight of swords. "This represents factors affecting the situation. You feel powerless, defeated, and overwhelmed. But the next card is outside influences and here I see help."

That card was the knight of wands. She continued, "This is someone strong and passionate with a sense of adventure and daring. This person will aid you."

Gavin, I thought at once. She described Gavin to a T.

"There's something else I sense about this card; I don't know quite what it is. It seems almost random." Her brow wrinkled as she tried to reach for it. Frowning, she shook her head as if tossing the stray thought away and went on to one of the two cards I dreaded in the layout. Death.

"Your hopes and fears rest in this spot. This isn't a bad card, dearie. It represents transformation. Things aren't always what they seem and what you think is bad may turn out to be wonderful."

Her eyes moved to the last card, the Tower, upside down, and her mouth set into a grim line. "Because of your fears, you think this could be the possible outcome. Destruction, a dark enemy rising against you. It doesn't necessarily mean it will come to pass. You are aware and that is a positive part."

"Well, it sure doesn't look good," I said, gazing forlornly at the spread. "To me, it looks like a battle brewing and I'm at the center." On an impulse I picked up the Tower card and gazed at it, willing it to tell me more, to be more specific.

"There is some good news in it, Gillian. The cards are confirming that Gavin is your mentor. Have you talked to him about it?" She replaced the rest of the cards in the deck, allowing me to hold onto the Tower for the moment, and she shuffled them again before she set them to her left side.

"Not quite. I found out a little more about him, although he's not telling me everything. He admits he's seen the shades. Only briefly in their dark form, he says, then they assume human forms."

"Interesting." Her eyes narrowed as she thought about it and I wondered if she was consulting with her spirit guide. "Even though he knows what they are, he doesn't appear to be able to see that form well, but he sees what most people see when one shows up on this plane... a human form."

"Oh. Maybe I wouldn't see one on Earth either," I said. "Although I saw them from the ring when Gavin didn't see them that way." To my thinking that was odd and I wondered about it. "But there's more. I had a dream Sunday morning with Zac, my guide."

I had Astrid's entire attention at that. As I told her about the dream and what Zac had said, she listened intently, eyes growing wider as I related his comments about the True Shades and what they were. I had the feeling this was news to her.

When I'd finished, she looked at the notes she'd made of the reading again and circled a few words. "This explains some of the vagueness of the reading. The dark enemy and destruction must relate to these True Shades. I thought that the shades couldn't possibly create as much chaos as this was suggesting, but if these other ones are as Zac says, this is something entirely different."

She paused to take a breath and think, her fingers tapping on the table in a staccato beat with a pause between each set of taps. "When I talked to Elias, he told me that the shades seemed to be on the rise and more aggressive than they usually are. From the other side, souls can get a glimpse of what is happening in the transitory zone. They're seeing more souls lingering behind and giving in to the shades. In spite of that, they haven't been lost."

"Are they sure?" I studied the Tower card still in my hand and a sense of dread filled me. "What would happen if a True Shade took a soul completely?"

"From Zac's implication, it sounds like they could be reborn on Earth with all the negative aspects of the shade dimension unless the captured soul is strong enough to fight it." She cast an intense, wide-eyed gaze my way that penetrated to my core and I shivered.

"It's like Armageddon," I whispered.

"Yes. It may well be." An eerie tone tainted her usually rich voice.

My mouth felt dry and I rose to get a bottle of water. I twisted the top off and drank deeply. My thoughts racing, I paced back and forth. "Are we expected to stop it? You, me, Gavin, a spirit guide, and maybe an angel? I can't even count on Zac!"

Astrid pursed her lips and her eyes looked sad. "Honey, I don't know if I will even be any help in whatever is to come. If I can, I am here. And yes, Elias is with us also.

"I think you need to make that connection with Gavin as soon as possible. Waste no more time in doing it. You need to establish the mentorship and learn everything you can in order to prepare."

My heart sank. I didn't want to be in the middle of this. How the hell did I get selected for this? A pure spirit, wasn't that what Zac called me? Like hell, I was.

"I'm sorry, Gillian. This is a lot to put on your shoulders." She shifted her eyes to the table where they focused on another card, the Jack of Cups sat on top of the shuffled deck. She brightened a little.

"However, my dear, I do sense that you have another ally around you. Perhaps someone you've known for a while?"

I stared at her and thought about Ferris and Digby. "Perhaps. I've put off telling my bandmates about this whole paranormal thing. I figured it would be too freaky for them. They know something is amiss and they've been pushing me to tell them. I want to do it. I just haven't been sure it's the right time."

Astrid took a deep breath, closed her eyes and concentrated while she mumbled a chant or a prayer under her breath. I couldn't make out the words and they sounded foreign. Eye still shut, she reached a hand to the Tarot deck and extracted a card somewhere from the middle of them.

Opening her eyes, she glanced at the card—the reversed five of cups—and nodded in satisfaction. "Yes. You should tell them. This card is a good omen for allies. They will support you even if they can't actually fight alongside you."

I blinked. "Why can't they fight with me? Won't they be able to see the shades or learn how to dispel them?"

In a patient voice, she explained, "The odds are you will be battling them on the spirit plane. Although they can't go there, they can guard your body while you're not in it."

"What?! Now, that sounds really twisted." Jumping to my feet, I spun away and paced back to the other end of the room. "I can't fight these things, especially not the True Shades."

"You can or you would not have been selected." Her voice carried conviction as she motioned for me to return to the table.

I sat, dropping my head on my arms on the table. My temples pounded as I considered all this. Barely lifting my eyes to look at her, I asked, "What about Gavin? Is he going to be able to help me?"

She shrugged. "You'll have to ask him, my dear. Only he can tell you if he can step into the transitional plane."

"Great." I sighed. "All this makes the real reason I wanted to talk to you today seem insignificant."

Her eyebrows rose in question. "What is that?"

"Zoe's murder. The simple task I have compared to what is dumping on me now. I located some personal items and I want to try psychometry on each of them. I hoped you could help me to get a clearer or more extensive reading from them."

I reached for the cloth bag I'd brought with me, set it on the table, and started to open it.

"Wait a moment. You are the one who has the gift. You can read those objects without any help. If they have something to show you, they will."

I had stopped fumbling with the bag when she'd said to wait, but my right hand still rested on the side. "I tried to read Zoe's hairbrush and I got nothing. An earring showed me a partial scene, just a little. How can I trigger them to show me everything? I hoped you could boost my power somehow."

Her eyes narrowed. "They aren't recorders, Gillian. It takes a large charge of emotion to imprint a memory into an object. You're only going to get a snippet or two. Sometimes it may last thirty seconds and other times, it may only be a few seconds. Your mind needs to be receptive and ready to take in everything the object will show you."

I thought about Gavin's ring and how much I'd seen from it. The long sequence when he was running must have been fueled by his fear or anxiety. But the others seemed pleasant, not too emotionally charged. Or maybe the kind of contentment the wearers got in the garden were strong emotions. "But Gavin's ring had several..."

Astrid's eyes almost crossed in her exasperation. "It's a very old ring. Think of how many hands might have handled it and how many emotions might have charged it. A ring is a powerful talisman. You can't compare these simple objects to the ring."

Scooting her chair back, she rose and walked to the shelf on the other side of the door where she kept her herbs, incense, candles, and other items. She picked up a packet of herbs, brought it back, and slid it across the table to me.

"These herbs will soothe your mind and open it to the images you'll receive. Put a pinch in a small bowl of warm water, stir them around with your finger—not a metal utensil—and breathe in the scent. When you feel relaxed, read an object. Only do one at a time and meditate on it before you touch it. If it has something to reveal, you will see it."

I nodded. "Okay. I got it. Thank you."

I started to pay her for the herbs except she waved it off. "My contribution to the cause," she said.

I hesitated to bring the last thing up; nonetheless, I wanted her opinion as well. "A television reporter has been bothering me to do an interview. She thinks the girl who sings at funerals is a novel, human-interest piece. My gut feeling is no, but–"

"Absolutely not! Do not call any extra attention to your gift. You do not need to become a beacon for any shades." Her face was as stern-looking as I'd ever seen it.

"You're right. Thank you."

As I rose to go, Astrid added one more thing. "Remember to use your protection spells. Whether you are visiting the transitional plane or are in your home, set the spells."

A pang of guilt shot through me. I didn't do them consistently. I needed to make it a habit.

After I pulled the Jeep into the driveway, I paused to call Janna before going in. I hadn't talked to her since our escapade and I wanted to bounce the Trumbull thing off her, although recent events had pretty much sealed it for me.

"Hey! There you are," she said when she answered. "What's up?"

"Just got back from Madame Astrid's and got some good advice, but I wanted to run something past you." I explained the offer from Gayle and asked her what she thought. I didn't add any opinions to it, just laid it out.

"Nope, Gilly. The woman turns things to suit her story and make her look like Ms. Super-journalist. She could mess up your life completely if she learns any of the real story. Don't do it."

"Got it. Pretty much what I think also."

"I'm on the desk here, so I'll get more details tomorrow, okay?" Janna spoke quickly and I figured she was pretty busy. If she was working the check-in desk, the hotel probably had a full load of tourists checking in.

"See you in the morning." I thumbed the phone off and got out, my bag of artifacts and the herbs clutched in my other hand.

Nygard greeted me with a concerned-sounding meow, a little louder and harsher than his usual tone. Maybe his food dish was empty, although I was sure I'd checked it before I left. Putting my things down, I turned toward the kitchen and, as I walked, the cat threaded himself through my feet the whole way.

"What are you doing?" I asked, afraid I was going to either step on him or trip over him. Once I got to the archway, I saw that his dry food dish still had food and the water bowl looked fine.

Maybe he wanted more moist food. I pulled out the can I'd opened earlier and put a tablespoon full onto his plate. I put it down, watched as he ran over and sniffed it. His head came up and he stared at me again, his slightly-crossed blue eyes seemed to be trying to tell me something. Tail twitching, he darted out of the kitchen toward the staircase.

What the heck? I followed him upstairs. As soon as I hit the top step, a cold, heavy feeling hit me. Nygard stood a few feet ahead with his back arched and hissed. Something was wrong. Heart pounding, I stepped onto the landing and gazed toward my bed area as I did a quick inventory. It didn't look disturbed. Still, I felt something not right and an odor similar to eggs wafted to my nose.

Nygard hissed again before he darted toward the bed and skidded under it. I heard his disturbed mrrow as his feet slapped at the floor.

Turning to my bedside table, I unlocked the drawer and opened it to pull out my gun. Hand shaking with nerves, I loaded it while I glanced nervously down the walkway toward the bathroom. With one side open to the staircase and the downstairs area, the loft had easy access from below and I never felt its open vulnerability as keenly as I did now.

I began muttering a protection spell for the house and its occupants as I snapped the magazine in the gun. The very spell Astrid warned me about and I hadn't been doing. I'd left the house wide open to danger.

My mouth felt dry as I eased my way to the bath. Although I didn't see anyone, it seemed too dark at that end. Putting the bathroom wall to my back, I spun into the entrance and pointed the gun toward every corner of the room in my best imitation of a television cop.

Nothing.

I stepped in and looked around, sliding the shower curtain aside and peering behind the door. All clear here, I thought and turned back toward the door and...

I shrieked in shock and fear.

A shade hovered right in front of me, human-shaped with unfathomable red eyes staring at me. Or into me. I felt like it peered into my soul, looking for weaknesses and things to exploit. It felt evil.

I stepped back and pointed my gun toward it as if it would do any good.

The smoky-looking blob emitted an eerie noise that sounded like a fast-speed human laugh.

I blurted out the protection spell as I thrust my left hand out, fingers spread wide to direct any magic I might be able to conjure to force the shade back.

It floated forward, moving without any sound, and continued to stare at me.

We have found you. Now, we can move forward.

It didn't actually speak, but the words formed in my mind, voiceless.

Then it disappeared, vanishing in an instant.

Knees going weak, I spun back to the bathroom. I needed it now.

Fifteen

"It was right there in my home, Janna. My house! Threatening me. When it looked at me, it felt like the creature oozed inside me."

I had talked almost non-stop since my friend had arrived for our Tuesday morning run at Virginia Lake. We'd covered half the lake when we'd paused for a break and I'd continued with my raving.

Janna nodded her understanding and a concerned look showed in her eyes. "I'm sorry this is happening to you, Gilly, but you need to get a handle on it. Have you called Madame Astrid?"

"Not yet. I'll call her later this morning. Honestly, I was a nervous wreck last night. I went through all the spells in the little book she gave me and performed any of them that I thought remotely hinted at giving protection. The house stinks from the mixed herb smell and candles. Problem is I don't know if any of them really work or if I even did them right."

I felt exhausted. If I'd slept at all, it had been in fits and starts. Knowing a shade had materialized in my house scared me more than I could put in words. Not knowing when another might come left me afraid to fall asleep. How did it get here? Was it like the ones that had pursued Gavin? Except those were True Shades—I was certain of it. Not the one in the bedroom. It appeared about the size of a human, like the ones I'd seen in the ethereal cemetery.

Janna twisted her upper body as she loosened her muscles. "Do you want to stay with me for a while until this is settled?"

I hesitated. While I would love to take up her offer, I feared the shade might be able to follow me, which would put Janna in danger. She misread my slow response.

"You can bring Nygard if that's what you're worried about."

"No, that's not it. Janna. As appealing as it sounds to spend a few days at your place, it might not be a good idea. I don't know how the shade found my home or if it's able to track me. I don't want it to find you."

She paused mid-twist and frowned. "Uh, do you think it followed you here?" She scanned the area, looking for any dark spots. "Like that black blob in the bushes over there."

She pointed to a thick hedge of japonicas that looked dark in the shadow of a tree in front of it.

"Shadow. The shades are much darker and they undulate, a little like a wave of water. Besides, you probably can't see them. If anything, they would look like a regular person."

"Oh. Well, that's no help, is it?" She turned and pointed back down the path we'd come up from the car park. "I need to get going. I have an early interview this morning. Want to come back with me?"

That interview came up without warning. I couldn't blame her for being nervous. I was. "No, you go on back, I'm going to jog a little more. Talk to you later."

"Yeah, let me know what Madame says, okay?"

I watched her run down the path, her speed faster than we usually did. I hoped I was worrying about her for no reason and the shades wouldn't include her in whatever dark plans they had. I'd practically screamed for Zac to make an appearance and give me some guidance before I'd left home. So far, no help came from that quarter either.

I finished my run and hurried home to shower and dress for work. On an impulse, I called Gavin. He picked up right away, which surprised me.

"Listen, I have something that I need to tell you about and I was wondering if we could meet tonight? It's really urgent." I hoped I didn't sound too pushy or too alarming.

"Good or bad?" he asked.

"Kind of on the bad side. I need to explain it though. It has to do with shades."

"Not the window variety, I assume?" His voice had grown serious and he spoke lower. "Gillian, what are you involved in?"

"I'll tell you everything when I see you." My voice almost broke with the fearful emotion I suddenly felt. I spun around expecting to find a shade behind me. But nothing was there. No dark spots even, just my nerves.

"Tonight. Say about six at my place?"

"I'll be there. Thanks, Prof." My body relaxed in relief and I dropped to the sofa before my knees gave out. The running was supposed to relieve the stress.

After a few more moments, I got up, picked up my things, put down food for Nygard, and instructed him to watch the house until I got home. Pausing at the door, I chanted one more protection charm before I left for work.

Our workload seemed a little light today as I came in. Only a few dogs in cages waited to be groomed. I picked up the shaggy gray, mixed-poodle pup and headed back to my station as I called out, "'Morning, Heeni. Do we have more dogs coming in later today?"

"Only a couple more appointments that haven't been dropped off yet. Unless we get a last minute call, this is it."

Cool. While it meant a little less money today, it also allowed me to leave work early and maybe get a nap in before I saw Gavin or try to read one or two of the objects I'd picked up. I hummed as I worked; it seemed to calm the dogs.

From across the room, Heeni called out. "Hey, Gillian. Did you see this?"

"See what?" I looked up to the flat screen TV on the wall and there was Gayle Trumbull yakking about something.

I moved closer and caught her words.

"...people I talked to have attended funerals where this young woman sang for the deceased. They all report that while she sang familiar melodies, the words had been changed to reflect the highlights and good qualities of the person's life. One even said that it sounded as if she knew them. While I would love to give you the singer's name, she has declined my requests for an interview and the chance to give you more insight on how she does this."

From under her dark bangs, Heeni's eyes grew wider as they rose toward me. "Is she talking about you? Do you do that when you sing at these funerals?"

I must have looked stricken as I stood there with my mouth gaping open. Dumfounded, I couldn't get any words to come out. *Oh. My. God. The bitch did it! She didn't wait for me to tell her no.*

"I told you not to do those," Heeni said, her voice yanking me back. "I told you it wasn't good for your career."

"I know, Heeni. I didn't give this woman permission to say anything. She went around me. At least, she didn't use my name, but anyone who knows me can put two and two together. This is a nightmare."

I turned and ran to the bathroom. Privacy, I needed a few moments to pull myself together. I turned on the faucet and splashed water all over my face. Ferris, Digby, Mark— If any of them heard this, they'd know it was me. Even Gavin. I hadn't told him about this aspect of my ability yet. I'd bet that Moss would be on it and maybe feel the pressure since he knew what I did. At least, Trumbull didn't have the whole story. Thank heavens. Would she keep at it until she did?

While only a select few people knew about the ethereal cemetery, anyone who'd been to any of the funerals knew that I looked spaced out when I sang those unique songs. Probably, they had told Trumbull about that while they were blabbing.

I swallowed a handful of water and splashed my face again. Taking my time, I dried off, took several deep breaths, and composed myself.

"Are you okay?" Heeni asked when I came back out.

I nodded. "I think so. It's just... unexpected. Let's get these dogs done."

I finished grooming my dogs in record time and left the shop by one-thirty with a plan in mind. Since I had the meeting with Gavin planned, I would tell him everything. Now, I really needed to talk to Ferris and Digby as soon as I could. I started to call Ferris when my phone rang. The number was Digby's.

"Hi, Dig—what's up?" I tried to sound nonchalant although my heart was pounding as I opened the Jeep's door.

"I saw something earlier today I wanted to ask you about. Those funerals that you've been singing for... Are you the only singer in town doing them?"

"Maybe. I don't know if anyone else does them." I entertained the notion I could avoid the issue until I could see him in person.

"Ah. Well, there's some news story that the reporter lady you were talking to over the weekend aired today. I just happened to catch it when I took my car in for servicing. Since you talked to her, I just wondered."

"You know, I want to talk to you and Ferris about that whole thing. But not over the phone. Can you meet me at my place about four?"

He barely hesitated. "Yeah. I'll be there. I'm assuming she is referring to you."

"I'll explain when you come over." I ended the call and dialed Ferris.

He hadn't heard the broadcast so I skimmed over it and just asked him to meet me at four. At this long pause as he probably tried to figure if he could, I added that it was important.

"Yah. Okay," he agreed and I sighed as I disconnected.

Two down. Maybe Mark hadn't heard anything about it. Probably he was working and not watching television. No one would be likely to mention it to him unless he had said something about his girlfriend singing at funerals.

As I thought about it, I grew furious again and my hands clenched the steering wheel with the urge to choke Gayle. I wanted to call her and tell her off, but a more sane part of my brain told me not to do it. It would only backfire if I did. I needed to think calmly and rationally when I confronted her.

The bag with my scrounged items sat on the passenger seat and I had an epiphany. Instead of going home, I decided to visit Zoe again. With luck, she might be able to enhance or add to any visions I might get from them if I tried to read them in her presence. To be honest, I wasn't sure how it would work, but I had a plan.

The parking area near Zoe's section was nearly empty and I didn't notice anyone in the vicinity of her grave as I approached it. Feeling more secure, I knelt in front of her marker and pulled out the object I thought might be the most likely to trigger a memory; the necklace with the Z pendant on it. I held it between my hands and focused, seeking any energy from it. Closing my eyes, I began to hum a bit of "Dante's Prayer". Why that song, I don't know, except it was what had popped into my mind at the time.

I slipped into the vision, arriving in a misty fog. I turned to look around me, marveling at this different aspect of the cemetery. The landmarks that rose above the mist appeared the same even though I'd not seen it like this before. I could see no sign of Zoe, so I called her name, hoping to draw her to me. I felt the necklace between my fingers and I looked down to see that even here, a representation of it sat in my hands.

I waited a short time before calling her again. Beginning to think she wouldn't show, I started walking along the silver path, and without warning, she appeared several yards away. Still as disheveled as she had been from the beginning of this, she ambled in my direction, unhurried and, apparently, oblivious to my presence.

When she almost reached me, I repeated her name and her head came up as if I'd startled her.

"Well, it's the not-an-angel girl again. Have you found out anything?"

"Maybe. I don't have anything specific yet. I did get a few items from your house and it occurred to me that you could help me read these better than I could on my own. Want to give it a try?"

Her dark eyes looked wary and somewhat confused. "What do you want me to do?"

"I've got this necklace in my hand in reality." I held up the illusionary chain with the Z dangling at the end. "I figured it might have some memories attached to it and you could help me draw them out. When did you first get it?"

"Eight years ago, on a trip to Greece with my parents." She didn't hesitate with that.

I felt a stab of disappointment. Not a gift from Nick, so it probably wouldn't help me with my quest. As I folded my hands back over it, a sudden vision popped into the area near us. In some ways, it was similar to what I had seen at Shiloh when I'd read the button with the memory appearing before me and not in my mind.

An almost black sand beach led to a sapphire blue ocean where white frothy waves rose and broke gently against the sand. Planted a few yards from the shoreline, a single beach umbrella and a pair of yellow and green striped towels were the sole spoilers on the beach. Not too much farther down the beach, a huge, black stone outcropping of rock straddled the sand and the ocean.

"Tenerife," Zoe said in a soft breath. "The beach is El Bollullo, a favorite place of Nick's. We went there on our honeymoon."

As if cued, a dark-haired man, wearing a skimpy, dark-blue bathing suit that displayed his trim physique well, ran into the image. I felt a moment of orientation adjustment as the vision shifted toward him. We were seeing this from Zoe's viewpoint. In the background, a short pier with a small boat tied to it thrust into the water. A handsome man, Nick looked fit and happy as he handed a bottled drink of some sort to Zoe. His eyes sparkled as he laughed with her.

"What happened that day that this memory impressed on your necklace?"

She shrugged. "It was the happiest day of my life to that point. I'd married the man I loved, and we were at one of the most beautiful places on Earth on a nearly private beach. We made love in the sand and washed off in the ocean with no one around to see us. We made plans for our life together and everything was perfect. It was a moment when my body and spirit radiated my joy."

"You weren't wearing it the night you died." I should have concluded that sooner. If she had been, it would have been around her neck and part of the police evidence instead of lying in the drawer.

She shook her head. "No. I didn't normally wear it to bed or when I was making love. In fact, I hadn't worn it much in the past year."

"So, that's likely to be the only image attached to this item." I closed my hands over it again, feeling the actual metal in my hands as my physical body complied.

"Probably. Although..." She paused to think and I waited, wondering what she might have from it. Then I saw it.

Projected the same way, I saw an angry Nick yelling at Zoe. They were dressed in evening clothes. He wore a dark suit with the tie loosened and hanging under the collar. I saw Zoe's image in a mirror as she removed a short burgundy-colored bolero top to reveal a matching evening gown that hugged her figure and flowed out from her knees. The Z of her necklace reflected in the glass, almost lost as it peeked out from under a blood garnet necklace. Nick spun her around to face him and he shouted. "You bitch! You could have cost me thousands of dollars tonight. I should—"

"Should what?" Zoe shouted back. "Leave me? Divorce me? Which threat is it this time? I'm always a disappointment to you, Nick."

Abruptly, he swung his arm around and his fist connected with Zoe's face. She stumbled; the image dipped, and she crashed toward the glass, shattering the mirror.

The image seemed to break apart at the same time. I turned my eyes back to the spirit standing near me, her eyes still watching the empty space. "Zoe? Are you okay?"

Her voice rasped as she answered, shifting her eyes to face me. "No. I am not all right. But I will be as soon as he is caught. He took me to boring business dinners and expected me to mingle and be charming to his potential clients and some of them were scum. I told one off that night and it didn't go well."

"What didn't you divorce him?"

Her lips tightened and she looked away from me. "My money was tied up in his business as well. If I left him, I'd lose everything my father had given me. Nick would rather kill me than let me leave, as you can see."

"Was that why he murdered you? You threatened his business."

She kicked at a small rock on the ground and hugged herself as if she'd felt a sudden chill. "Maybe. He and I had ceased to be a couple. We no longer slept together and he was angry that I'd found comfort in a relationship with a woman. I guess it threatened him and his business. I'm tired now."

On those words, she vanished, her spirit going wherever they went while they waited to move on. She wasn't the only one who felt tired.

The light had begun to diminish in the graveyard and the mist grew heavier. I felt something else as I turned to look around. Two *of them hovered on my side of the hedge line.*

Shades.

Not the big True Shades, rather the more human-shaped creatures.

"Stay away from me." *I stumbled back away from them.*

One of them seemed to ripple, the black shadows undulating as if it laughed at me.

Soon, Gillian Foster. It will come soon.

The words echoed in my head, weird sounds that weren't a voice, but the intent came through clearly enough. I yelled out a protection charm and willed myself back to my body.

Sixteen

Gasping, I caught my breath and dropped Zoe's necklace on the ground as I lurched forward. Still on my knees, I caught myself with my hands before I sprawled on top of her grave. Shivers of fear coursed through my body as I processed the threat in my mind. What would come soon? Was it to me, personally, or did it encompass much more?

I willed my fumbling fingers to pick up the chain and put it back into the bag I'd brought with me. I couldn't do any more readings now and Zoe wouldn't be there to help me out even if I had the guts to go back. One more thing to discuss with Gavin.

Hurrying back to the Beast, I flung myself in the driver's seat and slammed the door. I no longer discounted the shades being able to follow me in the real world. The one at my home had disproved that theory already.

More time had passed than I'd realized and I rushed to get back to my place before Ferris and Digby arrived. I didn't see either of their cars parked out front, so I zipped into my driveway and hurried into the house.

I paused as soon as I crossed the threshold, my senses on high alert. Everything seemed normal as I called for Nygard. Relief flowed as he came down the stairs roawing out his greeting. If he didn't sense anything, I felt the house was secure. I scooped him up, hugging him as I went to the kitchen. I found a piece of leftover salmon in the 'fridge and fed it to him before I set about performing another protection spell.

I preferred the lavender scent to some of the other ones. According to the description of its properties, it seemed to be as effective as the stinkier herbs. That done, I changed clothes to something less adorned with dog hair and sat down on the sofa with a pad and pencil to make notes on what I wanted to say to the guys. Just bullet points, they started with the accident, the cemetery, and so on until we reached the shades. The list for Gavin was almost identical except for expounding on the shades and their threats.

"I come bearing libation," Digby called out as he stepped through the door. He carried a six-pack of Victoria Bitter, an Australian brew that one of the local liquor stores imported. I think he talked them into it when he arrived in Reno 'cause it has always been his favorite beer choice.

He took the pack to the 'fridge after extracting a bottle and joined me in my petite living room, folding his tall frame into the arm chair. "So, what's got your knickers riding high?"

I chuckled a little, loving how he liked to cut right to the chase. "Let's wait until Ferris gets here. How did we do on album sales on Saturday?" He'd kept the tally and the money as it came in, and I hadn't gotten back to him for the final total.

"Really good. We sold almost all the ones we had with us, so two-hundred-forty-seven of them. I gave a copy to a local radio station that hadn't received a promo one. I think we autographed about half of them. You did fewer than that."

"Yeah, I'm sorry about that. The whole thing kind of blew up on Saturday night with that woman being there and other stuff. But the sales were fantastic. More than I expected."

"*Stuff* seems to be butting its head in more often this past year." He sipped his beer and raised an inquisitive eyebrow.

I retreated to the kitchen and poured a glass of white wine, taking my time to kill as many minutes as possible while waiting for Ferris. I hoped to avoid being pulled into discussing this with just Digby.

"Grab a beer for Ferry while you're in there," he called, well aware I was stalling.

I heard the car door slam about the same time and figured Ferris had arrived. Complying with the request, I grabbed one of the VBs, and went back to the living room at the same time Ferris opened the door.

After we got through the usual greeting and Ferris had moaned a bit about being late because of work, I cleared my throat to get their attention. I pulled out my notes and started the short version of my story. "I have something to tell you that is lengthy, complicated, and sounds like a fantasy. Please hear me out before you begin asking questions, okay?"

Ferris' brows drew closer together as he gave me his full attention. Digby leaned back, ready to listen, his eyes reflecting his curiosity with a questioning look.

"You recall that almost a year ago I fell on the ice and banged my head. Afterward, I started having some odd dreams about a beautiful park that I'd never seen. Eventually, this dream morphed into a cemetery instead of a park."

I caught the frown that formed on Ferris' forehead and the straight, tight lips. I hurried on. "Not long later, I got a phone call asking me to sing at a funeral. This is the part that you aren't familiar with and it sounds pretty weird. When I sang, my spirit left my body, transporting me to this dream cemetery, only it wasn't a dream. The person I sang for, a man who had died with Alzheimer's, waited there and he appeared to be confused. I still sang for him, but words appeared before me and I started reciting all the good things he'd done in his life, incorporating them into my song. I led him along a silver path to an opening in the surrounding wall and showed him the gate beyond where he would go to the next plane. As we walked, he grew younger, his memory returned, and he went through."

I could see the question forming on Digby's mouth and I held up my right hand. "Wait. Questions later."

I went on to tell them everything that had happened, how I'd dreamed an angel or a spirit guide named Zac, who offered me advice, and how I'd been guided by another spirit. I even told them I'd been to a doctor about it and I checked out fine. "The only explanation I have is that I have activated this extra-sensory ability to do this and to talk to the dead. And this has created additional problems."

Next, I explained about Marielle and my task to try to find her killer that led me to being abducted by her killer. Piece by piece, the story of the past year poured out of me as my two friends listened in complete disbelief. Finally, I got to the problem with Gayle Trumbull and the fear she might find out the whole story about the funerals and my strange ability.

"I've even been afraid to tell the two of you," I admitted. "I don't want you to think I'm crazy because this is really happening to me." My voice broke a bit and both of them stared at me in stunned silence.

Finally, Digby got to his feet, swirled his empty bottle around, glanced at Ferris, and said, "I could use another of these. How 'bout you, mate?"

Ferris nodded, leaning forward as Digby went to the kitchen. "All this has been going on for the past eleven months and you felt you couldn't tell us?"

I shifted uncomfortably and gazed at the carpet, not even able to look him in the eye.

"But you did tell Janna?"

"Yes. She believes in this stuff, so I figured she could explain it. Turns out, it even freaks her out some." I forced my head to come up to get a look at his face. His mouth was a straight line and his brow dropped down in a serious, unreadable expression. At least, he wasn't laughing at me.

Digby passed between us, handed Ferris a bottle, and dropped into the chair again. "It's a lot to take in, babe. Speakin' just for myself, I am stung that you didn't say anything about it until now."

"I was afraid." My voice squeaked, and I cleared my throat. "I thought you would think I'd taken a leap into the o-zone."

"Maybe we do." A big grin lit up his Aussie face as he spun his left middle finger in a circle around his head, like a crazy sign, then chuckled. "But you're our crazy girl and if you believe it is happening, who am I to say it isn't? I have an uncle who claims he talks to kangaroos and says they take him on spiritual journeys in the outback."

I narrowed my eyes at him, wondering if he was teasing me. He seemed perfectly serious.

"But you think I'm a little wacky?" A pang of disappointment touched my heart. I'd hoped they would believe me.

"Not wacky. As Dig said, if you believe, who are we to say differently? We shouldn't dispute it just 'cause we haven't seen it. Obviously, something is happening to you. If other people say you're writing unique lyrics about dead people you don't even know, I'd say something must be going on." Ferris flashed a supportive smile at me. "And talking to dead people, that's kinda cool. No matter how it's happening for you, it seems like you're drawing information from an otherworldly source. That being said, I am concerned about you trying to solve problems for the deceased. *That* has changed you."

I arched an eyebrow. Changed? I guess I had. "Maybe a little."

Ferris shot a glance at Digby before addressing me again. "You're getting stronger, slimmer, building up your body. You started taking self-defense classes. That wasn't something you would normally do. Dig and I figured you'd been really spooked by the abduction, but you never told us how bad that was. However, the bigger issue is that the music's been taking a back seat."

"No, not really," I started to object. Music was important to me; it was my greatest love.

"Not consciously, maybe, but you weren't totally into it a lot of the time like you had been. You were distracted and even getting the album together had become a tough process. There are a lot of little things."

Digby pointed at me with his bottle and added, "We were worried about your mental health after all that. After what you've told us now, I'm also concerned about your safety. It's like you've got this secret, supercharged life that is pulling you into danger. *That* worries me."

Ferris' head bobbed in agreement. "He said it. How can we help you? You're going places we can't go. So how can we support you?"

A glow spread through my spirit, lifting me with its warmth. I loved these guys. "True, you can't go where I am in the spiritual world. But you're here, anchoring me. I need that anchor and to know that I can turn to you for strength and advice."

Getting up, Ferris crossed to me and held out his arms to hug me. I jumped to my feet, flung my arms around his torso, and squeezed him, so grateful for this. As I pressed my face against his chest, his arms wrapped me in a cocoon of love and understanding. Oh, how I needed that. A few moments later, I felt the added weight and warmth of Digby adding his embrace to the mix.

"Thank you. Both of you," I murmured just loud enough for them to hear.

After that, I filled them in on the situation with Gayle Trumbull and the trouble she could cause for me. They gave me their complete support on it, telling me not to talk to her at all. Although I knew they'd stonewall her as well, I still had a feeling there would be more trouble to come from that front.

Thanking them again for being the staunch buddies they were, I ushered them to the front door, telling them I had a meeting with Gavin.

Ferris frowned. "You're not seeing him, are you? I mean, he's old enough to be your dad or uncle."

I shot an annoyed look at him. He had never liked Gavin. "Not that old. He's in his forties."

"The far end of them." Ferris' voice had a petulant tone like he was jealous or something.

"More mid," I snarked back at him. "Besides, this is all business. He's helping me with this spirit problem."

"What?" That got Digby's attention. "What does he know about it?"

"Quite a bit. Apparently, it turns out archeology is full of spiritual items and things that have power attached. And he knows about that." Okay, I exaggerated, but Gavin did have the knowledge and experience I needed.

"You told him?" Ferris groused, his eyes looking hurt.

"Only after I learned he knew about this stuff. Now, get going, so I can." I shooed them out the door and grabbed my purse. I paused, looking at the bag of found objects as I debated whether to take them. I decided against it and put them into a drawer in the side table. Murmuring a few more protective words, I headed out the door.

Just as I pulled up in front of Gavin's house, my phone rang; Janna calling. Thumbing it on, I said, "Hi, girlfriend. What's up?"

"What do you mean? I thought you would call me. Did you see that woman on TV? I mean, she was talking about you." She sounded excited.

"Yes, I saw her. And I'm trying to clean this up. I'm at Gavin's right now. I'll call you back later tonight, okay?"

I felt a twinge of guilt as I hung up. Although I had meant to phone her, I had decided talking to the guys and Gavin to be the bigger priority now.

I knocked on Gavin's door and he called out to come on in. The door was unlocked, something I had ceased doing these days. I stepped into the house and immediately detected the scent of an herb burning, something like licorice. Another aroma floated under it, something with garlic, oregano, and yeast. Pizza.

Gavin poked his head into the living room. "Hi. I didn't have time for dinner so I grabbed a pizza on the way home. You hungry? There's plenty for two."

"That sounds so good. I'd love a piece." I'd been so upset and nervous through most of the day that hadn't eaten anything since my yogurt at breakfast. I'd had coffee and soda, but those were temporary fill-ups. Even though I my nerves buzzed about telling Gavin my situation, my stomach, awakened by the delicious aromas, made its need for food clear now.

"So, what's the kind of burnt licorice smell in here?" I asked as I passed through the living room.

"I'm burning an anise candle." He'd brought the pizza to the kitchen table, a smaller and less formal one than the dining room. "Beer, soda, or –" He left it hanging.

"Soda. No, beer. I think I could use one after today."

He set a plate on the table for me and added a fork. Turning around, he pulled a salad out of the 'fridge while I sat at the indicated spot. He sat across from me and put the salad down.

As I loaded my plate with the good stuff and a large slice of the sausage and peppers pizza, I tried to recall all the bullet points on my list. Essentially the same as I'd gone over with Ferris and Digby, I did have a few additional things to discuss with Gavin as well as much more detail to add. I debated whether to bring any of it up while we were eating or to keep to idle chitchat. He solved that dilemma for me.

"You sounded upset on the phone and you needed to see me. What's happened?"

I took a big swallow of the beer. "I had my life blow up a bit today and I think you can help me. But it's a complicated story and I want to start at the beginning."

"Okay. It's your show." He waved his pizza slice in a motion to continue before he took a bite.

"About this time last year, I had a little accident, a slip on a patch of ice, and I hit my head." I proceeded to tell him the whole story, from small beginnings to the man with Alzheimer's.

Gavin stopped eating mid-way into the story and stared at me as if I was a strange creature, although I preferred to think of it as his intrigued expression. He set the pizza down and reached for his beer. "Go on."

I took a bite of my pizza, chewing it, and washing it down with another gulp of beer before I continued. I told him about the man regressing in age as his dementia disappeared as we drew closer along the silver path to the gate at the end. And I told him about the nothing beyond the gate except the light.

"So, do you think the light is the one to Heaven?"

"I don't know what to think, Gavin. I haven't been the biggest fan of God or any religion, but I have to question what I've seen. That man was only the first and I've sung for over a dozen funerals in the months since the accident. One thing I know is that where there's light, there's also dark. So maybe those inscriptions do tie in."

I told him about my dreams of the cemetery and the dark section with the tangled bushes, black roses, and thorns that I'd seen in one. And about the first, brief glimpses I'd gotten of the shades.

By this time, we had finished eating, popped open another round of beers, and moved to the living room with the more comfortable seating there. Gavin started up the fireplace and I filled him in on the special cases I'd had, the ones that involved me in their unfinished business, and the extra psychic abilities I'd discovered, such as psychometry and visions guided by the departed spirit. I even told him about Zac, something I'd not mentioned to my bandmates.

Gavin's right eyebrow lifted as I explained that I thought Zac was an angel, although he'd never confirmed it.

"I suppose he could be a spirit guide. Madame Astrid told me she had one, so maybe. But he looks like what I think an angel should."

"Madame Astrid? You're kidding." He laughed.

"Is there a problem there?" It seemed Gavin knew Astrid, but she hadn't mentioned that to me.

"No, probably not. She's just a little theatrical, but she does have a gift. Maybe you're seeing what you want to see. Even in your dreams, you might be controlling the vision. Have you ever seen Zac outside the dream state?"

I shook my head slowly as I thought about it. "No, I dreamed I saw him in my house and I thought I was awake, but I wasn't. So, you think I'm making it up?"

"I didn't say that, chica. I said you might be creating the illusion in your dream for that particular messenger. Our minds do odd things in dreams. How reliable is Zac? Does he respond to you?"

I chuckled derisively, "Not very. He is certainly not on-demand and there have been a few times that I've wanted him to show up and he hasn't. But sometimes, he does provide the answers I need and tells me other things. The shades seemed to surprise him when they showed up at Shiloh. And this last time, he told me something about your shades."

Gavin's eyes widened in surprise. "My shades? The ones from Syria?"

"Uh huh. He said they are True Shades – that's with caps. As if they are the actual race or beings versus the shades I have been seeing. They are the soul stealers."

Gavin dropped against the chair back and he took a long sip of beer. "Son-of-a... Is that why they seemed so big? You saw them in your vision and you said they were big black figures, not the human-looking ones I saw, right?"

"Yes."

"Do you always see them as they are? In their true form?"

I felt a prickling run across my shoulders as I answered. "So far, yes. They've had a more or less human shape, but they've been black or dark gray, and they undulate like a blob. They have a head shape and something that resembles red eyes but in a dark gray image. Some seem darker than others, and I think it's because they are taking over a lost soul."

His eyes grew wider as I'd spoken, and his lips tightened as he considered my words. "This is not good. The situation is escalating."

"Gavin, you seem to know more about this than Astrid or any of the spirits I've encountered. What's going on?"

Seventeen

"**I** wish I knew. I hate to see you tangled up in this whole situation, chica. But I'll tell you as much as I know, which is not enough."

Gavin rose and crossed to the bookcase again, this time pulling out a beat-up looking, leather-bound journal. He sat down and flipped it open about mid-way through. "This is from a dig I was on fifteen years ago. I was in India, working an exploration of a cavern there that had ancient buildings in it. While I'd done a few excavations before that, I hadn't encountered too many objects that were truly mystical. But this job was different. I found a bone carved puzzle box, not very big, only about three inches square."

He paused, looked down at the book. "You know, it was a puzzle. I had to try to solve it. Here's what I wrote:

'I've never seen a puzzle quite like this one. It doesn't seem like most Indian artifacts or from any of the neighboring areas. I can't know for sure if it's ancient until it's carbon-dated, but everything about the look of it suggests the box is authentic. The bone is discolored and worn, but with a little cleaning up, it still functions. Parts move as I shift sections trying to find the right combination.

Whoa! I didn't expect that. No problem figuring out the puzzle, only seven moves, but there was a spark of some sort when I moved the last piece. It flared up like a match or a flint but I couldn't find any evidence of a source for it. Just bone on bone. At the same time, I got the weirdest feeling. It felt like someone brushed past me. A spirit? But that made no sense. Inside, I only found a thimbleful of ashes that still held the scent of sandalwood. Why would anyone use a puzzle box to hold used incense? I can't wait to get this one to a lab.'"

He closed the book and stared at me.

"And?"

"I took it back with me to the University sponsoring the dig. I had to smuggle it out, in fact. We had it tested and the bone dated to almost four thousand years ago. We couldn't get a valid reading on the ashes within it, but we assumed they were contemporary with the box. No one could pull a match on anything other than the bones came from a monkey. Here's the real trick; after that, I began to have a sixth sense about unusual artifacts and experiences in ancient locations. I don't get a reading on them like you do, but I can sense when something is charged or has magic attached to it."

"Magic?"

"It's what I call it, but you might just label it the supernatural, something that isn't normal. Odd things happen around some of it. About a year later, I was on another dig in the Middle East when I sensed something in the rubble of a building that had been buried for centuries. A wisp of dark gray rose before me when I unearthed a large stone and for a few moments, I saw my first shade."

I blew my breath out. "So, that was about fourteen years ago. What did you do?"

"Nothing. Not that time, anyway. I thought it was an illusion, something from the light hitting a mirror or a shiny object. I wasn't about to tell anyone I might have seen a spirit. Did you?"

"Well, I did tell Janna, but she was the only one."

"Janna? The blond girl from the class?" His eyes crinkled at the corner in amusement.

I nodded. "Yeah. She's into hocus-pocus, so I figured she would understand if anyone did. But it's even out of her league."

"Well, to make a long story shorter, I began to encounter these shades more often on digs, or even visiting sites, so I started doing research on them. That led me to the paranormal experts, some of whom have at least heard of them, although none claimed to have had any personal acquaintance with them."

Disappointed, my shoulders drooped. "It sounds like you haven't encountered them that often either. I hoped that you would know more about them than I do. Excuse me." In need of the facilities, I rose and headed for the bathroom. I wanted to wash my face off and clear my mind for a few minutes. I'd caught the questioning look on Gavin's face and needed to think.

As I rinsed my hands, I went over the scant information he'd given me. The most significant fact, I thought, centered around his encounters being Earthbound. He'd touched them on this plane, not on the spirit level. Until the one in my home, I'd only encountered the shades in a transitional graveyard. Up to this point, the most aggressive ones had been at Shiloh.

Yet, Madame Astrid had seemed sure Gavin would be my mentor. Just because he hadn't been on the astral plane didn't mean he didn't know how to fight them or at least fend them off. Although the image of him running through a market to evade the True Shades did come to mind and caused me to question even that possibility. Did he know how to deal with them?

Time to find out. I wiped the moisture off my face and returned to the living room with a clearer head.

While I was gone, Gavin had brewed coffee and two cups sat on the table. I approved and grabbed a cup as I reclaimed my spot on the sofa. "Good idea."

"I thought it might help. I don't know exactly how much you know about the shades..." He picked up where we'd left off as he paced back and forth in front of the bookcase. "...but I do know they're dangerous. Not just on the spirit level, but on this one also. And one has threatened you. Why you? I've been encountering them for over a dozen years and they haven't threatened me. Mostly, they've cowered away. But they perceive you as a hindrance. Why were you chosen, Gillian?"

"What? Chosen? I have no idea. I didn't ask for it and, one day. Boom! This happened to me. No explanations other than I was given a gift. Some gift. It's altered my life and I don't seem to have any choice except to go along with it." My voice had skittered up a few notes in the abrupt tirade that his question had triggered.

He had come to a halt in the middle of it and gaped at me with concern giving his face a grave look. "Calm down. I didn't mean to set you off, chica. I'm just trying to figure this out. They... are afraid... of you. Something about you is different. Maybe it's because you can see them on the spiritual plane. But you're not the only one, are you?"

I really didn't like where his thinking was taking us. I couldn't be the only one. "Madame Astrid said she'd seen one from a distance while she was with her spirit guide. I think her guide has gotten closer, but I don't know about any others. I can't be the only spirit escort for the dead. I mean, there must be more. Wouldn't you think so?"

He shrugged his shoulders and paced some more.

"Do you know how to deal with them, Gavin? How can I protect myself?"

He gestured to the burning candle. "With spells. Magic. Mental strength. On one level, physical strength helps. On this plane, I can push them back, but it takes mental strength and incantations to repel them. So far, I can't destroy them. I burn protection oils and say spells to protect my house. I assume you do the same thing."

I lowered my head in acquiescence. No need telling him how lax I'd been on that score.

"Where did you learn them?"

"Madame Astrid gave me some protection spells and herbs."

"That's it? You need stronger incantations than ones in a witch's book! Is she the only person you've talked to about this?"

"Except for Janna, yes. Astrid's the one who told me to talk to you. She thinks you can mentor me." I barely got the words out. I felt like a total fool.

He stopped dead, crossed the room, and leaned over me. "Mentor you?"

My mouth tightened and my lips trembled as I fought back an emotional sob. "Zac called you a paladin and said you could help me. Astrid read my cards and they pointed to you. I'm an idiot."

He let out a deep breath and dropped onto the sofa next to me. "No, you're not. I'm the fool here. I'm trying to keep you safe and it sounds like that fruitcake of a psychic is tossing you into the fray."

"No, she's not." I opened my mouth to defend her and nothing came out. What was she doing? Did she knowingly send me into deeper trouble or was she just trying to guide me where I was going anyway? "I—think she's trying to help me, but this is out of her scope also. You said it earlier... I've been chosen. For whatever reason, the Supreme Being appears to have selected His champion in this fray and it's me. I don't understand the reasons and I don't have the tools

I need for it. That's why I need you." Hot tears spilled from my eyes, running down my cheeks as the overwhelming truth of the situation hit me.

Gavin's right arm slipped around my shoulders as he wiped at the tears with feather lightness. He pulled me into a hug as he stroked my hair.

"It's all right, chica. You've got me. If you're fighting this, so am I."

His lips pressed against my forehead in a reassuring kiss. I wrapped my arms around his chest, snuggling in tighter and reveling in the feeling of not being alone in this battle.

After several minutes had passed, I levered myself away and brushed the dampness from my face. I glanced at the grandfather clock next to the bookcase. Nearly ten-thirty.

"Is that clock right? I've gotta go. Can we meet again in a few days and put together a plan?"

"Sure. How about on the weekend?" He straightened up and stretched his arms over his head, his shirt rising a few inches to reveal his firm abdominal muscles. I tore my eyes away so he wouldn't think I was staring.

I mentally reviewed the schedule. The band had Roger's party on Saturday afternoon, so that was out. "I can do Sunday."

"Come over about one and I'll do a barbecue. In the meantime, I'm going to do some more research and checking around."

"Sounds good. I'll bring cheap wine."

He laughed.

"I'm serious."

He got to his feet as I did and walked to the door with me.

"Deal. As for you, don't do any more funeral singing until we figure this out."

"Like it's that easy to stop. I'm haunted if I don't." I still had Zoe to contend with if I didn't get that task resolved.

"It's not safe. I mean it, Gillian. You can get hurt on the spirit side." His eyes reflected his concern and it touched my heart. I'd had no idea he cared that much about me.

"I'll be careful."

He hugged me and kissed my cheek again, another friendly one. His eyes softened as his mouth shifted to mine and he planted a solid, non-platonic, kiss on me. I felt a jolt of desire shoot down the middle of my core as I yielded to him. I pressed closer, my eager lips working as hard as his to hold on to this fiery moment. Oh, my, I wanted this more than I realized.

With deep regret, I broke it off and pulled my head back. "I have to go. I need to be up early tomorrow." I had a twenty-minute drive to home, and another thirty minutes of spell casting to do before I went to bed.

"Call me tomorrow." His voice made it a command.

I nodded, turned away, and pressed the door control on my key ring as I marched to my Jeep.

As I pulled into my driveway, I thought about calling Janna. Almost eleven. She probably wouldn't be in bed, but I needed to be soon. I hesitated, then sent her a text message to let her know I was okay and I'd call her in the morning.

I'd barely sent it when the phone buzzed. "Were you sitting on it?"

"I was worried." Janna's voice showed her stress.

"I'm fine. I'll deal with the Trumbull bitch another day. For now, it's all okay. I still need to talk to Mark and that may be another whole ball game. At least, the guys are up to date and not freaked out, so that's good."

"Yay for that. I couldn't believe that woman pulled that B.S. on you. Thank goodness she didn't use your name."

"True, although some people can figure it out and there's still a real possibility one of the attendees might blab to her. People love to share gossip, especially if it can get them a minute of fame." I knew with a certainty that my name would get connected with that report eventually.

"That's a fact. Let's hope it's later rather than sooner."

"I'll drink to that... tomorrow. Let's get a drink after work and I'll fill you in on everything. I am so ready to collapse now."

"Make it about seven and I should be able to make it."

Late shift again for her, it seemed. Or she had a meeting. We set a place and I turned to my door. I hesitated before I opened it, pressed the wall light, and looked around to make sure it seemed normal. Curled up in the middle of the loveseat, Nygard raised his head and blinked at me. He seemed fine, unconcerned, which I took as a good sign.

Nonetheless, I moved warily through the downstairs, checking the spare room, and looking in the closets. Nervous? Not me. Not much.

Eighteen

I checked my phone messages as I settled into a booth at the Tipsy Topper, a quiet cocktail lounge not attached to a gaming establishment although poker machines did line the bar. In a town like Reno, almost every bar has some kind of gaming in it to help make ends meet.

A text from Janna informed me she had left work and would arrive soon. That had been about five minutes earlier. Another text came from Ferris checking on me and offering moral support if I needed it. One from Gavin wanting to know I made it home safely and asking me to acknowledge. I sent a quick text back to let him know everything was fine. Was he going to turn into a worrywart?

My agent's message was brief: *call me asap.* Well, that could be good or bad. Maybe she had a job for the band. I returned her call, got her voice mail, and left a message and followed up with a return text telling her I'd contact her in the morning.

And I had a missed phone call from Egan Moss. There was the problem with turning the phone to vibrate and not having it on me all day. However, I'd had a blissfully pleasant day with no interruptions or upsets and a dozen more-or-less cooperative dogs. After my conversation with Gavin, I had somehow managed a good night's sleep without any interruptions or peculiar dreams. I had really needed that. As a result, my outlook was more positive today than in the past few days. Amazing what a little therapeutic rest can do.

Janna breezed into the lounge, spotted me right off, and made a beeline across the room. She wore a dark red business suit, with a tight skirt slit to her knee that highlighted her figure.

"Business meeting?" I asked as soon as she sat down.

"Uh huh. One of the logistic people would not shut up even after he repeated his issue three times." She signaled a waitress and ordered a Mojito. "So, tell me everything. How the heck did this thing with Gayle Trumbull happen?"

"You know she wanted to do an interview, which I didn't want to do, but she pursued it. She caught me at the concert on Saturday night and tried to talk me into it." I hurriedly filled Janna in on the whole story and let her know I had clued in Ferris and Digby on the spirit escort thing.

"I held back a few things that they don't need to know about right now. For the most part, I laid it all on them and they're cool with it." I paused to sip some of my wine. "After that, I saw Gavin and we had a long talk. He's agreed to be my mentor and help me, but honestly, I'm not sure if he knows enough."

"What do you mean?"

"I mean, he has knowledge of the next plane and the shades, but he's never been to it. He's earthbound. He did say he's encountered some artifacts that have power and he can sense it, but he can't read them like I can. So is that going to be useful to me?" I shrugged my shoulders, the uncertainty showing.

"Well, his knowledge is something at least, and if he can sense things, that's useful. But if he's encountered the shades, he might have a better idea how to deal with them."

"Maybe." I signaled the waitress for another round of drinks. I refrained from telling Janna about the True Shades and that whole conversation with Zac. I found myself reluctant to add that to the pile of problems I'd already dumped on her. Gavin's questions about Zac bothered me and I needed to reassess every conversation I'd had with him. If I could just summon him to a dream meeting, I could ask him outright what exactly he was. But would he answer?

"So, what's been happening with you?" It was only fair to listen to her problems.

As I listened to Janna bring me up to date on her last few days, mostly work and an argument with her on-again, off-again boyfriend Justin, I made a few mental notes to discuss with Madame Astrid, like why she didn't tell me she knew Gavin or what I could do to protect my house more. For that matter, I still hadn't called her to make an appointment.

Nodding periodically while Janna talked didn't exactly do the trick as she stopped and stared intently at me.

"What?"

"You haven't been listening to me, have you? I asked you if you thought I should dye my hair blue and you just nodded."

"Well, blue is a good color." I put a sheepish smile on and batted my eyes at her. Busted. "No, my mind was drifting. There's just so much going on and I'm sorry, I let my own thoughts overtake your words."

She sighed. "I understand. You've got a shit storm happening in your life and my piddly problems are like ants in the jam."

"No, they're not. I am just not being a good friend at the moment. I just can't turn my thoughts off. I have some things I should be doing. I'll call you in a few days, okay? I promise I will be better."

"Yeah, okay." She watched as I put a tip on the table and grabbed my purse. "Gilly... Please be careful."

"I will." I flashed a small smile at her that I hoped suggested more confidence than I felt.

Once I got home, I rechecked the guards I'd cast on the house to attempt to detect any disturbances. Jeez, it would have helped if I had any clue what I was doing. I followed Gavin's instructions with little expectation that I performed any of the incantations or spells correctly. Nygard followed me around the house as I touched the walls and the doors and acted like I might know if anything felt off.

It didn't. I couldn't detect anything that gave off vibrations of any sort unless you counted the slight shudder by the heater. What was I doing? I never felt so out of my element as I did at that moment.

My cell phone rang and I jumped at the unexpected noise. Seeing Mark's name in the caller field, I picked it up and tried to sound normal. "Hi, Mark. How's everything?"

"Crazy, hectic. Same as always." He laughed a little, acknowledging that his life didn't vary much these days. His hours might be packed with interesting, intriguing, and challenging work, but he couldn't talk about it with me, so it came down to same-o, same-o when we talked. "And yours?"

"Usual routine. Busy most of the time, but not too much new."

Except for the things I couldn't tell him about.

"We're certainly an odd match, aren't we? Would you happen to have time for a late lunch on Friday? Say, around two? I'd like to talk to you." His voice held a more business tone than a "let's have a romantic interlude" vibe.

"Uh, yeah. I think I can do that. I mean, sure. Where?" I had an uneasy feeling about this.

"How about Miranda's?"

"Mexican lunch, yum. You bet. I'll meet you there at two."

"*Bueno*. See you there."

As I thumbed off the call, I wondered if he'd seen Gayle's report. I heard that it had been aired a couple of more times and Janna had mentioned that Gayle planned to talk to more funeral attendees.

I was in a quandary about that, not sure whether to call her out on bypassing my wishes or to continue to try to ignore it. I kicked off my shoes and sank into the sofa, putting my feet on the coffee table, and crossing my ankles. It felt good to just relax for a short time. Nygard jumped into my lap and curled into a cozy ball to take a nap. His purr started almost as soon as he settled.

The steady rumbling sound reassured me and tension snaked out of my neck and shoulders, almost visible tendrils slipping from me. I must be really tired if I'm seeing strands of tension, I thought, and suddenly realized that I was *seeing* it, not just visualizing it in my mind.

What the heck?

Even stranger, the coils of reddish-yellow seemed to lead to Nygard where they vanished. Indifferent to this activity, my cat appeared unaware, not even twitching a whisker.

Oh, boy! What was in those drinks tonight?

I closed my eyes and took several deep breaths. I wanted to just let everything drift for a while and not think about shades, spirits, reporters, or murderers. As if it was that easy...

"You can't stop now. You have to find out what happened to Saffi."

Zoe's voice came through loud and clear. My eyes popped open, expecting to see her standing in my living room, but nothing had changed. No indication that she'd spoken except in my mind.

Heaving a resigned sigh, I sat up, urged Nygard aside, and went to get the bag of artifacts I'd locked in the drawer upstairs. As I turned on the light switch, I paused at the top of the stairs and looked around the entire area, from the bed down to the end of the walkway and to the bathroom. No deep shadows or anything to indicate that something might be lurking in the corners.

Nygard shot between my feet, dashing into the room ahead of me as he hurried to leap on the bed, settling in the middle of it. That reassured me more than my own inspection of the room.

I unlocked the drawer, shifted my gun aside and pulled out the bag. I had two items in it that I hadn't read yet and I hoped one or both had impressions for me. One was the cufflink and the other was the key I'd found on the floor. Of the two, I thought the key might be the long shot. Anyone could have dropped it at any time, so it might not show anything about the night of the murder.

I picked up the cufflink and sat at my desk, clearing my mind as I handled the gold link. A smooth-edged square, the brushed face bore a script initial of S, presumably for Sarkis. I smoothed my right thumb over it and locked my fingers around it to form a cage. If it held a memory, it wouldn't escape me. At least, that was the thought that flitted through my mind as I prepared to search.

I closed my eyes and focused only on the feel of the object. Images swirled in my mind, flashes of parties and dinner occasions, although nothing paused for even a few moments. The visions stopped and I opened my eyes, thinking it didn't have more for me.

As I started to put it down, a nagging feeling pulled at me. I shifted the link in my hand, opening my fingers, and I stared at it. A moment of disorientation struck, as if I had fallen, before my vision filled with the dull gold color.

I felt movement as someone walked through a darkened house. Zoe's house, to be specific. I recognized the living room as the person turned to start up the steps. The cufflink had to be Nick's and I felt certain this image came from the night he murdered his wife.

As he reached the top of the stairs, the image turned and began to move slowly down the hall toward Zoe's room. The view dipped a moment and returned with an object held in his hand that blocked part of the view. His gun? It could be part of the handle.

He paused outside the door, close to it, and waited as if listening, then his free hand shoved the door open and he stepped inside. Briefly, I saw Saffi and Zoe entangled in each other's arms, faces touching, before they abruptly pulled apart.

The image tilted as Nick moved closer and apparently motioned at them with his gun hand. The girls moved apart, stark fear registered on Saffi's beautiful face, her eyes popping wide. By contrast, Zoe's face blazed with anger, rather than fright as she clambered off the bed. She shouted at Nick, waving her arms at him. She tilted her body toward her dressing table as if she was reaching for something to throw at him.

More motioning with the gun as Nick moved closer. Zoe's head snapped up, an easily-read expletive shaping her mouth. The gun swiveled toward Saffi, who had stepped to the right side of the bed, trying to move away from Nick. She froze, a hand reaching toward him as her mouth seemed to spout words to match the pleading look in her eyes.

In an instant, Zoe dashed in front of Saffi, her hands extended as if they would stop Nick from advancing. Abruptly, a burst of red blossomed on her chest. For a split second, she glanced down. Her eyes wide in surprise and shock. In what seemed like slow motion, her mouth opened in a cry as she folded to the floor when her body failed. She was dead before she hit the floor although her body spasmed a few times with sharp jerks.

Nick made a lunge for Saffi, but she back peddled, darting out of his reach. The vision shifted sharply, moving to follow a glimpse of Saffi's golden hair as she disappeared through the bathroom door and slammed it shut. Nick's free hand pounded on the door although the angle of the view suggested he might have used the gun hand as the image bounced and jerked with the link's motion.

He must have put the gun away or dropped it as a swish of movement made me lurch while the view rotated back to Zoe's body on the floor. Completely still, she had gone down into a small, folded heap. Nick went to the bedside table and opened a drawer, his hand rummaging through it until he located a switchblade knife.

Holding it in front of him, the link showed just the edge as it snapped into place. His hand didn't seem too steady, the image shaky, as he knelt beside Zoe. He reached for her neck and his hand closed on her necklace, a locket with a diamond mounted in the center. With a sharp tug, he yanked it from her throat. As he opened his hand, blood oozed from a cut in his palm. Apparently, he put the locket away and his hand shook in anger as he held the knife out. I could follow the movement as the blade crossed her throat, making that angry gash.

At that moment, Nick twisted sharply, the view rising high as he fell over and a swish of a gown broke the image, concealing the action behind it. I had a glimpse of Saffi's hair followed by her body partially on top of Nick and a struggle of some sort. The link's image changed to a blur of flight across the room, a landing on the carpet, and nothing after that.

The images stopped.

Stunned, I sat back, dropped the link on the desk, and shook my head as I caught my breath. Although from an odd perspective, the link had shown me the murder. Feeling lightheaded and a little nauseous, I hurried to the bathroom and splashed water on my face. Filling a glass with water, I drank it all in one long gulp, and refilled it before going back to the table.

I glared at the cufflink as if it had been responsible rather than the wearer. Snatching it up, I stuck it back in the bag along with the key and locked them away again. While the memories remained clear in my mind, I opened a new document on my computer and began recording as much of the detail as I could.

As I finished it, I considered what might have happened to Saffi. It seemed she'd emerged from the bathroom, perhaps with something she thought might be a weapon and had jumped Nick, trying to knock him out or something. In the struggle, the link had flown off his shirt and landed where I'd found it later. What happened to Saffi? Did she get away? Or did Nick kill her?

If he'd killed her, where was her body? From what had been reported publicly on the case, it didn't appear that she'd been at the scene of the crime let alone killed there. So had Nick knocked her out, taken her away, and killed her? Did he dump her body somewhere?

Whether the key held the final clue or not, it and the blood-stained carpet were all I had left. What could either of those tell me about what happened to the other girl?

Nineteen

I met Egan Moss at a Starbucks Coffee in Sparks after I finished grooming the last of my doggie clients. I picked up my latte and looked around. He'd claimed a small table at the back of the shop where no one else really wanted to sit. Dark, no windows, and pretty much out of sight also meant it provided a certain amount of privacy for our conversation.

"'Afternoon, Foster," he murmured, looking up from his cell phone, as I sat down. He tapped a message in before he set it down.

I nodded an acknowledgment. "I'm glad you called. I have something to tell you."

"Let me go first. I saw the show Trumbull did. Don't let it worry you. She didn't name you. Assuming she doesn't go any further, there's no real concern there."

"I've heard she's been talking to some of the people who were at those funerals. That does worry me." Like, him, I kept my voice low.

"So, what are they gonna say? They saw a singer perform at a funeral. She looked a little spacey. Maybe she does drugs."

"Oh, great. That would really spice things up for me. What if they say my name in an interview? Even if she hasn't said it, someone she talks to could very well blab it."

"Could happen. And you might actually get more business from it. Just for the novelty. People do strange things." He took a sip of his coffee and leaned forward a little. "Unless she flat out suggests that you're crazy, involved in the murders, or calls you a psychic, there isn't a lot you can do about it. You can't go to a judge to get a restraining order without proof, so the less you react to it, the better for you. If your name does get out, don't talk to the press about it."

"This is not helping, Moss."

He chuckled. "You know, you're not the only one who could have a problem with this. Hernandez and I really don't want anyone to know that we're getting information from a loony who sings at funerals. How would that look?"

"Thanks for the compliment." I could see I wouldn't get any help from him on this. I changed subjects.

"I took your advice and sent the information to RPD."

His left eyebrow lifted and he waited for me to continue.

"Now, I have more. I am picking up information from a few of the items I – acquired a few days ago."

He nodded, still saying nothing.

"For one thing, Saffi Alden was definitely at the house with Zoe. I got visions from a cufflink. She and Zoe were together when Nick came into the room. They argued briefly before he turned the gun toward Saffi. Zoe darted in front and he killed her."

"A cufflink told you that?" Moss frowned. "Do you know how insane that sounds?"

I shrugged, sipped my latte, and looked away. Of course, I knew. How could I not know? "It didn't talk to me. It showed me images, but only from the point of view of the cufflink."

"What?"

"I can't explain it, Moss. I don't know how these impressions get into an object. They seem to imprint from either the holder's point of view or the object's. In this case, it was the object."

His eyes shifted to look behind me, scanning the space to see if we were secure, I guessed. Satisfied, he said, "Okay. Tell me exactly what you saw in this vision."

I leaned closer, as did he, until our heads almost touched, then I told him everything. I kept my voice low, as worried as he was that someone might overhear. Moss listened without interrupting, making notes into his phone as I gave him the details.

When I stopped talking, he leaned back and read through his notes before saying, "So, you saw the Alden woman go into the bathroom, but you didn't see when she came back out? And you didn't see if she had anything in her hands?"

"Right. Like I said, I only saw it from the cufflink's view." I shuddered at the thought. The cufflink had a view? Jeez, that sounded so lame.

"And you're sure this was Saffi Alden?"

"Pretty sure. She looked like the picture on her Facebook page."

"When did you look at it?"

"This morning. Only a little is available if you're not a friend."

He considered that a moment, his eyes looking past me again. "Could you tell when she'd last posted anything?"

"It looked like her last entry was on a cat video a couple of weeks ago."

He rolled his eyes. "That figures. Okay, so you've given me a lot of information about a possible victim we don't know about. Problem is, it's still Reno's case."

I sucked at my lower lip. "Yeah, I get that. Isn't there something you can do?"

"I don't know. I'll look into this as much as I can, talk it over with my partner, and maybe we can come up with something. Do you happen to know where Ms. Alden lived? If her home is in the county, we could start by checking on her safety."

Damn. I didn't think about looking up her address. I shook my head.

"Okay. Don't worry about it. I'll take it from here. You just stay out of that house and don't get into any trouble." He rose to leave, paused a moment more, adding, "And don't talk to Gayle Trumbull."

I finished my coffee, giving him plenty of time to leave, dumped the cup, and strolled out the door.

My next stop was Madame Astrid's place. Although she had a tight schedule, she did manage to give me about ten minutes and I had exactly seventeen minutes to get there. I knew it would be close and I did push the speed limit a bit to make it on time.

Her previous client came out the door as I pulled up and parked. The woman ducked her head a bit as if I might recognize her and report her to someone. I found it funny how people responded to seeing a psychic as if it was a stigma. I felt less uncomfortable about this than the possibility of being spotted coming out of the psychiatrist's office.

On a perverse whim, I tossed a little wave at her as she passed by me. I caught just the hint of a head shift as she tried to look at me without actually looking. I hurried up the steps and into Astrid's parlor.

She was tidying up a little, putting her Tarot cards back into a deck. She glanced up at me. "Good afternoon. Can I get your anything? Water?"

"No, thanks. I'm good."

She nodded and motioned me to the chair at the left of the window. She disappeared behind the curtain with her customary tea service tray and returned a few minutes later. With a big smile, she sat in the other window chair. "Okay, what is so urgent that you had to see me today?"

Now that I was here, I questioned whether it was as urgent as I'd thought, but I did want to clear the air, so to speak. "I don't know if you heard that Gayle Trumbull did a report about me a couple of days ago."

Her smile vanished. "What kind of report?"

"Maybe not so serious," I admitted. "She talked about a woman who sang at funerals and mentioned the unique lyrics. She's been at a few of the ones I've done. While she didn't reveal my name, she claims to have been talking to people who were at the services."

"Oh, I see. And you're worried that your name might get out and people will think you're an oddity."

"Well, yes. To some extent, that is a concern. I'm more worried that if she digs deep enough she'll find out about the other aspect of my gift. She's hasn't contacted you, has she?"

"Oh, my goodness, no! I've never met her or talked to her. We talked about this a few days ago. I assure you, there's no need to worry about my discretion. I'm like a lawyer; you have client privilege, you know. I don't divulge who sees me professionally or what I talk about with my clients." She waved her hands around as she spoke until one hand, with pinched fingers, flashed across her mouth indicating zipped closed.

"I didn't think you would. I was just worried that she might have traced me to here." As I said it, I had a sudden urge to check that I hadn't been followed. I hadn't considered that until now.

"But, on a similar note of client privilege, I suppose, why didn't you tell me that you knew Gavin Haines?" That still bugged me. She could have given me a warning.

She shrugged her shoulders as her lips twitched into an

indecisive smile. "Whether I knew him or not had no bearing on your future partnership with him. If my name came up, I'm sure you know that I am not at the top of his preferred people list. We have met a few times amicably, but he clearly doubts my talent. Nonetheless, I am aware of his and its limitations."

"I see. I did speak to him and he has agreed to be my mentor. To be frank, I have some reservations about *his* limitations. He's never been to the next plane. How is he going to help me?"

"Just because he has not stepped into the existential plane doesn't mean that he isn't aware of it or hasn't interacted with it. I only travel there with my spirit guide. In many ways, your gift is way beyond mine. You have gone there not just a couple of times, but many times. And you've been granted access in more than one way. You have been chosen, Gillian."

As I took a breath to ask what she meant, she held up her hand to wait. "I don't know what you've been selected to do, but your gift is steadily growing. Therefore, you must be a champion—someone the Almighty has selected for a special task."

A shudder of fear shook my shoulders as the words sank in. They echoed my own thoughts and I hadn't wanted any confirmation. "But I never asked for this!"

"None of us do. We are chosen to serve as needed. It is clear that you have an important task and one that the Almighty has given you gifts to handle. He's led you to me and to Gavin Haines. In some way, He must have been preparing you for this task as He has put people in your path to prepare and help you."

"Prepare? I'm not prepared. I'm agnostic, a Pacifist, and just a singer. I don't have any special skills for this and it sounds like I may be the sacrificial lamb in some battle I don't understand."

She shifted her chair closer to me, leaned across, and caught my right hand in both her hands, turning it palm up to face her. She studied it, her eyes growing deeper and more intense as she focused on the network of lines across the surface. I felt uncomfortable, wanting to pull my hand back, yet I resisted and allowed her to scrutinize it.

In a few moments, she straightened up, released my hand, and sat back. "You have a long lifeline, and I see struggles in it. I also see where you overcome adversity. You are a strong person, Gillian. You are being called upon to serve humanity. You can deny it, but you can't walk away from it."

I was horrified. I didn't want this task. Why would anyone, let alone the Divine Being, choose me? This deal was getting worse and worse.

"Perhaps you can talk to Zac about it," Astrid suggested, her eyes wide with sympathy.

"Yeah, that's another thing. Gavin asked me if I was sure he was an angel." I dropped my voice to a low tone that matched my uncertainty. "I had to say no. I don't know for sure. He's never said as much and I just assumed with the way he looks and talks that he is an angel. I mean, who else would be talking to me and encouraging me?"

"Hmm, that is a question." Astrid frowned. "Perhaps he's your spirit guide."

"If he is, he doesn't do much guiding. I can't just summon him. He shows up in my dreams when he chooses." I was beginning to have some serious doubts about Zac and the possibility of him not being on my side made me uneasy. "Could he be aligned with the shades?"

Astrid stared at me for a long moment, at a loss for words, apparently. Her voice rasped a little when she finally said, "You need to find out, Gillian. Soon."

Twenty

On Friday morning, I sat at my dining room table and studied the small key I'd found. It looked like one that would fit a padlock rather than a lock box or a mailbox. Who had dropped it and when? Was it even from the night of the murder?

I took a deep breath and focused on the object. I tried to keep my mind clear of any thoughts so that I could pick up any images from the key. I sensed nothing from it, not even an owner vibration. If it had been used on a lock, I didn't get any kind of a hint of what kind or where it might be.

After ten minutes of trying to conjure something, I sat back and let out a disappointed breath. Even though I knew it would be a long shot, I'd hoped it would reveal at least a small clue.

"That was a bust, Nygard." The cat had sat on the chair opposite me and watched as I tried to make something happen. Now he flicked an ear and blinked his blue eyes, a query of some sort in them.

I glanced at the little plastic baggie with the carpet piece in it. I'd only cut about an inch of the fibers from the rug, so it wasn't much. I didn't know if it could even pick up an impression and the blood itself would be Zoe's. Still, I deemed it worth a try and opened the baggie, dumping the fibers on a paper napkin in front of me.

Nygard peered at the dried-out, rust-colored shag pieces and let out a low growl. He rarely used that voice and I cast a sharp look at him. Both ears were back and he showed his teeth as his howling voice cut in before he jumped down and ran toward the stairs.

Odd, I thought. Perhaps it was the scent of the blood. Clearly, he didn't like this. With a touch of trepidation, I picked up the clump of strands.

My stomach wrenched as a distasteful odor assaulted my senses, followed by the metallic taste of the blood. A flash of crimson filled my mind, followed by the sensation of falling and I clutched the table with both hands even though I was sitting.

After a few moments of blackness in my mind, a swirl of images–clothes, arms, legs–crossed back and forth in the vision. A clear profile view of Saffi's face peered up from the floor as Nick hovered over her. He leaned toward her, his face closing in on hers until their lips met. As he pulled back, he reached a hand to her and everything tilted again.

The vision cleared leaving me stunned and nauseous from the uneven and constant movement of the images. I took several deep breaths and tried to piece together what I'd seen. It didn't seem to be from any particular point of view, perhaps just emotions tied to the carpet. Or enough charged energy in Zoe's blood to store a disjointed record of the events.

Reflecting on it, I conjectured that Saffi had jumped Nick after he killed Zoe. They'd fought, struggling as the images had jumped around. Nick had got the upper hand and kissed Saffi. Could that be right? A show of defiance or superiority before he killed her perhaps.

Or did he kill her? Saffi didn't appear too frightened. Was she in on it with Nick? Did she set Zoe up? Had I sent Moss off to look for a dead body when she might very well be with Nick wherever he'd gone to hide?

When my phone rang, I jumped at the sound. Snatching it up, I read the caller name. Mark. Was he canceling lunch again? I swiped my finger across the screen and answered with a terse "hi".

It turned out he only wanted to move lunch back an hour. Of course, something had come up in emergency, but he was sure it would be cleared up by two if I could make it later. I agreed and hung up, actually happy to have a little extra time to pull myself together.

Handling the carpet fibers with caution, I pushed them back into the baggie and sealed it. Perhaps Nygard had been wise to run from this particular reading.

I'd just gotten seated at the restaurant and ordered a mango margarita when Mark breezed through the door looking like the high winds buffeting Reno this afternoon had blown him in. I waved to get his attention and he skirted around the tables to the booth and slid into the bench across from me

"Rough day?" I asked as I took in his frazzled look. His eyes drooped with weariness.

"One of many. Had three emergencies at one time, so we were all rushing from one to another. I'm sorry I had to set this back." He flashed an apologetic smile that quickly vanished as he picked up the menu.

Catching the cue that he didn't plan a leisurely lunch, I quickly scanned mine and settled on the chimichanga, a favorite dish of mine. When the waitress brought my drink, Mark ordered an iced tea and said we were ready to order. Once that one was done, he turned his attention to me.

"You look great. How is everything going for you?"

"Pretty good. Keeping busy. Not as busy as you, obviously."

"This has been pretty insane for the past month or so. I thought it would be getting easier in the third year, but it seems to be the opposite." He brushed a hand through his hair to push the overlong front locks back. It appeared he hadn't had time for a haircut either.

"Yeah, I figured it was rough. I wanted to talk to you about something. You know I've been singing at funerals – those odd gigs I get occasionally?"

He nodded, "Yeah. I heard that some reporter had a story on the news about a woman who sang at funerals. One of the nurses mentioned it to me and asked if I was still dating the girl who'd done that. Was that story about you?"

"Yes... and no," I hedged and gave him the same line about her doing it without permission. I dipped a chip into the salsa and took a bite as I steeled myself to tell him the whole story.

Mark put a few chips on his little plate and spooned the salsa over them, added salt, and used his fork to eat them. Hmmm, I hadn't noticed that little quirk before. Maybe he didn't want to drip on his clothes. He'd taken off his medical coat and wore a blue and white, thinly-striped shirt, no tie.

"What's the big deal?" he asked after he chewed the first forkful.

"Well, it's the insinuation in her story. She's trying to make it sound like I'm a little off or misleading people. Or... I don't know exactly what she's after with this. She told me she thought it was a good community interest story, but she had a lot of questions."

Mark looked up, his eyebrows arching with the question in his eyes. God, he looked adorable and I was afraid to see that look change when I told him the truth.

"Here, the thing, Mark. When I sing, I change the lyrics to the song to personalize it for the deceased." There, I said it. At least, I got the first part out.

"Really? That sounds pretty awesome. So, why the concern?"

"The truth is that I don't know that much about the person, but I alter the lyrics from a paranormal state. When I start to sing, I get information– That is, my spirit form goes to another place where I learn the good qualities of the person, and I somehow turn it into the song."

That came out in little spurts and I noticed mid-way through that Mark was staring at me with his mouth open.

"Surprised a little?"

"You're kidding me, right?" He looked around as if someone had a camera on him and this was a practical joke.

I pinched my lips together, shrugged, and said, "No. Not a joke. This has been happening to me since I hit my head last winter."

He took a deep breath. "For real? You're getting lyric input while in a spirit form?"

I nodded just as the waitress brought our food and I felt so grateful to have that plate in front of me.

"Let's eat, okay? I'll tell you more if you want to know after we eat." Picking up my fork, I cut off a piece of the fried tortilla and jammed it into my mouth.

Mark hesitated before he, too, shoveled a forkful of taco salad into his mouth. I could see he wanted to talk more, although the intense-looking, pulled-together eyebrows suggested he really didn't want to know. I wasn't doing the best job of explaining it either. I seemed to blurt it out more than the thought-out approach I'd originally intended. When you got right down to it, there was no easy way.

We ate mostly in silence until he set his fork down. "This is awkward, Gillian. I am surprised by what you're telling me and I don't... know what to make of it. It's not unheard of that people can develop some extrasensory faculty after a head injury, but this is unusual. Uh, maybe you're hallucinating?"

Awkward? Is that really *what he was thinking?*

"Nope, I've been checked out." My voice came out in a dull, flat tone. He was trying to rationalize it. I set my fork down, my dominant hand resting on the table as I fought the urge to tap my fingers.

He nodded, took a deep breath and said, "I see. Actually, what makes this peculiar is that I wanted to talk to you to more or less end our relationship."

I felt my face crumple, falling into a surprised frown, as he said it. My immediate thoughts went to that poorly stated confession. Shit! Why did this catch me off guard? I'd been expecting it or maybe I had hoped he would be more understanding.

He reached for my hand. I pulled it back from the table, not wanting him to touch me.

He swallowed hard, his eyes softening. "It's nothing to do with what you just told me. It's nothing to do with you either. It's my crazy schedule and the complete lack of time I have to properly have a relationship with anybody, let alone a romantic one. I mean, I keep looking at the number of times I've had to cancel on you. It's not fair to either of us."

I fought the trembling in my lower lip. While I had expected it would come to this, it still hurt when Mark said it. Could I believe it had nothing to do with my weirdness? Fighting for a steady voice, I asked, "So, what I said made no difference?"

"No. None at all. Although on a professional level, it's certainly intriguing." He winked at me and grinned as if it was a joke.

I looked away from him, my eyes scoping out the details of the restaurant with the Mexican decorations—serapes, sombreros, and the brightly-colored piñatas creating a festive atmosphere. My vision blurred, running the colors together, as tears filled my eyes.

"I'm sorry, Gillian. I didn't want to hurt you. It wasn't my intent.

I do care a great deal about you and I have enjoyed being with you. But my life just isn't my own right now. You understand, don't you?"

"I guess," I muttered, not knowing what I should say at this point. Even when you expect it to happen, it still hurts to hear the words.

"Look, I'm sorry, but I have to get back to the hospital. You can call me if you want to. I would still like to talk to you now and then. We can be friends, can't we?"

"Right. Sure." I stared at the table rather than meeting his eyes. I heard the scrape of his chair as he rose, followed by footsteps as he left. I didn't turn to look, couldn't. I wouldn't be able to hold it together if I did.

Hell, the relationship had been going nowhere anyway and I knew it. Besides with everything that was going on in my life, who had time for a boyfriend? To cap it off, would I have let Gavin slip into my life so easily if there had been more happening with Mark?

Sorry, Mom. I let the doctor slip away. On the other hand, the archeologist has a Ph.D.

When I looked back to the table, I saw that he'd left money to cover the lunch check, even mine. Nice. To the very end, nice.

Twenty-One

As I walked into my house that evening, I immediately had a sense that something wasn't right. I stood barely inside the door and gazed around the living room. Everything seemed in place, nothing disturbed.

I thought back to earlier in the day. Had I set the protection spell before I'd left that afternoon? Hell, did they even work or was I simply hoping that they did? I moved a little further into the house and closed the door behind me. I ran my eyes up the staircase and stepped closer to it so I could peer up to the loft from there. I couldn't see anything in the immediate area, but much of it wasn't visible until you were almost all the way to the top.

Nygard... where was Nygard?

Normally, he would be in the living room when I came home. "Nygard? Where are you, little guy? Come on, Nygard."

I waited a few moments before I went to the kitchen to see if he hid there. As I walked, I checked that the windows looked secure. The two front ones didn't open at all, so those were intact and no problem. The one on the south side could slide open and had a screen; that looked fine. That just left the kitchen window to the east and the one in the door. Seeing they were okay, I looked around for my cat.

Going back to the living room, I opened the door to my music room, which was just at the bottom of the stairs. Nothing out of order in there and no sign of Nygard.

Nerves twitching, I went up the steps and called out to Nygard again. I hesitated about midway up as I heard a faint meow. I hustled the rest of the way, pausing only to peer into the corners at the end of the room to be sure a shade didn't wait for me there. Nothing.

And no cat on the bed, either. However, the room looked, and felt, disturbed. A prickle of alarm tickled the back of my neck as I sensed that someone had been in the room. I turned my eyes to the locked drawer where I kept my gun. Although I didn't see anything alarming there, I went in for a closer view to see if it looked like someone had tampered with the lock. I saw no scratches on the wood around it and only a couple of old marks showed on the metal. It didn't appear there was anything new. That didn't mean that someone couldn't have picked the lock without leaving evidence.

Turning to my computer and desk, I noticed at once that the mouse wasn't in its usual place and things had been disturbed. As I took a step toward it, I heard Nygard's deep meow again. It sounded muffled but close. I circled around the banister, past the bed, and turned right to face the closet.

"Nygard?"

"Merroow." His voice came from behind the shut door and I yanked it open. A cream and brown streak of Himalayan feline shot out of the closet and across the room to the bed.

How did he get shut in the closet? I thought back to when I'd left. While I wasn't sure I'd even closed the door, I did recall seeing him downstairs before I'd left. Someone had shut him in.

I called him to me and he worked his way across the bed as I sat down. Scratching his ears and chin, I thought about the situation. Someone had broken into my house; someone who could get in without breaking a lock or a window. That person may have tried my secure drawer in the nightstand and even tried to find information on my computer. Who would—or could-- do that?

My mouth felt a little dry as I gave Nygard a comforting hug before I crossed to my computer. I booted it up, looking for anything unusual in it. I called up my word processor and looked down the list of recently opened documents. Nothing that alarmed me; they seemed to be exactly what I'd done recently. I hadn't even saved the letter to RPD on the hard drive and it was coded with a dumb name when I backed it up to the flash drive I'd used.

Could the police have gotten a clue that I sent the letter and come looking for proof? No, that wouldn't have been it. They would have had a warrant. This had to be someone else. Who would want information about me or my business and would be sneaky enough to do this?

Gayle Trumbull came to mind. She might think she could find

more dirt for her story in my house and my computer. Damn!

Before I leaped across the assumption chasm, I wanted to see if I could get a little proof of my own. I called my landlady, Mrs. Roche, who lived in the front house on the lot.

"No, Gillian," she said as I asked about her coming into the house. "You know I would only come in if there was any emergency. I strictly respect your privacy, dear."

"I know. But I thought that maybe something had happened. Did you notice anybody looking around my place? Maybe trying the door or going around back."

"Oh, no, I can't say that I did. However, I was out for most of the afternoon today. Shopping and having a nice dinner with Simon, so I didn't get home until about forty minutes ago. Is something wrong?" Her voice took on that worried-mother tone she could get.

"Not anything serious. It just looks like someone was in the house. It doesn't look like they took anything and they didn't make a mess. Like they were just looking around with no intent on stealing."

I heard her gasp through the phone. "Oh, my goodness. You need to notify the police. A burglar might have been casing out your place. And maybe mine. You know, there's been a string of burglaries recently."

She went to panic mode quickly, I thought, as I tried to reassure her. "I will give them a call. It may be nothing, but best to report it, huh?"

Report it? I couldn't even prove anyone had been in the house. It was a feeling and knowing things were out of place, yet nothing I could point out to a police officer and say someone had absolutely disturbed my stuff. Instead, I called Gavin.

After I'd told him the whole story, he said, "Are you certain you cast a protection spell before you left?"

"Yes. At least three of them."

"Then your intruder is more likely to be human than a shade."

"I figured that much out, Prof. Now what?"

"I'm coming over. We may not be able to find much out, but we can give it a go. I'll see you in about twenty." He didn't wait for a response before he hung up.

I stared at my silent phone and frowned. Did he even know where I lived?

A minute later, it buzzed. Gavin calling. "Uh, what's your address, *chica*?"

True to his word, Gavin arrived within twenty minutes and immediately went through my little house from bottom to top with a gadget in his hand that I'd never seen before. I tagged along behind him and noted that he stopped at various places to look at the instrument that looked like a light meter and had a little needle on it that fluctuated around the middle.

"What is that?" I tried to get a glimpse of the reading as he pointed it at the corner where I'd seen the shade. The needle eased up a little into the red zone, though not enough to conclude anything.

"Residual energy there. Is that where you spotted your shade the other day?"

I nodded.

He held the device up and answered my question. "This is a unique gadget I managed to put together that registers abnormal vibrations or power. In short, spirits or other supernatural beings."

"You made it? How?" I'd never heard of such a thing.

He grinned and pointed it at me. A glow came from it, casting a blue light over his hand.

"What does that mean?"

"It means, chica, that you have an above average reading in the positive zone, which is those of us who are not on the side of the demons," he chuckled.

"Believe it or not, I found a simple reference in a very old book on the occult. Not everyone can use it, even if they can build it right. It takes one of us, a paranormal, to power it."

"You mean I could use it?" Excitement at the prospect shot through me.

He nodded. "I think so. Try it."

He held it out to me and I took it carefully, studying it a little more closely now that it was in my hands. "Huh? It looks like my guitar tuner. Only they're yellow for sharp, green for on the mark, and red for flat."

"Yeah, I adapted a tuner and adjusted it accordingly. I changed out the lights and adjusted the insides to pick up paranormal vibrations rather than music."

"I get that, but how?" I pointed it at him and my eyes popped as the needle dropped into the blue zone lighting up a string of small lights. "That's you! It shows you're really strong."

He laughed. "Uh huh, a little bit. Just because I don't go waltzing between this plane and the next doesn't mean I don't have big juju in the metaphysical world."

I pursed my lips. Had Astrid said something to him about my doubts? "Oh, I didn't think –"

"Sure you did. I saw it on your face. You wondered how powerful I could be if I didn't move onto the next level. We each have our gifts, Gillian, and they're not exactly the same. But never underestimate my ability."

I handed the gadget back to him and headed back down the stairs. Now, I felt properly chastised. He'd known exactly what I'd thought.

As Gavin stepped off the steps behind me, I got a glimpse of Nygard's head peeping out from the kitchen. His eyes were wide as they intently watched the professor.

I called to the cat and waited a little bit as he tried to decide if it was prudent to come out. "C'mon, kit," I added and sat in my comfy chair next to the sofa. I patted my lap, providing the incentive to Nygard to run and jump onto it.

"This is my cat, Nygard," I told Gavin as I glanced up at him while petting my buddy.

"Hello, Nygard. You're a fine-looking fellow." Gavin wisely gave him space, not even attempting to touch him, as he circled around and sat on the sofa. "Is he sensitive to the paranormal?"

"I don't know for sure, but he seems to be." I decided to tell Gavin about my vision the previous day; the one with the odd golden strands that seemed to connect me with Nygard.

He cocked an eyebrow and gazed at my cat for almost a minute without saying anything. "Can you get up and leave him in the chair? I want to try a reading on him."

"I'll try." I shifted Nygard from my lap to the arm of the chair, and got up. Sometimes the cat didn't stay put when I moved, but this appeared to be a lucky time. He returned to the cushion and sat with his tail curled around him.

Gavin pointed the device at him, and we watched in amazement as the pointer shifted through six blue lights to nearly the same strength Gavin had shown.

"Wow. What does that mean?"

"That your cat is a powerful medium, I think. He's definitely on our side. It's possible he was either channeling energy from you or to you when you saw the connection. You've never seen it before?"

"Are you kidding? No!" Stunned, I dropped onto the couch next to Gavin and rubbed my eyes. I thought back to the incidents with Nygard. Had he given me any indication before? "You know, sometimes, when I've had some psychic-type dreams, Nygard has awakened me and been right on top of me while I was dreaming. I just thought I must have made noises that disturbed him."

"Interesting and puzzling. Witches use animals as familiars and have a psychic link with them. Or so I'm told."

"Are you calling me a witch?"

He caught my nearest hand, rubbing the back of my fingers as his lips formed a lop-sided grin. "No, I'm just saying that there might be some truth to the practice. That animals are sensitive to the other planes and the paranormal. Cats, in particular, may be able to sense things that we can't. Probably the reason that many who practice witchcraft choose them. Although I know a witch whose familiar is a chicken."

Nygard seemed to have listened to enough of the conversation as he blinked, jumped down, and boogied off to the kitchen. "Guess he's not worried about me being with you," I quipped. "So what have we discovered with that gadget of yours?"

"That nothing abnormal has been in your house. At least not from the supernatural category."

"But we don't have any indication of anyone being here except for my observations that things have been moved and my cat was shut in the closet." This hadn't helped me with that concern at all and I still had no proof that someone had broken into the house.

"No, you don't. But you're sure of what you know and for certain, Nygard didn't shut himself into the closet. You're positive he was out when you left the house?"

"Yes, one-hundred-percent. I saw him before I left and he was downstairs."

"Do you feel comfortable sleeping here tonight? Are you concerned whoever broke in might come back?" I detected a touch of worry in his voice.

"I'm a little nervous, I admit it. But I don't think anyone will come back while I'm here. I suspect it could have been someone Gayle Trumbull hired to try to get some information on me. But I don't have any way to prove that."

"Would you like me to stay here tonight?"

I turned to gaze into his eyes. I saw concern in them, but no suggestion of anything more than a friend wanting to help out. No ulterior motives in the suggestion.

"No, thanks for the offer though. I think I'll be all right. I fear the supernatural visitors more than the human ones. I'll put up my wards and keep my gun handy."

"Right. Call me tomorrow and we'll make a plan for your training, okay?"

I agreed and rose as he did to see him out. He hesitated at the door, turned, and pulled me into a tight hug.

"If anything else happens, call me. Understand? Anything."

"Got it. You're on my quick dial."

After he left, I double locked the front door, went to the kitchen, and set the deadbolt on the back door. Next, I sat at the table, pulled out my dragon oil burner, put a little water in the bowl, added a few drops of sandalwood, and lit the candle in the base. Even though I didn't need to say the words out loud, I did, calling for good spirits to help protect my house and those of us in it.

If that kept the shades out, I could deal with any human intruders.

I pulled my gun out of the drawer and loaded it. Although it made me nervous to have the gun, I felt more confident about it now and the likelihood a friend would creep in on me while I slept was nil.

In spite of that, I left my lamp near the television on and snuggled down under the covers. Nygard bounced over me and curled up on my right side. He was a good watch-cat, and I knew for certain that if anyone tried to break in, he'd hear them before I did.

Twenty-Two

I reached up for my keyboard case as Ferris handed it down to me from the back of his van. I'd ridden with him to the park that Roger had rented for his engagement party. Frankly, I felt exhausted, my eyelids drooping and shadowed in spite of the half pot of coffee I'd downed once I'd dragged myself out of bed. I'd slept poorly, waking up several times with a jerk thinking I'd heard a sound downstairs.

To top it off, I had a weird, anxiety-induced dream that involved Zac. I was talking to him, although I couldn't remember now what we'd talked about. As he talked, he kept flashing from a positive to a negative image, white to black, and back again. His face had been like the theater masks going from happy to sad, smiling to frowning. I didn't think it meant anything except my subconscious mind was reacting to my second thoughts about him. Curse Gavin for even putting that idea into my head.

As I took my instrument to the small stage that had been set up on the grass, Digby met me and took the keyboard to set up on the stand he'd already positioned. We were using the battery power units today; no city power available at the park. Roger had dropped that bombshell on me this morning. We were lucky that Ferris had them charged up. What would I do without my two guys? I wasn't up to a screaming acoustic set today.

"Have you spotted Roger yet?" I asked stepping up onto the stage to check out the microphone set-ups.

"No, but there haven't been too many people around yet. When is this gig supposed to start?" He flipped the power switch for the amplifier and a pop of static burst out from the mic I'd just tapped.

"In about twenty minutes. I thought he'd be here by now. Must be running late or maybe his fiancée wasn't ready on time. I'm looking forward to meeting her." Even though Roger had seemed like a stalker, he wasn't a bad guy, and I was curious what the girl he'd chosen to marry was like.

Ferris came up with the first load of his drum kit and Digby turned to helping him get those in place. I went back to the van to get the iced coffees we'd picked up on the way over. Man, I really needed a jolt and this probably wouldn't do it.

More people began to pour into the park, most dressed casually in jeans and sweaters for the cool, although sunny, day. A few hardy souls wore shorts and knit shirts. I felt overdressed in the country skirt and blouse that I'd chosen for the day, thinking it might be a little more dress up than a picnic. Apparently, I was wrong.

Once Ferris was set up, we started our sound check, and people began to meander our way. Mid-way through, I spotted Roger weaving his way toward the stage. Oddly, he came alone. Where was his intended? He waved at me and ambled to the edge of the short stage, putting us about eye to eye.

"Hey, Gillian. I'm sorry I'm a little late. Last minute things to pick up and my timing was off."

"Yeah, that happens." I peered behind him looking to see if a woman was making her way toward him. No one seemed to be. "Where's your fiancée?"

"Oh, Sonya is still getting some stuff from the car. I wanted to let you know we're here. You guys can start whenever you're ready." He grinned up at me with that same silly look he got when he was around me.

"Right. We're ready to go now. So, bring your lady over and we'll chat at the end of the first set, okay?"

He nodded and I tossed a little hand wave after him as he started back through the folks moving toward us. It looked like nearly a hundred people now. Not all of these were there for his party, were they? If so, he must be more popular than I thought.

I gave Ferris the high sign and we kicked off our set with our rendition of the Beatles "I Saw Her Standing There." We played another twelve songs ranging from romantic ballads to rowdy rock, all with a love theme to celebrate the happy couple, although I still didn't see them in the people dancing in front of the stage. As I began the last number of the set, I spotted Roger coming toward the front holding the hand of a woman wearing a blue jean skirt, western shirt, and a sunhat. Perhaps the mysterious fiancée finally showed up.

We finished that set, telling everyone we'd be back in about fifteen minutes. I jumped down the four-inch elevation from the stage to greet Roger and his intended. He grinned at me and pulled her a little to the front.

"Gillian, this is Sonya. Honey, meet my former crush."

I felt my eyebrow twitch as he said that, put on a friendly smile, and offered my hand to Sonya. She was about my height and build, and under the hat, I could see her hair color was almost the same hue of golden brown. In fact, she was a pretty close look-alike for me. Same facial shape and similar eye color.

"Pleased to meet you," she said. "Roger's told me so much about you." She glanced at him. "You're right, honey, I do look a lot like her."

Behind me, I heard Ferris catch his breath as he came out to greet the couple. I could guess that he was thinking the same thing I was.

"Yeah, there does seem to be a resemblance." A little too much of one as far as I was concerned. I had an uneasy feeling about this. "So, do you want us to say anything in particular or should I just call you on stage?"

"Yeah, I'll come up and say a few words after a couple of songs into your next set." Roger put an arm around Sonya and hugged her. "I won't take long."

"Oh, that's fine, Roger. You're the boss today. Congratulations to both of you." I excused myself and headed for the ladies' room. Ferris followed, catching up with me before we got there.

"I don't like that guy." His voice carried that annoyed tone he could get. "I mean, that girl looks a lot like you and it's not a coincidence. He picked someone who was like you. I think he's trying to turn her into you."

"I noticed. It is a little creepy, but it could be just a fluke. Since he asked her to marry him, I assume he's in love with her."

"Maybe." He turned toward the men's room when we got to the building. I continued around the corner to the ladies.

What game was Roger playing here? Did he deliberately look for someone who resembled me? Was he so infatuated with me that he thought he could make someone else into my duplicate or was he trying to make me jealous?

Shaking my head, I started back to the stage and spotted a bright-blue plastic bucket filled with ice and cold drinks. I made a detour that direction and snagged a trio of icy cold sodas. A few people came up and commented on how they were enjoying the music and how cool it was to have a live band at the party. A couple of them even asked for a business card, which I gave them with a smile and a promise of a discount on our fee if they decided to use the band.

I handed a soda to Digby when I got back to the stage. He grinned, popping it open, and asked, "Did you notice how much that chick looked like you?"

"Yeah, I did. So did Ferris and probably everybody else here." My happy face went south as I thought about it.

"It's weird, don't ya think?"

I nodded. End of story. I filled him in on the slight change in the second set to give Roger the microphone for a few minutes after we did "My Girl."

Ferris came back a minute later, grabbed his soda with a word of thanks, and settled behind the drums. He tapped the cymbal, his code that we were starting soon. I flipped the switch on my keyboard and played a couple of chords to be sure it was still on the amp. Digby fingered a little of a Spanish rhythm on his guitar, and we were set.

Roger's guests, and possibly a few strays, gathered around again as we launched our second set with a rocking version of "You're the One" that had them bouncing in place and singing along. Ferris took the lead on "My Girl" and after he finished, I took the mic. "Thanks, everyone. We are having a great time here today. How about you?"

Some cheered, some clapped, and some whistled—just the kind of reaction we wanted. "Before we go on, we are going to pause for a word from our sponsor." A few laughs from those who caught it, so I went on. "Your host is here to say a few words as we celebrate his engagement. So come on up, Roger."

He'd been waiting right at the stage and only had a little hop up onto it. He hugged me, kissing my cheek as he took the microphone.

"Thanks, Gillian. Isn't she terrific? And this band is just awesome. Thanks so much for playing for this amazing day." He waved his arms to everyone gathered in the area and continued, "Friends, thank all of you for coming out to help us celebrate my getting the lovely Sonya to say yes to me."

He reached down for Sonya's hand and helped her onto the stage. Wolf whistles and cheers went up as Sonya shyly ducked her head. She took her hat off and snuggled up alongside Roger as several people snapped photos and videos of the occasion.

With her face more visible and the golden brown hair obvious under the sunny day, she looked even more like me. I caught Digby's look as he rolled his eyes toward her and raised his eyebrows. I glanced behind me to see that Ferris frowned, a decidedly unhappy look. Coincidence, I told myself. I was sure Roger didn't go looking for my doppelganger.

"Okay. We are officially inviting all of you to the wedding... which we haven't set the date for yet. We have decided it will be in the spring, probably late April and as soon as we lock it in, we will be sending out the invites. So, we expect to see all of you there. Now, let's get back to the music with my favorite group and good friends, Spicy Jam."

Good friends? My left eyebrow twitched upward and Digby turned to adjust the sound on his mic. That was taking a bit of liberty with our relationship, I thought. Sure, he'd been at a lot of concerts, but he was far from a good friend. Still, we were professionals and let it slide as we started the next song in the set.

After we'd finished, we began packing up our equipment as the party got a steadily rowdier. I realized Roger had brought champagne and beer so people, including Roger, were getting happier with each toast. Once we were done and Ferris took the last load of his drums to the van, I motioned to Roger to ask about our fee.

He floated over in a silly little half-dance step and his face split into a big grin. He flung an arm around my shoulders and yanked me closer to him. "What can I do for you, darlin'?"

Cringing, I said, "Uh, you have some money for us, right?"

His eyes narrowed a little as he seemed to puzzle over it, then he replied, "Oh yeah, of course." He dug into his pocket, pulled out five Ben Franklins, and pressed them into my hand.

Cash. Great, I wouldn't have to worry about a bad check. I stuck them in my skirt pocket and started to pull away from him. That's when he tightened his grip and moved in to try to kiss me as I tried to push him away from me. What the hell?!

A moment or two later, I felt someone grab me and Ferris' arm shot forward shoving Roger away. Ferris guided me away from Roger as he placed himself between us, hands raised and ready to strike at Roger, who had stumbled back a couple of feet and looked stunned.

"Are you nuts, man? Your fiancée is right over there and you're trying to make out with Gillian—what's up with that?" Ferris kept his voice low enough that only the three of us could hear.

Roger raised his hands in submission and shook his head. "Look, man, I just wanted to thank her with a friendly little kiss. I didn't think it would be a big deal. I mean, we're friends, right?" His voice slurred and he had trouble getting the words out.

"No, fella. We're a professional band and while we appreciate our fans, it doesn't give you the right to step out of line around Gillian. From now on, you stay away from us. You got it?"

I think my mouth must have dropped open as Ferris issued this verdict. While I didn't appreciate Roger taking advantage of the situation, Ferris was right that it was totally inappropriate, although he was a little harsher than I would have been. I turned my gaze to Sonya, who stood not more than five feet away staring at us in shock. She appeared frozen, unable to move or tear her eyes away from the altercation.

I found my voice again and stepped around Ferris to speak to Roger. "Look, let's forget this ever happened and it will not occur again. Right now, you better take care of Sonya 'cause she is sure confused by what you just did. Blame the alcohol, but you go make it right."

Ferris slid his arm around my shoulder, pulling me toward him in a purely possessive gesture as if he wanted to send a clear message to Roger that I was off limits. Although a little more territorial than I would have expected, he didn't hesitate to protect me.

Roger managed a shaky nod, turned around, and wobbled back to Sonya, reaching a hand out to her and presumably apologizing for his drunkenness. Poor girl. She may not have realized that Roger had that much of a thing for me, so this might have been a real eye-opener. For that matter, I'd tagged him a harmless stalker, and I might have to revise that assessment.

Arm still around me, Ferris guided me back to the van and opened the door for me. Digby stood next to his beat-up-looking car watching until I got in. He gave us a nod and went around to the driver's side.

"Thanks for rescue," I said as Ferris pulled the van onto the street to head up to McCarran Blvd to circle back toward his house. Dig's car edged out right behind us. "Man, Roger was so stinkin' drunk..."

"Yeah, I could smell it. I couldn't fuckin' believe he would be that ballsy."

I gaped at him in surprise, my eyes wide. I rarely heard Ferris talk like that, especially not around me. "You might have over-reacted a little back there."

He shook his head, taking his eyes off the road for only a second or so. "No, I didn't. That guy has a thing for you and it's pretty damn obvious. He started making moves as soon as he saw you and a couple of those remarks were out of line. I feel bad for his girl. If she's smart, she'll dump him."

"He'd been drinking, Ferris." I don't know why I felt I should defend Roger. Maybe I thought a stalker was kind of cool, but it was also creepy, and Roger had taken it too far today. Drunk or not, he really disrespected Sonya. That was a fact.

"No excuse. He wants her to be you and that is just plain sick." Ferris made the turn onto the freeway and we pointed back to the northwest side of Reno.

"I know. Like I said, thanks for coming to the rescue." While I could have flipped Roger myself, it was nice to have my band mate step in to do it instead.

"No problem. You know I'm there for you." He flashed a gentle smile at me and his eyes radiated a tender look that I hadn't seen since we had dated that brief time back in college.

Once we got to his house, Ferris got my keyboard and stand out and took them to my Jeep. As he loaded them in the back, he asked, "D'ya want to come in for a bit?"

"Not today. I have a few things to do before it gets too late. Another time, maybe?"

"Sure. Anytime."

He hesitated a moment, pulled me into his arms, and rested his chin on top of my head as he rocked me in his embrace. It felt good, another flash from the past. But where was this coming from now?

He shifted his head a little and his mouth grazed my forehead with a light kiss as he brought a gentle hand under my chin to tilt my head up. His eyes gazed at me, long eyelashes closing partially, as he moved in to press his lips against mine. Without thinking, I opened my lips slightly, and we merged in a deep, breathtaking kiss that set a small fire burning through my body.

When he released me, I was trembling. With a light touch, he ran his fingers along the side of my face and smoothed his thumb over the edge of my mouth. I gazed at him, my mind not quite grasping what had just happened.

"You sure you don't want to come in?" he asked.

Twenty-Three

I leaned against the door of my Jeep as I caught my breath. Janna sat sideways in the drivers' seat of her car and sipped from her water bottle. We'd done a fast half mile run this Sunday morning although neither of us had felt up to it. I'd filled her in on the events at Roger's party, telling her that Ferris had shoved him pretty hard and ready to fight.

"I still can't quite believe he came to my defense like that. It's like he was jealous or something."

I hadn't told her about the kiss later in front of his house, keeping it to myself for now. While I had been tempted to go inside with him and see where this sudden mood of his was going, I did have things to do at home, like laundry and catching up on some housework that I'd been neglecting for a few weeks. At least, that was what I'd told myself as I'd declined.

Her head came up and a half smile crossed her lips. "Come on, Gilly. You have to know he's had a crush on you ever since college."

"What? No. We broke off on dating after a month because it wasn't working for us." We'd found we weren't getting our work done, and we kept getting distracted while we dated. Plus we quarreled a lot. We were better as friends.

"That was in school. Now you've been away from it and things have changed. Isn't the attraction still there?"

"He's a friend. I don't see him as a romantic interest anymore." I paused to take a sip of my energy drink.

"Don't see it? Or haven't looked?" She pursed her lips into a smug, crooked smile and raised her eyebrows.

"Neither one. It was a mutual agreement and I moved on."

"Uh huh." She dismissed it with a shoulder shrug. "So, what are you up to today?"

"For one thing, I'm heading to the cemetery soon to contact Zoe. I have some questions for her. My last reading revealed some interesting things, although I'm not clear on how I'm interpreting them. I'd like Zoe's input."

"Jeez, that sounds so weird. You make it sound like you're picking up the phone to call her."

"Yeah, it is pretty strange. And you know what? I'm not even considering it all that odd anymore. I guess that's a sign I'm adapting pretty well to this peculiar situation I've been tossed into. I don't know if that's a good thing or not."

Her eyes took on a worried look. "To be honest, I don't know either." She stood up to give me a hug. "I gotta go. I need to be at work soon."

I embraced her back, waiting as she slipped into her car and pulled out of the parking area. I turned back to my Jeep and paused to gaze at the lake just beyond the lot. With autumn well underway, the duck population had dwindled quite a bit although they never completely left the area. Leaves had turned to red and gold, some still clinging to the branches while others had fallen to the ground. Mustiness from the moist leaves touched my nose and I breathed it in. I always found it a peaceful time of year, a time for reflection and recharging my energy before winter arrived. I had a felling I might need it.

I climbed into The Beast and pointed it toward home.

Less than an hour later, I made my way through the headstones to Zoe's grave. Although fallen leaves clustered on several graves in the area, hers remained barren of Nature's decorations. Tufts of new grass grew on the slight mound and flowers from the funeral had been blown away or removed long ago. With nearly a month gone since she'd died, I speculated I visited her more than any of her family did.

I bowed my head a moment reciting a prayer for safety as I made this excursion to the other side. I started singing a tune I called "Sad Broken Doll"—the one I'd written a few days earlier. Zoe had provided the inspiration if you could call it that.

The words flowed as the song poured out from my soul, tearing their way into the ether to summon the broken woman on the other side. I sang my heart out while I called to her and expected the ethereal graveyard to materialize around me at any moment.

Nothing happened.

I made it all the way to the end, tears rolling down my cheeks in an emotional flood. However, I still stood at the foot of the grave. I caught my breath, pulled out a tissue, and wiped my eyes and nose. Why hadn't I connected? Maybe I had gotten too caught up in the song and the lyrics or maybe it hadn't resonated with the next plane. I had no idea how this thing worked. I seldom failed to connect to it.

Unless Zoe had moved on. Perhaps she'd given up on seeing Nick apprehended and had gone on through the gate. I found that hard to believe though. She'd been so angry and dead set on making him pay as well as finding Saffi that I didn't think she'd abandon the option.

I decided to try another song, something that I could sing without involving my brain so that I could easily drift. I settled on "Purple Rain" and began singing again.

Come the end of the song, I still stood in the same spot. No contact at all. Even if Zoe wasn't there or didn't want to talk to me, I thought I would at least make it to the other cemetery. Come on, I'd done it before and in my dreams. Now it was like I was shut out. Had my gift failed me? Had I lost it somehow?

I dropped my shoulders to release the tension and trudged back to the Jeep. Now what? Try to figure this out on my own or just turn it all over to Egan Moss?

As I pondered this, my phone buzzed with a text message from Gavin.

U doing anything? he asked.

No. What's up? I replied.

Got sumthin u need 2 see.

My lips twitched into an amused smile. Nice to know the Prof used shortcuts in his text like the rest of us.

Now?

Yep.

Your house? Be there in 40, I sent back. I needed a quick stop and something for lunch before I headed over.

Although I was curious about his message, I still took the time to zip into a fast food restaurant, park, and hurry in to use the ladies room. Coming out, I ordered a burger and a soda to go. I could eat once I got to Gavin's. Just didn't want him to think I expected him to feed me.

On the way over, my thoughts drifted back to the failure at the cemetery. Maybe I should have sung the song Zoe liked and that would have triggered it. Or maybe I should have sung a hymn since it was Sunday. I didn't gain anything by questioning it now. I somehow hoped it didn't mean I'd lost the ability; something I found ironic since I hadn't been overjoyed when I got it. Now, I was in the middle of solving a mystery and I needed the input.

Or did I? Could I puzzle this out without Zoe's help? I knew Saffi was alive when she and Nick left Zoe's bedroom. Nick had lost the cufflink in the room, so that was where it ended. As Saffi had left, she seemed to be somewhat calm, not frightened of Nick even though he'd killed his wife. Did that mean that Saffi was in on the plan? Or was that simply the secretary trying to appear to be on his side? Then again, it looked like she had attacked Nick when she exited the bathroom.

I didn't have any more of an answer than I had before when I parked the Jeep in front of Gavin's house. I only made it partway up the walk before he came out and down the steps to meet me.

He grinned and pointed at the food bag in my hand. "Bring any for me?"

"No, but I'll share my burger."

He laughed and hugged me. "Not necessary. I have sandwich makings in the house. Come on in."

He ushered me through the door, closing and locking it behind me. Was he worried about someone—or something—coming inside? As I shot a questioning look at him, he ignored it and led the way to the kitchen.

"Grab a seat. Do you need anything else? Plate, fork?"

I shook my head and took the chair across from the main part of the kitchen and set my bag down. He fetched a beer and slid into the seat across from me.

While I unwrapped my burger, I asked, "What is so important that you wanted me to see?"

He flashed a brief grin. "Actually, it's more that I want you to touch it."

"Huh? Are you asking me to try to read an object?"

"Sort of."

"Uh, I think that's a yes or a no question. Either I am or I'm not." I bit into the burger, started to chew, and waited for his reply.

"Not a reading so much as just seeing what kind of impression you get from it." He winked and sipped his beer.

I swallowed, took a sip of my soda. "That's a reading in my book, Professor. But I'll try it." I judged it might be a fair test of my ability to read objects although I might also fail.

"Great. Finish your food and we'll do it."

Less than ten minutes later, Gavin took me to the living room where a bamboo-looking wooden box, about six inches by ten inches, sat in the middle of the coffee table. I took a seat on the sofa across from it. Sliding in close to me, Gavin pulled on a pair of gloves and leaned forward to open the box revealing light tan, fur-looking liners on the inside cover and bottom. In the middle, an apple-sized, not-quite-round ball rested on the cushion formed by the fur. He picked it up and held it up to me.

"I found this item twelve years ago in a remote part of Cambodia near Prasat Bakan on a dig. It actually belongs to a Seattle Museum that financed the expedition. I borrowed it back from them for a few days to do a little more research on it."

As he spoke, I gazed at the ball. It appeared to be carved out of a slightly yellowed ivory, although the designs worked into it didn't look Asian to me. In fact, a few images appeared to be demonic in nature—distorted faces, horned heads, a gaping mouth. I shivered as a feeling of something evil touched me.

"You want me to touch that?" I turned my gaze to him.

"Yep. Just hold it for a minute to see if you pick up anything from it." He offered it to me.

I shook my head slowly. "I dunno. I don't like what I'm feeling about it."

"It won't hurt you. Just try for a moment or two."

I held my palm out flat and let him set the thing in the middle of my hand.

Zap!

If I hadn't been sitting down, I might have stumbled at the transition. As it was, I felt disoriented and with some sense of preservation for the artifact I held, I curled my hand around the ball to avoid dropping it. My mind filled with images of dark green foliage, colorful blossoms in various bright hues, and a creature that looked neither human nor animal.

Dark skinned, the body was lithe and flexible, gyrating at odd angles as it seemed to dance around a fire where some kind of meat roasted on a stick. The creature tossed a wad of herbs or powder into the flames and they shot skyward with a flare of dark green, followed by a deep red pillar of fire. In a cage made of smaller tree limbs laced together with vines, I could make out the faces of two brown-skinned children, their eyes wide in horror as they watched the bizarre actions of the creature. One reached a hand through an open space in the cage and her mouth formed the shape of a cry for her mother.

I forced my hand open to toss the vile object from my grasp. Instead, I lurched forward and my head smacked against the coffee table as the ivory ball vanished from my hand.

"Ow," I complained as I brought my head up and pressed my left hand against my forehead to feel for a bump before I began rubbing at it. I shifted my head to view Gavin with the ball still in his gloved hands about to return it to its storage box.

"That thing is totally awful." I felt like it had invaded my guts, oozing through me with pure evil from its core.

He slipped it into the box and closed it again before he removed his gloves. He slid a comforting hand on my back and rubbed. "It's all right now, chica. Just take a few deep breaths. It can't hurt you."

"That's what you say. I feel like it snaked all through me with nothing but evil. That was god-awful." I coughed, burping as if I might eject my lunch.

Gavin left for about a minute, returning with a glass of water that he held out to me. "Drink this. A little hydration will help."

I gulped half of it down at one time, feeling the cool liquid going into what seemed like a sizzling hot stomach. I had never experienced such a ghastly sensation from touching an object. "What the hell is that thing?"

His eyes seemed a little worried as he shook his head. "Truth? I don't know. It isn't consistent with the other artifacts from Prasat Bakan, and I've never seen anything like it before. I found it about a kilometer from the Buddhist Temple in an underground cell where some urns containing dried food and herbs were stored. The box had been tucked into an alcove with ivory bars across the front. I thought it was something important and possibly sacred to them."

"Not sacred, unless they were Satanists." I finished the water and held up the glass. "More, please."

"Need anything stronger?"

"No." I stared at the box as if it might burst into flames and consume us and the house at any moment.

From the kitchen, I heard the clink of ice hitting glass, followed by a glug as water from the dispenser poured out. Gavin returned with a pitcher of water and refilled my glass before setting it down on a pad on the table.

I leaned back against a cushion. "Did you feel anything when you picked it up?"

"Not at first. I wore gloves when I first opened the box, as I did this time. When I got it back to our dig tent, I pulled it out and touched it for the first time without gloves. I got the impression of something dark and foreboding, a flashing image of a triangular face, black with red eyes, and a spiral-shaped horn sprouting from the top of the head. Also black."

"That was it?"

"Pretty much. I just had a sense of it being somewhat demonic and I figured it was stored away from the monastery for safekeeping. Although I searched for more information, I could find no mention in any of the writings, glyphs, or reports from Prasat Bakan that referenced it in any way. So, I packed it up with the rest of the artifacts destined for the museum and shipped it to Washington."

"And that seemed like a good idea to you?" I frowned at him. If the monks had hidden it away, they probably had a good reason to keep it out of anyone's hands.

"Yeah, it did. I wanted to know more about it and I thought I'd have better luck with the resources here. So, I've told you. Now you tell me what you got from touching it."

I did. I described everything in as much detail as I could down to the look of the strange creature dancing and the frightened looks of the two children. As I spoke, his face grew grimmer and paled.

"What?"

He ran his hand across his jaw and mouth, got to his feet, and strode across the room. Going to the bookcase, he searched for a book and pulled out one. As he flipped through it, he paced back and forth until he found something. He came over to me, holding the book open to where I could see. "Did it look like this?"

I gazed intently at the page he indicated, seeing what looked like a woodcut illustration that looked very much like the creature I'd seen. Beneath it, a succinct caption declared it to be a *daemonium anima*. My mouth felt dry as I shifted my gaze to meet his eyes.

"Soul demon," he translated. "Possibly a rendition of a True Shade."

My stomach plummeted. What was the purpose of the relic? Had it recorded what the ghoul was doing? Had it been a possession of the thing?

"What are they, Gavin? Are they what we're facing now?"

"Could be."

"I think..." My voice wavered as I started to speak. I drank more water. "I think you made a mistake removing it from the alcove. A big mistake."

"Maybe," he conceded. "Or maybe not. Maybe it had nothing to do with the recent appearance of the shades on this plane."

"Or maybe you opened a pathway for them by removing it." I might be leaping to a conclusion; however, if this allowed them to gain entry, how did we stop it? Put it back?

Gavin shook his head, picked the box up, and took it to a wall safe at the back of a cabinet with a false front. It didn't bother him that I saw where he put it, so I had to wonder how secure it was.

"There's more to it than an old ivory relic. It may hold additional information if I can decipher it."

"Just don't ask me to touch it again." I rose, picked up my purse, and started for the door.

"Wait. You don't have to go. We still need to talk about your training. We can get started—"

I paused and turned to him. "I have to go. As long as that thing is in your house, I don't want to be in the same space."

"That bad, huh? Okay, I'm sorry. I had no idea..." Although he sounded sincere, his apology wouldn't change my mind.

"Catch you later."

"Gillian, we need to plan..." His voice faded as I scurried out the door as briskly as I could without breaking into a run. I still felt as if a malicious bug crawled inside my skin.

Twenty-Four

The ominous feeling I'd left Gavin's house with stayed with me all the way home. A horrified part of me trembled in fear at the prospect of facing off with a shade, let alone a True Shade if they were as powerful as they seemed to be. I knew I was woefully inadequate to subdue such a strong creature.

Where there is good, there is also evil. I'd heard that all my life. I'd never fully felt it until I saw the vile images from that cursed object.

Oh, sure, intellectually, I knew the shades I'd seen in the cemeteries were the guides to hell fires, so to speak, although I didn't believe in Hell. What I'd seen did suggest that a purgatory existed and an unsettled and broken soul could end up there. Perhaps naively, I didn't think it was the Hell of the Bible.

The fact that the shades were identified in an ancient book as "soul demons" suggested something far more terrifying to me. If a true description, they represented the destruction of the soul. No chance for an afterlife or a next life or whatever came next. Even for an agnostic like me, it meant the slim shred of hope and faith I had in soul survival could be in danger.

I pulled into my driveway, hurried into my snug house, and proceeded to throw up more protection spells. Aware they constituted little more than ritual and a prayer to the forces of the Universe or God to provide protection, I nonetheless said them with the hope that Madame Astrid and Gavin were right that they would work. Was unwavering faith a necessary component? If so, I was already in deep trouble.

Nygard moseyed down from upstairs and sat on the steps just above the sofa level to watch me. "I'm not nuts, kit. I need all the help I can get."

In his unique, deep voice, he offered a supportive meow before he came over to rub against my legs and purr. In his book, that made everything right. I reached down, scratched his ears, then offered dinner. Together, we entered the kitchen, checked out the locks on the door, and satisfied ourselves that it was secure.

To say my nerves were stretched to the limit would be an understatement. As I got Nygard's food, I muttered aloud to my so-called angel. "Zac, I really need some guidance here. If you're supposed to help me, you'd better show up soon. Otherwise, I'm beginning to think you might work for the opposition. So, if you can hear me, please make contact."

I nearly jumped out of my skin when the landline rang. Certain Zac hadn't started using a phone, I pulled myself together and went to check the caller id. Gayle Trumbull. Oh, great. Perfectly bad timing, Gayle. I let it go to the answering machine.

"Hey, Gillian. This is Gayle Trumbull. I haven't heard from you about doing that interview we discussed so I wanted to touch bases. I know there's a lot of interest for this story and I think we should do it soon. Call me back."

A lot of interest that she'd drummed up, I thought. That woman had a lot of nerve. This was turning into the worst weekend I'd had in a long time. I poured a glass of wine and sat on the couch with a notepad to try to make some sense of what had happened today.

First off, although I couldn't contact Zoe, I had been able to pick up images from Gavin's object. From that, I gathered that I hadn't lost my ability to communicate, so something else must have blocked me at the cemetery. Either my song choice or some action on Zoe's part might have been the problem. Perhaps she wasn't where she could hear me or she just didn't want to come. I recalled Marielle saying something about certain things draining energy and she needed to recharge in order to come talk to me. That could be the problem, although what Zoe might be doing other than talking to me, I had no idea.

Next, I needed to figure out what exactly I'd seen in the vision from the cufflink. So, I started there and made notes as I replayed the scene in my mind. Nick had been bending over Zoe, whom he'd shot and was already dead. He'd pulled out a knife and cut her throat. Why? Was it anger or was there some other reason? Not just the necklace. He yanked that off easily. Whatever he did, it wasn't something I could see from the view I had. Next, Saffi jumped him and they rolled on the floor. Had she attacked him or was it a more friendly romp? But over Zoe's dead body? I couldn't accept that they were so callous about it. Yet, she didn't seem frightened by Nick's threat and the knife he held. They argued, that much I could see, so what were they saying?

I rubbed my temples as I felt a headache starting. I'd had enough for one day. Taking my wine, I went upstairs and filled my Jacuzzi bath, adding in lavender oil to relax me. I set the glass on the slim ledge at the top, stripped off my clothes, and slipped into the warm, swirling waters to relax. I closed my eyes as I slid down to my neck with my head resting on an inflated pillow at the back and breathed in the soothing scent, letting my mind drift with the sound of the water jets.

I conjured an aquamarine blue sea with light sand beaches and big boulders along the shoreline. No one else appeared to be around, so I seemed to have it to myself. I shifted my eyes to my feet and the crimson-colored flip-flops I wore. Stepping out of them, I strolled to the shoreline, letting the warm, soothing waters lap against my toes and up to my ankles. I felt so relaxed and secure at this moment.

"Hey, not-an-angel. I need to talk to you."

A familiar woman's voice called from near me. I turned toward her and gaped at Zoe standing in the middle of the beach, still bloodied with torn nightclothes and looking even worse for the wear since I'd last seen her.

"Zoe, how did you get here?" I gasped.

Her face reflected her confusion as a light crease formed between her brows and her eyes narrowed. "Well, you called me, didn't you? I've been trying to come to you."

"That was hours ago. I went to the cemetery and couldn't make contact. Where were you?" I started walking toward her, curious how she managed to materialize on this beach. For that matter,

where was I?

Just realizing that she stood on a beach, Zoe turned in a circle, hand above her eyes to block the sun, and seemed to study her surroundings. "Yeah, this is strange. Nice beach and secluded. How did I get here?"

"Good question and I don't know. Why didn't you come earlier?"

She gazed at me, eyes locked on mine. "That was really weird. I heard you singing and could hear your whisper above it, calling me. When I tried to get to you, I couldn't. No matter how I tried, I couldn't make the connection. Something was blocking me, something that felt..." She paused, searching for the word. "...vile. Really off and just vile. I tried to push through it, but it resisted and I couldn't break past."

I didn't like the sound of that. Did that mean the shades could block her? Or did they block me? Were they interfering now? "Were you in the cemetery?"

"No, I'd gone somewhere else."

What? Did the souls leave the cemetery when I wasn't talking to them? They didn't go through the gate, so where did they go? "Where? I didn't know that you could leave the graveyard except to the gate?"

"Well, yeah. Of course, I can. I'm a ghost, aren't I?"

"Not exactly. At least, I don't think so. You're a transitional soul preparing to move to the next plane. A ghost is an unsettled spirit that lingers around the location where it died."

Her eyes widened and a slight smile broke from her lips as she said, "Oops."

"Zoe, where were you?" I had a sneaky suspicion, but I wanted to hear it.

"At my house. In my bedroom." Her face grew sad. "I knew our marriage had deteriorated and Nick on-again, off-again about divorce. Honestly, I never thought he would kill me."

"Would he have killed Saffi?"

She shrugged. "I didn't think so. Maybe."

"He aimed at her. You got in the way. So, it seems like she was the target. Unless..."

Her eyes turned toward me, prompting me to continue.

"Unless he believed you would move to protect her. Was he testing you, Zoe? Did he want to see if your relationship with her was strong enough for you to risk yourself?"

Her lips tightened and she looked away from me. "It was complicated. He'd had an affair with Saffi before she and I got together. Ironic that we wouldn't have if he hadn't hurt me."

I saw a nearby boulder where the water just lapped around the edge and made my way there to sit and think about this. "You know, I have a theory and you're not going to like it."

She strolled over to lean against the boulder. The water brushed up against her legs and appeared to soak the bottom of her gown, but the blood didn't wash off. Even here, in this vision, she wasn't corporeal.

"What?"

"I think that he and Saffi might have planned your murder."

"No."

"Hear me out, Zoe. I saw what happened after your death and even through Saffi initially retreated to the bathroom, she came back out. At first, I thought she attacked Nick, but she wasn't afraid of him and they left your room together. While she did seem to be arguing with him, she didn't try to get away."

She kept shaking her head no. "Not Saffi. She wouldn't betray me. I know that for a certainty. She was probably trying to find a way out of the situation. Play along with Nick. Do whatever he says while looking for an opportunity to get away."

"Do you really believe that?"

"Yes. No..." Her face fell, sadness clouding her eyes. "I don't know. I just can't see her doing it to me."

"Maybe you're right. Here's something else puzzling me. I found a key on the floor in your house. It's made by Master, so I would guess it opens a padlock. I tried to get a reading from it, but couldn't get even a blink. Any idea what it unlocks?"

"Yeah, Nick has a storage unit in Sun Valley; I'm not sure where exactly. I don't know what he keeps in it and he doesn't—didn't—tell me."

My interest perked. "Maybe he's stored more documents in it or there's something else that might incriminate him. Although the case belongs to Reno PD, it's possible we could find evidence in it and that would pull in the sheriff's department. If you and I can figure out where he's fled, my friend at the sheriff's department might find a way to get him back in the country to arrest."

As she turned to gaze around the area again, a smile wormed its way across her face. "Either you or I chose this particular location for this meeting, my friend. Unless you've been here, I think it must have come from me because this is the exact beach that Nick and went to on our honeymoon. It's in the Canary Islands and this particular beach is pretty remote. It's on La Palma Island and the nearest town is Santa Cruz. Remote and quiet—a good hideaway. That could be where he went."

"You're right. I saw the travel brochures and this was one of them. Now, all we need is a way to lure him back."

"Think, woman. You may already have that. Didn't you find records in the crawlspace in the office? He wouldn't have put them there if they weren't important."

I snapped my fingers as I thought about the double books. "That's it. I forgot about those. If I—"

A big wash of water interrupted me as a wave splashed over the boulder I was sitting on. I sputtered...

And woke up splashing with my face underwater in my Jacuzzi where I'd slid down while I slept. Coughing and spitting water, I sat up and reached for my towel. I had been dreaming; however, these days, I didn't discount a dream for a lack of evidence. I had been talking to Zoe; I was certain.

I climbed out of the tub, dried off, and put on my pajamas. As I opened the bathroom door, I nearly tripped over Nygard who was crouched down next to it. I scooped him up, giving him an affectionate squeeze. "Were you watching out for me, Ny?"

He tucked his head against my chest, rubbing it back and forth, and purred. I'd probably scared him with my coughing and splashing. Petting him, I carried him back to my bed and settled on it.

As I sifted through the information I'd gotten in that vision, I decided I'd visit Moss after work tomorrow and see if he could use the key as an excuse to locate and investigate Nick's storage unit. I still had reservations about Saffi and wondered if she might not be sunning herself in the Canary Islands right now.

Putting my gun under my bed, just where my hand could easily reach it, I turned off the light and made one last plea to Zac to get in touch. My faith in that spirit continued on a steady decline.

Twenty-Five

I woke early the next morning, thinking I'd heard a noise in the house. Nygard curled at the end of the bed and seemed unconcerned. I reached under the bed for my gun, took the safety off, and slipped out of bed to go downstairs.

Nightlights in the living room and kitchen cast enough illumination that I could make it down the stairs without stumbling on anything. Even though I detected no movement, I remained cautious. I made my way through the living room seeing nothing amiss and poked my head around the corner into the kitchen entry.

Still nothing. No signs of movement in the shadows or anything disturbed. I turned on the kitchen light and looked around. It looked normal. Maybe it had been my imagination or nerves or maybe some animal had attempted to come in the cat door. While I kept it closed at night, sometimes another cat or even a raccoon tried to get in.

I glanced at the clock on the stove. Six-thirty. I could go back to bed or start my day early. I opted for the second choice. It would take longer to fall back asleep than it was worth. I headed back upstairs to get dressed.

A hiss came from the end of the walkway to the bathroom and Nygard stood, fur bristling up, in front of the closed door. I froze for a moment and an icicle of fear shot up my spine. Bringing my gun up, I walked as silently as possible toward the door even as I knew if what I feared was behind the door, the gun would be useless.

Using my foot to nudge the cat away, I opened the door with a quick flip and crouched low, grasping the weapon with both hands. I couldn't see anything in the dark, so I used my shoulder to press the light switch up. With determination, I kept my eyes from blinking as I peered in. A sudden movement, then a black streak of shadow shot through the ceiling.

Another damn shade in my house. I lowered the Luger and leaned against the doorjamb as I sagged. So much for the wards. I definitely needed something stronger against them.

Shaking a little, I bent to rub Nygard's ears. "Good job, watch-cat. It's gone now."

I turned on all the lights upstairs and went in to shower. It felt creepy to stand naked in my own bathroom and know that one of those things could show up at any time. On edge, I pushed my back against the shower wall as if it might offer protection from a rear attack. The water cascaded down my face as I rinsed shampoo from my hair and I kept blinking it away so I could keep an eye open the whole time. Nothing leisurely in this shower, I finished up in about five minutes, snatched the towel from the bar across the door and dried off as I scurried back to my closet.

Ten minutes later, I'd dressed and sat on the edge of my bed. As I returned the gun to the locked drawer, I gazed at the little bag of objects I'd purloined from Zoe's house. The key kept coming into my mind and I felt it might hold the clue I needed to find Nick Sarkis. While I couldn't find out what it opened, perhaps Moss might find some other clue from it.

Hell, I thought, why not take all of my finds to him? I'd gotten what I could from them. I tucked them into my work bag with a change of shirt and a snack bar. I'd call him from the shop and set up a meeting.

Evidently, I also needed to talk to Madame Astrid again about the wards and why they didn't keep the shades out. Maybe she knew a stronger chant, potion, or herb. Possibly Gavin had some ideas. I'd talk to him later also.

Work went by in spurts of busy and times of not so much. In those slower periods, my mind went back to the dream meeting I'd had with Zoe. Even though it had been a curious meeting, I felt certain it had been real. At least as real as the excursions in the cemetery were. If the shades were blocking me from Zoe, they were becoming stronger and more dangerous. A sinking feeling told me that I might lose her if I couldn't get her problem resolved so she would cross soon.

At my noon break, I called Madame Astrid for an appointment, then called Moss to set a meeting for later in the day. With that done, I called and left a message for Gavin, hoping he would pick it up sometime during the day.

"Tell me again what you saw," Astrid said. I'd already told her about the shade twice. "Only this time, take a deep breath, close your eyes, and tell your mind to slow down."

Right, that would work fine, or it did last time I tried. I followed instructions, drew in a deep breath that smelled like oranges—she'd opened an herb—and instructed my mind to show me slow-mo. Seeing again from my view in the bathroom doorway, I flipped the light on, and the shade drifted forward from just above the Jacuzzi. I had the impression it was startled as it jerked forward, condensed into an elongated black streak, and zipped for the ceiling where it slipped through around the inset lighting fixture.

Well, that had slowed it considerably. So, why was the shade in my bathroom? If it waited for me, why was it surprised when I showed up?

"You have a weak spot somewhere on your roof," Astrid pronounced. "You need to seal all the doorways in the house and cast a ward to protect the roof. It found a way past them. I have another essence that might provide stronger protection."

Rising, she scurried to her store of herbs, candles, oils, and incense on the shelf next to the curtained door. Shifting a few around as she hunted, she located a small bottle of oil, popped the top to sniff, and turned to me with a satisfied smirk. "This should do it. Nutmeg oil is very good against evil."

Why did I feel like I was enrolled in Witchcraft 101? I sighed and took the oil from her.

"What else is troubling you?"

I looked up. Why not ask for help? "Would you be willing to boost my object reading? I have this key that keeps bothering me and I can't seem to get anything from it."

An eyebrow rose in question. "As I said, psychometry is your gift, not mine. I can try to give you an energy boost, but not all objects have a story to tell. Perhaps I can call in Elias for a little more power." She leaned back and closed her eyes.

Elias served as her spirit guide and helped her to see the other side if I understood her explanation correctly. I felt the reading might be successful with that much power behind it. Getting out my evidence bag, I pulled out the little pouch with the key and slid the object into my hand.

"He's here," Astrid said, and she reached across to touch my left wrist. She took another deep breath and nodded for me to begin.

I rubbed at the key, my thumb gliding smoothly in a circular motion as I focused on it and Nick's name in my mind. If there was a connection, I willed it to show me.

At first, I saw nothing, just an empty screen waiting for a picture to play. Gradually, I noticed a glimmer of something that grew into a road off a big street or highway, and the image of a storage facility. The area looked familiar and the signage had a bright red background with faded letters I couldn't quite make out. The vision shifted to one of the long buildings housing garage-sized storage units and I could read the number six on the outside. We turned to the left and traveled down two doors to a unit marked B. 6B—that was it. That had to be the unit the key opened.

The vision broke and I opened my eyes. Almost certain, I knew where that storage place was in the Sun Valley area. "I've got it!" I told Astrid and she released my wrist, taking a deep breath.

"So, it worked. I could see nothing, but if you got the information, all is good." She peered at the larger bag as I put the key back in the pouch. She pointed to it. "Something in there is calling me. I can feel a pull. A tug. May I?"

I nodded.

Astrid pulled the bag to her, stuck her hand in, digging around in it as if she sought something. She pulled out the little plastic bag with Saffi's earring in it."

"That's—"

"No, don't tell me. Just take my hand again and let me sense what I can from it."

She offered her open palm with the ruby earring in the middle and I pressed my hand over it and closed my fingers around hers so that we locked the stone into the pocket of flesh. She closed her eyes and reached for Elias again.

At first, I felt nothing, just a tingling along my arm. I received no images from it, not even a suggestion of what I'd seen before. We sat like that for a minute or two, neither speaking as Astrid appeared to be in a trance state. Out of the blue, I sensed anxiety, fear, and grief coming from it. I heard Astrid murmuring something in a soft voice and figured she spoke to Elias.

She jerked and lurched forward before snapping back in her chair and her eyes shot wide open. Her pupils were huge, spooking me, and sending an uncomfortable tremble along my backbone. She blinked, breaking the tension, and said, "I fear the owner of this earring is dead. Elias saw something on the other side. It isn't very specific, but this is what he showed me. There is a grave in the desert, not far from a huge rock pile near a road. It lies perhaps another half mile into the desert to the northeast. Mountains surround the area although they are somewhat distant from the rocks. I can't tell you more than that. He is quite certain the person who wore this stone is dead."

I stared at her for a moment, taking in what she'd said and searching my mind for an elusive memory to do with a rock pile. What was it? There was a huge pile of rocks, a natural formation, off the Pyramid Lake Highway. That could be it. "Did Elias see anything else around it? A lake or a pyramid?"

She seemed to consult him for a moment before she shook her head. "No, just what I told you. Wait! He saw a blue haze nearby. Does it make any sense to you?"

"Yes, I think it does. You and Elias might have solved a mystery in the case I'm working on. If this works out, I might be able to help my spirit client." I slipped the earring back into the pouch and put it back with the rest of the evidence.

"Thank you so much, Madame. I have more information than I

had before. Now, I have to hurry to another meeting." I jumped to my feet, ready to bolt out the door.

Astrid rose also, leaning forward on her table. "Gillian, be careful. Don't go rushing into anything. Pay attention to the signs. You've caught the attention of the shades and that is not a good thing."

I grew more serious. "I understand. I hope that Gavin and I can handle that problem."

"As do I. But know, I am here and will help where I can. Don't hesitate."

As I got in my car, I thought about the key and the storage unit. I pulled out my phone and did a search on Sun Valley storage buildings. Close to a dozen listings came up. I clicked on the first few, looking for a sign or a logo that resembled what I'd seen. I found it on the fourth try—Store-It-Away, and it was only a few miles beyond the Sheriff's office. I had a little over an hour before my appointment with Moss. If I could open the unit with the key, I'd feel more confident about telling Moss it was related to Nick Sarkis.

Decision made, I headed out toward US395 north and the turnoff to the unit. Within fifteen minutes, I pulled into the small parking lot at a gate to the units. A business office sat on the lot side of the gate with six rows of storage units behind the chain link fence. A sign indicating the open hours hung on the fence with a card reader next to it for after-hours use.

I walked through the gate with confidence in my stride like any other paying renter. I went to the side and glanced at the end of the buildings enough to see the numbers on the end. Of course, it would be building six, the one furthest from the parking. As I went, I noticed a couple of people at their units and they had driven in rather than parking out front. I should have done that, I reflected, thinking that it made me look like a visitor.

I reached the building and turned to the left, happy to see a B on the second unit in. Garage doors that lifted up covered the fronts of each unit and the locks looked like standard ones. I pulled out my key, took a deep breath, and put it in the niche. As it slid in without resistance, I let my breath out and turned it. The lock clicked and I removed it from the slider. I grabbed for the handle, lifted, and the door went upward, rolling back into the ceiling rack.

"Can I help you, miss? Is this your unit?"

The voice startled me and I turned to face the speaker, a sturdily-built fellow with a retreating hairline peppered with gray. Dark brown eyes regarded me from his weathered face and the hint of a smile seemed less than welcoming.

"Uh, no, it's not my unit. I'm a friend of the owner and I'm just checking on something for him."

A look of confusion and suspicion wrinkled his brow as his eyes narrowed. "He told me this was for his aunt."

Thinking fast, I replied, "Yeah, right. His aunt. He wanted me to get a box out of storage for her. He's out of town and I work for him, so he called me. He even left me the key so I could help out." I held it up like a magic ticket as I hoped he would buy the story.

A disgruntled-sounding exclamation of annoyance burst from his throat like a growl, and he said, "Whatever. When you talk to Barnet next, tell him his monthly payment is overdue. He needs to pay up in the next week or I'll lock him out."

"Okay. I'm sure that's just an oversight and I'll let him know. I know he'll take care of it." I flashed my best smile.

He nodded, spun around, and marched back out to a motorized golf cart. I hadn't even heard it come up. I watched as he turned it around to head back to the office and let out a sigh of relief.

I pulled out my phone and made note of the name he'd given me. Barnet. Was Nick using an alias or was someone helping him?

I turned back to the building and went inside to look around. For the most part, there was office furniture—a few chairs and a pair of desks shoved into one corner. Two file cabinets stood stacked on top of each other. Going to the lower one, I pulled on the handle. Locked. Glancing up, I suspected the other one to be as well. I moved to the desks, pulling open drawer after drawer, all empty.

A three-level shelf leaned against the opposite wall and several boxes sat on them. Deciding I should find a lightweight box to take to my Jeep in case the manager watched me, I approached them. The first box felt heavy, maybe papers or books. The second box was a little lighter but still more than I wanted to carry back to my car. I couldn't even budge the third and fourth boxes. The fifth one, a smaller one, lifted with little effort, so I picked that one up and moved it to the top of the desk. I'd noticed a gray metal object out of the corner of my eye and stepped around the desk to see a squat safe shoved up against the back wall.

Kneeling, I studied the combination lock and considered trying to open it. I decided it would be better not to touch it. Bad enough that I'd broken into place. Moss would never let me hear the end of it if I tampered with the safe and it had evidence in it.

I straightened up. I'd seen enough, even though I hadn't seen anything that directly tied it to Nick other than the key. I'd leave it to Moss from here. I picked up the box, closed the door, and locked it again. Hurrying back to my car, I slowed to a normal pace when I came to the edge of the first building before I crossed to my Jeep. I slid the box into the front seat, climbed in, and backed out. Next stop was the Sheriff's Office.

I pulled into a close parking space with a little over ten minutes to spare. Curious about the box I'd chosen, I decided it wouldn't hurt to take a peek inside it before I handed it over to the detective. Besides, it might be something I could definitely connect to Nick. I pulled it closer and used a little pocketknife to cut through the tape binding it.

I felt like I was on a treasure hunt as I lifted the lid and gaped at the contents. Clothes. Not just any clothes, but a blood drenched shirt and a torn, stained frilly top that I'd last seen in a vision. Using my thumb and middle fingertips, I tweezed it up so I could see under it. A plastic bag and—

I gagged and slapped my hand over my mouth as I felt like I might be sick.

Twenty-Six

I sat in a barely cushioned chair across a plain wooden table from Moss and stared at the damn box. If the manager hadn't caught me, I wouldn't have picked one up to take back to the car and now it would land me in a mess.

I'd somehow managed to close the lid and secure it enough that I felt safe walking into the Sheriff's office with it in my arms. I'd calmly asked for Egan Moss, signed in on the visitor log, and waited in the lobby until he came out to get me. I'd told him there might be evidence in the box and we needed to speak privately.

To his credit, he'd given me a short nod and taken me to his office upstairs where he guided me to an interrogation room. While some of the officers had glanced at me with curiosity, no one said anything.

"Sorry we don't have a non-secure room up here, so this room will have to do for privacy." He'd grabbed a bottle of water from his desk on the way past it and set it down next to me before going to the opposite side to face me.

I'd nodded and set the box in the middle of the table as I had sat down across from him. I'd pointed to it, not saying anything.

Now, Moss pushed back the flaps on the top and peered into it, a frown crossing his face and pulling the corners of his lips down as he saw the contents. He raised an eyebrow at me and said, "Wait. I'll be back in a few moments."

He stepped out of the room for a short time, then came back, pulling on a pair of latex gloves. Lifting the box flaps again, he reached in, moving the contents around, and lifted the plastic bag out, holding it where I could see it.

"Whose?" he asked.

Revulsed, I dropped my gaze to the table, not wanting to see the bloody finger again. I shook my head slowly, "I don't know. I'm guessing it's Saffi Alden's. Zoe told me she'd been at the house and if those bloody clothes belong to her husband, it would be probable that the..." I hesitated a moment before saying, "...finger would be Saffi's."

"Okay. We'll start there and see if we can get a match on it. How did you get this?" He put the evidence back in the box and closed it up. "You know I'll need to file a report on it."

I nodded, drew in a nervous breath, and told him about the incident at the storage locker. He listened quietly, making notes and not interrupting me.

"I wouldn't have taken the box at all if the manager hadn't questioned what I was doing there. I had to grab something to take back to the car in case he was watching. I just went for the lightest box."

"Okay. Let's backtrack some more on this story. How did you get the key to the storage locker? Was the name of the business on it?"

"No." I pulled my plastic bag of evidence I'd collected out of my purse and set it in front of me. "These are all the items I gathered on my foray into Zoe's house. They were all in her bedroom except the key. I found that on the floor downstairs as I was leaving. The police didn't find any of this and the evidence tape was down when I snuck into the house."

He gave me a hard look. "You mean broke in and entered."

"She gave me permission," I shot back.

"I don't think that permission from a dead person will carry much weight in our legal system." He pulled the bag toward him and opened it, pulling out the smaller bags inside, each holding an item I'd collected. He paused at the earring, frowned at the bloody carpet fibers, and found the key. "I suppose your fingerprints are on all of this."

"It's hard to read an object without actually touching it. So, yeah. They're on there."

Moss shook his head and sighed, "Now, tell me what you think you know from all this."

"Right, let me start at the beginning and it'll make more sense."

"Frankly, I don't think it will ever make sense, but give it a try, Ms. Foster. I'm going to record this for me and whether it ends up on an official report depends on how much I have to reveal."

He pulled his phone out and set it to record so I knew it wasn't going on an official police recording. I started my story at the beginning with my first encounter with Zoe Sarkis and ended with my dream visit with her.

"That's what led me to go to Madame Astrid to try to learn more about the key. With her help, I was able to visualize the storage facility and the number of the unit that the key fit." I sat back and reached for the bottle of water he'd brought me earlier. "There's more. Astrid felt something from the earring. As I said, it was Saffi's and I've told you all I could get from reading it. Somehow a connection to Saffi existed to it and Astrid's spirit guide could pick up on her frequency or something like that and he saw her grave. He's certain she's dead."

Moss shot an incredulous look at me, his eyes wide, and mouth slack as if a question perched on the edge of his tongue and backed away like a scared driver. At last, words tumbled out. "You just can't keep your nose out of it, can you? I thought I made it pretty clear—"

"It's not my choice! I didn't ask for this stupid gift. In spite of that, I have it and I have to help those who are on the other side. I don't know why I was given this task. If I try to avoid it, it finds me anyway." My voice escalated to a near shout and I was glad the room was soundproof. "I need to help Zoe get to the other side soon. She's in danger."

"What do you mean? She's dead. How can she be in danger?" He was clearly confused by this and I guess I couldn't blame him.

"Things aren't rosy in this in-between area where her spirit is. There are other spirits that are trying to capture her soul. There's a dark side to it. I can't explain it, but I've seen them in my visions."

"Lady, you are Looney-Tunes." He leaned forward in his chair, folded his left arm into an L, and dropped his jaw onto the heel of his hand.

"Maybe, but someone else pulls the strings. Whether you want to believe me or not doesn't matter 'cause you'll find out I'm right."

He raised his free hand in surrender. "All right. So where is this supposed grave?"

"Astrid's guide didn't know exactly—"

His mouth took on that skeptical smirk he got when he thought this was utter nonsense.

I hurried on. "He described the area and I think it may be out toward Pyramid Lake. He mentioned a big rock pile and I seem to recall reading something about a rock formation—"

"George Washington Rock Pile." Moss' head came up as he jumped in. "It's on reservation land about fifteen miles from Sutcliffe. I've been by it a few times."

"That's it! I couldn't remember the name. Anyway, the body is near there. I want to go out and look."

"Oh, no! You've already done enough and I have no proof of it. Let me investigate this storage unit where you've found evidence that may pertain to the Sarkis murder, then we'll see if I can get an official connect to the case. Otherwise, I'm turning it over to Reno. If the body's on Native American land, the tribal police will be involved."

"How long will that take? I can find her body. I know I can and a lot faster than you or the tribal police. Time is running out..." I pleaded with him now, anxious to tie the pieces together.

"All right. Settle down, Foster. Look, I'll talk to my partner and we'll see what we get from this..." He slapped the side of the box. "If it ties into the Sarkis case, we'll get a warrant and check out the storage unit. Then, we can proceed with the body possibly being where you say it is."

"Look, I need to find her soon. I'm going to get a friend and take a drive tomorrow. I'll let you know when I locate her body." I started to get to my feet.

"Sit. I'm not done here. Look, you've just handed me evidence that could incriminate you in this case. I'm still trying to figure how I can explain this and keep you out of it without getting myself into deep water. I sure as hell can't tell my superiors and colleagues that I'm getting my information from a girl who sees dead people!"

"It's the truth," I replied in a small voice. I understood what he was saying and I knew he wanted to protect me. If this got out, Gayle Trumbull would be the least of my worries.

Moss ran a hand through his hair, dropping it down to rub at the back of his neck as he thought for a moment. "Okay. Let's try this. We'll try to get the warrant in the morning and check out the storage unit. Maybe we can get into the safe. If there is anything to indicate that the locker was Sarkis' or if that finger can be identified as belonging to Saffi Alden, we'll contact the reservation police and go out with them. But it will take time."

I started to object and drew in a breath.

"Wait a minute. I know that doesn't satisfy you," Moss went on. "How about if I go out with you in an unofficial capacity? Strictly as a friend and not as a detective. Should we find signs of a body, we call the locals in."

Stunned by the offer, I sat back and thought about it. Did I want to go out with him? What if I couldn't find the grave site right off? If I failed, it could cost me any credibility I'd managed to gain with the detective. On the other hand, when, or if, I found Saffi, he'd be right with me and it would ease the way with the tribal authorities.

"Okay. It's a deal. When?" I still wanted to do it as soon as possible.

Moss glanced at his phone, possibly checking his calendar, and replied, "Can we make it Wednesday afternoon? About three?"

I thought about my work schedule at the shop and thought I could manage to get done with the dogs by that time if I started an hour earlier. "Yeah, that will work. Should I meet you here?"

"Out front. We'll take your Jeep."

On an overcast and dreary-looking afternoon, I picked Moss up and we headed out on Pyramid Lake Highway toward the lake. In fact, the area we set out to investigate was well past the usual lake cut-offs, continuing to where it split with Highway 446, or so Moss informed me when we'd gotten a few miles out onto Pyramid.

On the way, I asked Moss how things were going with his son. He and his wife had filed for divorce and she had attempted to hold

FUNERAL SINGER: A Song of Betrayal

their child hostage in the arrangements. At least, that's how I interpreted it.

Moss flashed a grin. "Not bad, Foster. I have joint custody and while he lives with his mother during the week, I get him on the weekends, two nights a week, and two full vacation weeks in the summer. We went camping at Yosemite at the end of July. We had a great time."

"That's wonderful. So your ex is cool with this arrangement."

"Not really, but I don't give a rat's ass. I won in court and she can just live with it. She has plenty of time with him throughout the year. The irony is that her schedule is just as screwy as mine so she's in no better position to provide full-time care than I am."

I knew that was a sore spot. Peg, the about to be ex-wife, worked as a dispatcher and sometimes worked extra shifts or covered an off shift for a co-worker.

"Anyway, it's working out and that's all that matters now. I thought you were bringing a friend along this afternoon."

"I planned to, but he couldn't make it. He had another commitment." Gavin had a lecture for his class that he couldn't hand off to a TA. His main advice was to be sure to say a protection spell before I began searching for the grave and to anchor myself in our world. How I accomplished that I wasn't sure. He suggested holding a person's hand or a rock or some other physical object. I didn't see myself grabbing Moss' hand while I went on an astral trip.

"Did you and Hernandez get the warrant for the storage unit?" I asked as we passed by the last of the housing developments on the right and the land gave way to more small ranches and open desert spaces. While it often seemed a bleak-looking desert, at certain times of the year, it could be beautiful. Under the overcast sky, the colors seemed more intense than in bright sunshine and the shadows gave it an otherworldly look.

The turnoff for the regional shooting range was only a little further down the road, then another eight or so miles beyond that to the lake.

"Yeah. We got it." His voice sounded flat with that official sound.

I bobbed my head a couple of times in acknowledgment figuring he wasn't going to tell me anything. I asked anyway. "Did you find anything to tie it to Nick?"

"We're still examining everything we found and if there's a tie to the Sarkis murder, we'll pull in Reno PD on it. As of now, it's all evidence in connection with that finger."

"What about that? Could you id it?"

"Uh huh. Belonged to Ms. Alden. We have her fingerprints on file."

"Well, since Hernandez didn't join us today, I assume that this isn't an official search for her body."

Moss chuckled. "Nope. I want to see just how good you really are, Foster. Take a look around. That's a lot of desert out there."

I'd been considering that as we'd driven along. Thousands of acres of places where a person could bury a body and it wouldn't be found for years if at all. Finding Saffi would be a daunting task. I swallowed my sudden nervousness to answer. "I've thought about that. But I have clues and a little help, I hope."

"We'll see," he said. "Okay, our turn is coming up just after this next rise, as we go down to the lake. Then turn left at the junction."

I guided the Jeep up the incline, after which the road dipped and revealed the deep cobalt blue of Pyramid Lake. A huge desert lake, it stretched about eight miles across at its widest point and almost four times that long. I knew it was a remnant of an ice age lake that had one filled the entire Washoe Valley and a good portion of northwestern Nevada. Fed by Lake Tahoe via the Truckee River, the entry point was somewhere at the southern end.

"We're on Paiute land now," Moss commented, letting me know that we'd entered the reservation.

"Now what?" I asked as I made the turn and the road paralleled the lake on our right.

"We go through Sutcliffe and about another fifteen miles beyond."

This was a longer drive than I had expected. It was almost four now and it would likely be getting dark before we could do too much exploring. I began doubting I would be able to locate Saffi before dark.

Sutcliffe came and went almost as fast as I only slowed to pass through the town. We went a few miles on the other side before the road changed to a dirt road and became Surprise Valley Road.

"It's still Pyramid," Moss said. "It just leads to Surprise Valley from here."

"Never heard of it." I had never been out this far on the highway. When I'd gone to the lake, I'd gone to one of the shore turn-offs from the other direction at the south end. I knew there was a marina of sorts in Sutcliffe and we might have taken a boat out from there once or twice when I was a kid. I didn't remember much about it.

"It's on the California side." Moss dismissed it as of no concern to him.

A short way ahead on the right I spotted a big rock formation that looked like a fortress. "Is that the rock pile?"

"Nope. That's Monument Rock. The one we want is a little further up the road."

He was right about that. The first indication of a big stack of rocks came into view and we soon came to it. It was bigger than I thought it would be "I don't see any resemblance to George Washington in that heap of rubble."

Moss laughed. "Not from this side. Drive on up the road another half-mile or so, then pull over to the side."

I did as he said, stopped the Jeep, and climbed out to look back at the rugged-looking stones. He stood beside me, pulled me slightly to one side and pointed. "Now look. You can get the impression of a forehead and beak of a nose as if he was reclining."

At first, I frowned trying to see what he described. The afternoon sun cast shadows against it and I couldn't make it out. All at once, I saw it. It did look like a profile of the first president. "I'll be darned. Well, if you can see Elvis in a potato chip, why not?"

Better than that revelation, the jog up the road another half mile put us in the vicinity of the grave, provided Astrid had Elias' information right. He said it was to the northeast of the rock pile, so that would put it toward the lake. I looked at the open area of desert and my heart sank. It was a huge sandbox to dig in.

"Now what?" Moss asked.

"I guess I try to do my thing." I reached in the Jeep for my bag and pulled out a little vial of incense oil. I poured a couple of drops in my hand and began saying my protection charm in a low voice. Out of the corner of my eye, I caught Moss' raised eyebrow. Cynical. The man was definitely cynical.

I looked around for an anchor, spotted a small rock, and picked it up. Taking a deep breath, I faced toward the east in the direction I believed she was buried. Closing my eyes, I focused on the image of Saffi's missing finger and hoped I could connect through that. With still slitted eyes, I began walking slowly across the open desert. I heard Moss' footsteps as he fell in behind me.

After about fifty paces, I felt a pull to my right side and adjusted my direction a little. Brush and small cacti covered the ground in places. For the most part, walking was easy. In the back of my mind, I hoped no rattlesnakes remained in the area. As late in October as it was, they should be hibernating, I reasoned.

I pressed on and followed the little tingling sensation I felt tugging at me. A black fog appeared in my mind. It seemed to sit on the land, dense and obscuring the view. I quit walking and stood rooted to the spot as I tried to see into the darkness. Had the shades already claimed Saffi? Were they trying to hide her from me?

I reached out for Zoe's help. I began singing her favorite song, or at least the one she wanted. My voice rose across the desert, carried by a breeze that stirred from the lake.

I heard Zoe's voice responding as she called out, "Sing louder."

I did, putting more power into the song. Through the dark haze, I saw a blonde woman trying to walk toward me. Her hair appeared tangled and dirty along with the gown she wore. As she came closer, I looked at her right hand and saw the bloody stub where her ring finger had been severed.

"Where are you?" I asked her, my voice echoing in my ears as I said it aloud.

She motioned to me, her left hand curling her fingers and beckoning me forward. I stepped that direction, following her continuing motions toward the illusion. After several steps, I put my foot down and nearly tripped over a stone in the path.

My vision focused entirely on the apparition in front of me as I continued to move as she guided me. Coming to a halt, she pointed down. The black mist swam over the area, obscuring a clear view. I moved forward and felt a subtle change in the ground. Not even looking down as I'd walked, I had become oblivious to the terrain.

A hand grabbed my arm, pulling me backward.

"Whoa, Foster," Moss said. "You're almost in the lake."

"What?" I snapped back to myself and opened my eyes to the reality. The lake lapped at my feet and I became aware of the subtle swish of ripples hitting the shore. Behind me, the sun was beginning to dip toward the mountain peaks. We had about an hour until twilight. I didn't understand. Saffi had pointed down to a spot not far from where I stood.

"You're walking into the lake," Moss repeated, answering my question. "Didn't you notice?"

"No, I followed Saffi in a vision. She was guiding me to her grave." I sounded as dazed as I felt. Had I imagined it? In a blink, it dawned on me. I shifted my vision to the water in front of me and about where I thought she had pointed. Was something floating in the water there?

I turned to Moss. "He didn't bury her. He dumped her in the lake. I think I see something floating about twenty-five feet out."

He squinted in the direction I pointed and shook his head. "I don't see anything." He pulled his phone out, pointed it toward the water, and pressed the zoom on the camera app to bring it up larger. Using it like binoculars, he scanned the water as I peeked at the screen behind him.

"There! See that's something floating. Maybe it's some of her clothing or just a piece of sail. But it's something in the water."

He increased the size until he hit the maximum magnification on the phone. "I don't know. It could be anything. What makes you so sure?" He looked again, then swore. "Sonuvabitch! I think that's a body!"

My mouth went dry as I realized we might have found her. I had been right. I turned away from the lake and started back to my Jeep, which was now about a half mile west, off the dirt road. I glimpsed back over my shoulder to see Moss lift his phone, hunting for a signal. He turned and motioned for me to continue toward my vehicle as he hurried to catch up.

We walked back and he kept checking as he went. Near the car, he got a weak signal and called as I went on. Drained by the experience, I sat in the Jeep and gulped half a bottle of water before I slowed to a sip. As Moss came over, I handed him a bottle and my eyes asked the question my mouth didn't.

"I don't know. There's something out in the water. It could be her or it could be a big fish. I called the res officers out. It's going to be a while."

I nodded. Had I really found Saffi that easily? What about that black mist? Even if I wasn't sure her soul was free or not, at least, we might have located her body. Still, I had a nagging feeling the battle was far from over.

Twenty-Seven

The low light of dusk settled as the scene along the shore grew busier. Two WCSO officers had arrived minutes after a pair of reservation police officers. All four of them stood with Moss along the beach, discussing who knows what as they peered out toward the lake and the boat arriving from Sutcliffe. I leaned against the fender of my Jeep and watched from a distance. The boat, a speedboat with a small cabin, dropped anchor near the floating body and began the process of recovering it.

One officer used a big pole hook to try to pull the corpse closer to him and seemed to have trouble moving it very far. Another donned diving gear and jumped into the water as they turned a spotlight on the area.

Moss and another officer detached themselves from the group at the shore and worked their way up the shallow slope to me. As soon as the officers had arrived, Moss had identified himself and filled them in on everything that had happened; however, they hadn't spoken to me yet. I suspected that was about to change. I trusted Moss hadn't said anything about the weird portion of this discovery and I planned to tell the bare minimum.

"Gillian, this is Officer Clayton, who is assigned to the reservation. Bill, this is my friend, Gillian Foster." Moss kept the introduction simple, but calling me a friend—really? I guess he had to say something to not make it seem odd that we were out here together while he was off duty.

I shook hands with Clayton as I greeted him and waited.

"Miss Foster, I have a few questions. They won't take long," Clayton assured me. "Can you tell me how you discovered the body?"

"Sure. I was walking along the shoreline admiring the view and happened to spot something floating on top of the water. I told Moss it looked like a dress or a sail floating, but when we looked at it through the magnification on his camera, we saw it looked like a body."

Clayton made a note on his iPad and nodded. "This is kind of a long way out on this road, so why did you decide to come this far?"

I cracked a sheepish smile, "I'd heard about a big pile of rocks on the road called the George Washington Rock Pile and I'd never seen it. Moss knew right where it was and offered to come out with me. I didn't believe it actually looked like our first president and, of course, it didn't. Until we drove past it. Then we stopped and the lake looked so pretty, I decided to walk along the shore."

Moss half-smiled and dropped his gaze to the ground for a few moments.

"So then Lt. Moss called the reservation police. Is that correct?"

"Yes. After that, we came back up here to my Jeep to wait."

"Seems pretty straightforward," Clayton said as he made one last note and turned back toward the beach. "It looks like they might have gotten the body cut loose."

I peered around him in time to see the diver pushing the body to the boat where they could lift it aboard. Clayton started back to the beach and Moss lingered a moment.

"Hernandez is on his way out to get me. We'll be here for a while still. Go home. They have your statement and that's all they need from you. Good job, Foster."

I gnawed at my lower lip a moment. "Do we know for certain that it's Saffi Alden? I mean, I am pretty sure it is. But—?"

He shook his head. "We can't confirm until we've gotten a positive id on her. Go on home. I'll let you know what I can tomorrow. Besides, news media is on the way and you don't want to be here for that. I'll try to keep your name out of it."

He'd spoken the truth; I didn't want to be there when the news arrived. If Trumbull happened to be among them, she would be like a pit bull on this and my flimsy story wouldn't hold up. "Thanks, Moss. For everything...believing me and covering for me."

"Hey, weird asset or not, you're one of my best informants." He made light of it as he flashed a grin.

Wasting no more time, I got in the Beast, pointed it toward Sparks and started on the trek back to town.

As I drove, I thought about the odd way things had connected on this case. First, there had been the objects that led me to the storage unit, followed by the connection through Elias and Astrid. I'd had nothing tied to Saffi other than her earring, so I hadn't gotten anything from her directly, yet somehow Elias could locate her. Once I'd gotten here and tried singing for her, it had reached Zoe. Although distant, she'd seemed to know what was happening and that linked me to Saffi somehow.

All in all, it was a strange connection and I failed to understand how it worked. For that matter, my whole gift puzzled me. It seemed to keep evolving, growing more expansive as I went along. One thing for certain, it appeared to bind me to whichever spirit I needed to help and if it involved other spirits, I could interact with them as well.

Were there other spirit guides? I didn't think I could be the only one, so there had to be, right? If so, how could I connect with them? I didn't think an ad on Craig's List would be the answer. I could just imagine the kooks that would produce, all claiming to have who-knows-what abilities. Still, there had to be a way. If a battle with the True Shades was brewing, I needed an army capable of repelling them.

Gavin and I planned to get the training started right away and somehow, we had to learn more about the nature of our adversaries. So, first was training; second finding our allies; third understanding the nature of the Shades. And where the heck was Zac and did he fit into this plan at all?

Almost two hours and a swing through a burger take-out later, I pulled into my driveway. First stop was to feed Nygard, then I sat to eat my dinner as if I could get through it without my furry friend demanding a portion. Then I called Gavin and told him we needed to get the training started.

"I'm willing," he replied. "Let's meet tomorrow and put together a plan, okay? How about my office at UNR? It's evil relic free."

"Deal. I'll see you there at what time?"

"Is three too early?"

"Make it three-thirty." That would give me time to get my quota of dogs groomed and get to the campus.

Still holding my smartphone, I thought about the photos I took in the secret room at the Sarkis house and decided I needed to upload those to my computer. I locked up downstairs, bounded up the steps, and hunted for the connector to attach my phone. After a search through three drawers, I finally found it and transferred the images.

Once I could view them bigger, I looked at the records I'd photographed in more detail. Lots of numbers in columns with adjustments to one side that looked like a good percentage skimmed off the income. I think Zoe had it right that Nick was embezzling clients' funds and these books would prove it. Did the Reno police have them and were they doing anything with the information? I hoped my message to them made it to the right person and gave them enough information to act.

I flipped to another photo and I caught my breath. A familiar name popped from the page. A copy of the identification page of a passport, it showed issued to Robert N. Barnet and the photo on it, although a smudged black and white copy, looked like Nick Sarkis. Wasn't that the name he'd used to rent the storage unit in Sun Valley? The issue date indicated it had been obtained three months earlier. So Nick had been planning this for a while.

I clicked to the next photo, which was an email that Nick had sent to RNBarnet and mentioned a code for an account with a series of eight numbers. Had he sent it to himself and was it part of a cover-up? Or was Nick working with someone else?

I saw two scenarios here. In one, Nick was Barnet and he'd built a second identification. The passport had his picture on it, so it seemed likely that was the case. Although in scenario two, he had an accomplice who was Barnet, who allowed Nick to use his name and id to obtain a passport. The numbers could link to a Swiss account for either one of them. Personally, I thought the first scenario seemed more likely.

With this information, I could probably lure Nick back to this country. All I needed was a good plan to ensure he returned to Nevada where he could be arrested. Maybe I could pretend to blackmail him for the files. Or maybe I could hint that I knew something about Saffi. On the other hand, that might just chase him further away. No, the duplicate books were the key. Why did he leave them behind?

A gentle butt of the head against my arm brought my attention to Nygard. I'd been ignoring him too long, in his opinion. As I stroked his fur, I thought about what Gavin had said about our energies connecting. Did it run both ways? I squinted my eyes partially closed and gazed at him, looking for those golden lines I'd noticed before.

Indifferent, the cat curled into a circle on my lap with his head resting against my idle arm. His purr rumbled and sent a buzz into my flesh that had a soothing effect. His deep blue eyes blinked once, and he nudged his jaw and cheekbone on my arm again, content. I'd read somewhere that the blink and the purr meant a cat accepted you and loved you. The feeling was mutual.

I gave up squinting after a minute since I wasn't seeing anything except a slight halo of bluish light around Nygard. An aura maybe, although I thought they were multicolored. I yawned, suddenly feeling exhausted. It had been a long day. As I looked at the cat again to urge him out of my lap, I caught a glimpse of a spray of golden threads rising toward me and a return line of them from my hand where I stroked him. Energy exchange...did this happen all the time and people don't normally see it? Or was it just me?

Heeni raised a questioning eyebrow when I waltzed through the door an hour earlier than usual. Most times, my workday didn't start until nine or so. That was one perk of being an independent contractor in the shop.

"I have an appointment this afternoon so I'll need to leave at three," I explained. "So, I wanted to give myself plenty of time. Are any of my pups in yet?"

With a slight frown crunching up her happy face, she shook her head. "Nope. You can start on Mister Frump there." She pointed to a medium-sized, tan-colored shaggy dog of dubious bloodlines.

As I approached the cage, he looked up at me through barely visible and woeful eyes, defying me to touch him. I could see his fur was tangled into knots. This would be a challenge. I started humming to him as soon as I opened the cage, let him sniff me, and patted his head a few times to reassure him. This job was going to take some scissoring before I could do anything else.

An hour later, I had Frump's hair cleared of the knots and took him to the bathing station. As I worked, I thought more about how I'd connected with Nygard and wondered if it extended to any animal. I tried to focus on the dog, hoping to detect some kind of indication that I could share energy with him also. He seemed to get a little nervous and I resumed humming to him. As he calmed down again, I concluded that humming them to a comfort zone might be the only connection I had with dogs.

Not that I didn't try again later with the next two dogs I groomed. If I made a connection, I couldn't detect it. Bitsy Poo, a toy poodle, whined at me while I tried, so I thought it might be annoying her. Okay, if I was entertaining the idea that animals might be useful in a battle against the shades, I scored a fail on that test.

By noon, I was getting antsy. I'd groomed five dogs and had two more on my list for the day, so I should be done in plenty of time to get to the university. So far, I hadn't heard anything from Moss. I hoped for a confirmation of Saffi Alden's identity even though I knew it was her body. I also wanted to see if he would buy off on any of my ideas to lure Nick Sarkis back to Reno.

When my phone buzzed with a text message a little after one, I jumped to get it. Yes, it came from Moss. He wanted to meet me outside the shop in fifteen minutes. What the heck? He hadn't shown up at my job since he'd first thought I might be involved in Marielle's death.

I finished the golden retriever I was grooming and wandered out to the parking lot to wait. Shortly, Moss' car came around the corner of the lot and pulled into a nearby parking space. Hernandez, his partner, stepped out of the passenger side as Moss came around the rear.

"Haven't seen you in a while, Hernandez," I said. "How have you been? How's the family?" I liked the detective. He'd believed me when I'd told my fantastic story even though his partner was skeptical. I'm not sure Moss would have given me a chance if it hadn't been for Hernandez.

"I'm good and the family is doing fine," he answered with a broad smile.

Moss leaned against the fender of the car, indicating we were having a parking lot discussion.

"What's up, Moss?" I asked.

"I promised you an update so here we are. The body has been identified as the Alden woman. She'd been secured to an old outboard engine, then dropped into the lake a short distance from where the beach dropped into a trench under the water. The ropes holding her had frayed, probably cut by the engine blades as the water shifted it, until the strands broke enough to allow her body to drift to the top."

"Oh, God, was she alive when..." I couldn't even say the rest I was so repulsed by the idea he might have drowned her like an unwanted cat.

"No, he shot her. She was dead before he dumped her body."

I felt oddly relieved that her last moments of life were quicker than drowning. Although I couldn't be sure of that either. It must have been a nightmare from the time she left the house with Nick unless she truly believed she could manipulate him into letting her go.

I shook those thoughts from my mind and said, "I want Nick Sarkis to pay for what he did to his wife and Saffi. I think I know where he is and I have an email address that I think will reach him. He's using an alias—"

"Robert Barnet," Moss said. "Yeah, we know. That's the name on the storage unit as well."

"Right. He also has a passport in that name and I'm pretty sure he fled to the Canary Islands. I have an idea on how to lure him back—" I was ready to launch into my grand plan that would involve me sending a bogus email.

"No need, Foster. RPD picked up on the leads from the materials they found at Sarkis' house, thanks to an anonymous tip. They'd begun to track him down, but with Alden's murder added to it, the Feds are in on it. Since it's international, they are working with Interpol to arrest him and extradite him back here for trial."

"Oh, so there's nothing more to be done?" I sounded a bit stupid as I said it. Of course not. They had the evidence, the trail to Nick, and the means to grab him. What was I thinking?

Moss chuckled. "Nope, you have done all you can. I can't tell you any more than that except that Sarkis will be punished for his crimes. All of them."

"Great. Thanks for telling me. Now maybe I can get my spirit to move on."

"Right. See you later, maybe," Moss said, making it clear this case had closed.

Hernandez winked at me and mouthed out "thank you" before he slid back into the car.

I lingered to watch them drive out of the lot before I went back into the shop. That would close out part of my problems although I felt let down by not being involved in the final solution.

Almost two hours later, I leaned over the dismally small chart spread out on Gavin's desk and frowned. Designed in columns, it showed me just how little we knew about the shades, true or regular. Gavin had listed sighting, location, duration, and outcome as the headers. Each column had about a dozen entries in it.

"Are these all the ones you've had over the years?" I asked as I thought it seemed a small number compared to the encounters I'd had in just the last seven months.

"Not all. Just the ones from the point that I actually realized what they were. Remember, my sightings are all earth-bound, so it could be a significant number with that consideration."

I detected a tone of irritation as he spoke and I realized I might have made his sightings seem trivial. "I understand. It just seems like so little information about them. And you first encountered them after you opened that box in India, right?"

He nodded and took a sip of the coffee I'd brought him.

"What about communication? Have you conversed with them in any way? What was said?"

"Talked to 'em?" His eyes widened and he looked startled as if I'd asked if he'd had sex with one.

"Yeah. I mean, they don't actually speak. They communicate telepathically or something similar."

"You've heard them? They actually communicated with you"

He reached for another chart-sized piece of paper and a ruler. "Okay, we need to do another chart for your encounters and I'll add that column."

He quickly drew and labeled the chart, then said, "Okay, let's start with your first experience. Date, if you remember it."

"Sure, it was in April, around the fifth. I'd done a funeral for a car accident victim and I got my first look at a shade. It lingered in the background and didn't communicate with me. In fact, it just watched as I interacted with another spirit in the ethereal cemetery."

"Just watched?" He looked up and arched an eyebrow.

"Yep. Like it was scoping me out, watching everything I did."

"Did it send you any message that time?"

"No. The first time that happened was at Shiloh when one challenged me for a spirit I was helping."

One by one, I filled Gavin in on the details of each encounter I'd had with a shade or True Shade, where it was, and what it had said to me. When he'd finished making the notes, he dropped into his chair and stared at the chart. I'd encountered them a little more than half the times he had.

"Mostly, I've seen them in human form, rather than as a shade, but they never spoke to me or anyone that I knew about."

"How could you tell they were shades?" I asked, taking the seat at the side of the desk where I could lean my elbows on it as we talked.

"Sometimes I got a brief flash of a shadow before I saw the person. I think they might be taking over humans for a short time. There's something zombie-like in their eyes like they're not really seeing me. The ones chasing me never said anything, although they were more animated than the others I've encountered. If those are True Shades, they may have human forms they shift to versus borrowing them."

"That's not encouraging, Gavin." I shuddered at the thought that shades could be walking around anywhere on Earth and look just like a neighbor. "So, how do we fight them?"

"Well, that's the real question. I don't exactly have a plan or a method for doing this. So we need to figure out what we each did to combat them so we can build on those skills."

I thought about that a moment as I realized I hadn't actually done anything to combat them. I only repelled the one in my house. I don't know how I did it or even if it was something I did. I just instinctively threw out my hands and light seemed to burst from them."

"That sounds like something." He made a note of that on the chart. He sat back and stared at the wall for a few minutes in thought. "Okay, I have a few contacts I can tap for some information that might help us. If anyone knows anything more about these shades, I'll find out. So, I'll be going out of town for a few days. You have my number. If anything comes up, you can call. In the meantime, try practicing that light-flinging thing."

I shot an exasperated look at him. "Sure. I'll do that."

He waggled his eyebrows and grinned. "Want to get dinner?"

Twenty-Eight

Saffi's funeral drew very few friends or family. She'd not been a native of the area and had only lived in Reno a couple of years. Most of the attendees were co-workers at Sarkis' financial firm—all three of them—, a couple of reporters, who hoped a story might arise from it, and Egan Moss.

Extradition of Nick Sarkis from the Canary Islands was underway, although it could take some time. The Feds were handling that now. At least, Zoe could rest assured that he would be punished for his crimes. I hoped I could assure Saffi Alden as well and that she would cross the gate with no reservations.

At the front of the small chapel, a gold-painted pillar supported a large brass urn that held Saffi's ashes. I thought her Viking blood would approve of a cremation in lieu of a burning barge. In a quiet whisper, I said a little protection chant as the service started and hoped that this would be an easy transition that would include Zoe as well.

On my cue, I started to play the introduction for "Cast Me On Your Shore", a song I'd found in an old book and rewritten a little to suit Saffi. I was swept away before I got through the first line of the song.

I knew something felt wrong as soon as I arrived in the ethereal cemetery. Dull yellowish light gave the impression of late afternoon and cast its glow over the entire place. The ever-present sense of peace I usually sensed failed to assure me and my pulse quickened in apprehension. I cast my gaze around to look for Saffi, not sure what sad state I might find her apparition wearing, but I didn't see her.

Had she not come here? Was she still lost because of the lake burial or had she gone on ahead? I felt certain she had been at the lake and guided me to her body. Could she have moved on after that? With all that had happened, I felt it unlikely that she hadn't lingered behind at all. But if she was here, she hadn't stayed in the vicinity of her grave marker.

As I surveyed the area and moved around a line of hedges that blocked the view to the eastern side, I noticed a roiling black haze in the distance. It looked like a storm of black sand whirling around in the area beyond the mausoleum. In my dark dream, that area had been ringed in thorny black bushes and sinister grabbing vines reaching out for me.

My heart sank. I had a foreboding feeling that this was associated with the shades. With reluctant steps, I started on the path toward the disturbance. As I spotted a figure running toward me, I quickened my pace, breaking into a sprint.

"Hurry, angel-girl," Zoe's voice cried out. She waved her arms as she closed the distance, motioning me toward her. "She can't resist them. You have to help her!"

I didn't have to ask who pursued her. I knew they were here and they were trying to claim Saffi. How could I fight them? What could I do to pull her free of their clutches?

Light will conquer darkness.

Wasn't that what the symbols had alluded to in my dream? If I could just get Saffi to the gate and the light, she would be free of the shades.

I'd caught up with Zoe and we both raced to the wall of swirling black. I noticed that she looked pretty good—her body image returning to its normal state. I considered that a good sign.

In another minute, we were close enough that I could see Saffi struggling to hold back from the sucking center of the whirling black. Her tattered dress whipped around her body trying to wrap her in a cocoon. Her long blonde hair swirled around her head forming a misshapen halo as she stumbled backward from the suction tearing at her.

I had no idea what I could do to stop the darkness from grabbing her. Why couldn't she and Zoe just teleport to the gate? They were spirits, yet it occurred to me that every spirit I'd dealt with in this way station had acted as if bound by human constraints. *Did they not have the power to move as a spirit within it? I knew they could vanish from it when their energy ran low.* "Zoe, can't you and Saffi just transport to the gate?"

She paused as we came to only a few feet from Saffi. "I—I don't know. We just arrive here when we come across and we leave to another place to rest. When you called me, I just popped in."

"What about when you went to your house?"

"I thought about it and that I wanted to go there and I materialized there."

"Think about the gate and take Saffi's hand in your mind. See if that will pull you to the other side of this cemetery."

"I don't know if I can touch her..." *Zoe turned desperate-looking eyes at her lover and her mouth trembled with fear as Saffi slipped a foot or more toward the dark cloud.*

"Just do it!"

She nodded and reached her hand toward Saffi as she ran the short distance between them.

"Visualize it!" *I called to her and concentrated on holding back the darkness that threatened to engulf Saffi. On some instinct or just channeling my inner Gandolf, I thrust my hands forward, palms outward and screamed,* "Release her. She is not yours!"

At that moment, I saw Zoe and Saffi appear to touch hands and they both vanished in a blink. A beam of white light burst from my palms and shot forward into the dark cloud. The whirling stopped and it broke apart.

Light will conquer darkness.

I spun around and ran toward the gate. Great, they could transport on a thought. I couldn't. When I came around the curve toward it, relief flowed over me as I saw both women standing in front of it.

"You need to go through and into the light." *I gasped as soon as I got close enough.* "I don't know how long we have before the shades try again."

Zoe frowned, a protest starting to build in her. Saffi just looked confused. While both of them didn't look as gruesome as they first had, neither looked ready to transition.

"Zoe, you can't stay here any longer. You both have to go through."

"But Nick—"

"Will be arrested," I interrupted and waved toward the open portal. "The extradition papers are started and he will be punished for both of you. Saffi, you need to find peace now and both of you need to let go of this realm. Go through."

I heard Saffi gasp and watched Zoe's face shift to a look of fear. Before I turned, I knew what came up behind me.

"Go!" I screamed and turned to face the pair of True Shades that were nearly on top of me.

"Ours," one of them said in an eerie whistle of a voice that irritated my hearing and they came closer to claim their victims.

"Oh, God and angels, please help me," I prayed and raised my hands again in a rejection position. Where the hell was Zac when I needed him? Would my fighting skills do me any good here?

"You cannot have these two innocents." I thrust my hands forward and a ball of white light sped toward the closer shade. It exploded and seemed to stun the creature for a moment. In no time, the shade regrouped and came forward, angling to go past me to reach either Zoe or Saffi.

I heard Saffi scream followed by Zoe yelling, "We're going!"

I glanced back to see Zoe pulling Saffi into the light. Their hands didn't touch, but a silver cord connected them to each other. The shade made a last-moment lunge coming up just a split-second too late as they vanished in a burst of golden light from the tunnel.

"You are interfering, Gillian Foster," a deep voice resonated in my head as I realized the other ghoul communicated via telepathy.

I shouted my defiance. "You're overstepping your bounds! These people don't belong to you. They aren't lost and desolate and they haven't given up." I shot an angry look at the shade that was face to face with me. I brought my hands up and poked a left hook at it. My hand went right through it, nothing to resist at all. Where my skin touched it, I felt an icy chill that shot through my spirit.

A laugh tinged with angry malice echoed in my mind, and I felt myself drowning in it. I shook my head, trying to focus. Call the light, a small voice seemed to say, and I tried again to blast the shade with light. I twisted my palms toward it and visualized a silver spray encompassing the shade. Light burst from my hand and spread into an array of light spikes shooting into the apparition.

A sudden chill shot through me and I realized the one behind me had touched me. I screamed as I fell to my knees, weakened by the touch. Horrified, I knew it would try to devour me. "Zac, please help me," I moaned as I tried to project light all around me.

Out of nowhere, a familiar shape appeared and leaped over the shade in front of me to attack the one behind me. With shock and amazement, I realized it was a cat form. Not just any cat, but Nygard's spirit, appearing at least ten times larger than his real body, and his fierce lynx-like face focused on the threat to me.

The chill left me and encouraged by the aid, I centered my strength and shot another repelling blast at the one in front of me. Getting the hang of it now, I climbed to my feet and shot bolt after bolt of my energy at it until it broke apart and disappeared.

I turned to see Nygard facing off with the remaining shade, his teeth bared and a deep, rumble of a growl rolled out of his throat as he vaulted toward it, front paws flailing into the inkiness of the creature he fought. The shade barely blinked, if you could call the slight flash of red in its eyes that, and flung Nygard across the grass toward the gate.

"No! Nygard!" My scream rolled around the clearing as all the anguish poured out of me and into the fireball I launched from my hands.

The golden red ball of light flew into the shade and broke apart into hundreds of needles of burning light. It shrieked out a shrill whine that pierced into my brain and made me stumble back even as I prepared another fireball. Recovering in a moment, I readied my hands to fling it when the shade blinked out. Gone in an instant. I released the energy I had built up and numbly made my way to the inert form of my over-sized cat.

Tears welled in my eyes as I knelt by him, reaching to stroke his silky fur that I couldn't actually touch, although it felt like it. I feared the worst. "Nygard?" My voice rasped as I called his name and tried to see if he was alive. If he died here, did he die in reality?

For that matter, if I died here, did I physically die? Could the True Shades claim my soul?

I dug my fingers into my cat's fur, pressing my head against him...

Something bounded into me and I screamed as a chill shot through me...

Noise went on around me; voices babbling; someone touching me; none of it made sense. Confusion muddled my mind and I tried to get a grasp on where I was. Something poked my cheek and I lifted my head a little to see as my eyes focused on the golden letters in front of them...e—i—n. Piano keys, my face was resting on the piano keys.

A man put his arm around my shoulders lifting me from my slumped position. I stared at him, my mind struggling to connect to the moment. Slowly, I realized Egan Moss held me upright at the piano and a woman hurried over with a cup of water. Had I passed out? What had happened?

"I've called for an EMT," Moss said as I nodded my head numbly and sipped at the water until the words registered.

"No, no. I'm all right. I just fainted." I had to get home. I needed to get to my cat.

"Are you sure? They'll be here in a few minutes. Just let them check you out." Moss' eyes held a worried look that made me wonder what exactly had happened here while I was fighting the shades.

I swallowed the rest of the water and straightened up, partly to convince myself that I was fine, but also to show Moss and the others around me that I had just fainted, nothing more serious. "I'm okay, really. I just got a little overwhelmed and probably forgot to breathe. It happens sometimes."

Moss shot a cockeyed look my way, his eyebrows almost twisting in confusion.

I gathered my music and got to my feet. "Look. I'm okay now. I can walk and I'll be fine. I need to go."

Before he could say anything else, I turned and started a fairly brisk pace toward the chapel exit. Although my knees felt a little shaky, I kept walking, determination keeping me from wobbling on the way out.

Moss followed me out. "What happened back there? You were singing, switched to humming, then boom! Out like a light. I know you were in a trance state of some sort. So what happened?"

"I'll tell you later. I need to sort through it all in my mind. Right now, I have to get home." I opened the door to the Beast and started to slide in.

Moss caught my left arm. "Are you sure you're okay to drive? I feel like I shouldn't let you."

I met his eyes, seeing the concern in them, and nodded. "Yes, I'm fine. I'm not dizzy or anything. I'll be okay."

"Let me drive you."

"Honestly. Thanks for the offer, but I can do it. You'd better cancel the EMTs." I slid behind the wheel and closed the door as he stepped back, pulling out his phone as he did.

I fought every urge to speed out of the chapel parking lot and onto the street. Dread filled me as I thought of my cat possibly dying at home and it would be because of me.

I'd gotten Nygard as a three-month-old kitten, a gift from one of my clients at the shop. He'd become my little buddy instantly, a warm body that slept by me at night. I loved him as much as you could love anything or anyone. Over the past four years, he was my daily companion, my sounding board, and guardian of my sleep. I hadn't ever thought he would also be my defender. How had he made that connection to the ethereal cemetery? Through me? I couldn't bear it if I lost him.

Tears leaked down my cheeks as I thought about him and what had happened. I pulled into the driveway and rushed to my front door, fumbling with the keys to unlock it. As I pushed inside, I called his name and looked wildly around the living and dining room area. He wasn't there. I went to the kitchen and checked into the closet there before I turned my head to look at the staircase.

I rushed up the steps, my heart pounding as I went. At first, I didn't see him. I scanned the room, eyes darting around until I saw the dark brown of his tail sticking out at the end of the platform bed. I approached him more slowly, fearful of what I would find.

"Nygard? Hey, kitty? I'm here." I came around the edge of the bed and saw him. He sprawled across the floor, his body stretched to its full length as if he'd been leaping when he collapsed.

"Oh, no, no, nooo..." Wailing, I knelt to touch him, to feel for any sign of life.

There... a faint heartbeat. His body rose ever so slightly with shallow breaths. I scooped him up, wrapped him in a towel, and bounded down the stairs. I called my vet as I went, alerting her that he might have had a stroke.

Please let him be all right, I pleaded with the God I barely believed in. *I can't lose him.*

Twenty-Nine

Blinking back my tears, I fidgeted in the veterinarian's waiting area and stared at the floor. In the back of the clinic, Dr. Bindhi held Nygard's life in her hands and I hoped they were skilled enough to save him. The only thing I could do was continue to mumble little prayers over and over, pleading that he would survive.

In my mind, I replayed the attack in the ethereal cemetery, visualizing the super-sized spirit feline that had leaped to my rescue. I knew it was Nygard even though his spirit was many times his actual size. How had he gotten there? Was that energy connection we'd experienced more than a power link? Did it somehow allow him to come to me on the next level?

I sniffled and wiped at my nose with a tissue as tears gathered again at the edges of my eyes. Too clearly, I saw my cat's limp body at the foot of my bed. He'd been unconscious, barely breathing, and I almost wrecked my Jeep getting him to the vet's office. She had taken one look, told me to wait, and whisked him away to her emergency room.

That had been almost thirty minutes earlier, and I was on edge, fearing the worst. Even though some might say he was just a cat, he was so much more to me. Ever since I'd gotten him as a kitten, he was attached to me, becoming my companion and sounding board. He was my furry child—sweet, inquisitive, and loving. I couldn't bear the thought of losing him. Not now. Not so young.

The front door squeaked open and I looked up as Ferris stepped inside. I'd called him as soon as I'd handed Nygard over. He'd often watched my furry baby when I was out of town so I knew he would come. Of all my friends, he had the closest attachment to him. Besides, *I needed* him with me.

"What happened, Gillian?" he asked as he opened his arms wide and I flew into them. They closed around me, pulling me close. I breathed in the spiced scent of his aftershave, a counterbalance to the antiseptic odor of the clinic, and it offered an odd comfort.

In a choking voice, I told him how I'd found my cat after I got home from singing at Saffi Alden's funeral. In response, his arms tightened around me, rocking me back and forth in a soothing motion. His eyebrows drew together in concern. "Did he have a stroke or did something hit him?"

"No," I answered, shaking my head slowly. "He was attacked."

"By what? How?" he asked, his face reflecting his confusion. He guided me back to the chairs as he talked.

"Do you remember everything I told you about the cemetery I go to when I sing and about the shades I encountered there?" I asked as I sank into the chair.

He nodded.

"They attacked at the funeral, trying to trap the women I needed to escort across. I intervened so Zoe and Saffi could get to the gate and cross. As they started to go through, two shades attacked me and I tried to fight them off. It was terrible, Ferris. They're bone-chillingly cold when they touch you. It just saps your strength. I couldn't fight like I can on a physical plane, but I discovered I could use energy blasts against them. Somehow– I don't know how I did it, I could fling light and energy in bolts and balls of power. I barely had any grasp of what I was doing. I'd been fighting with one of them when the other started to attack behind me." I paused, closing my eyes as I recalled the moment when I thought I would lose the battle.

"Suddenly, Nygard was there and he was huge. I mean, he was the size of a panther. He flew into the ghoulish creature, claws out, and shredded it. The shade retaliated..." My voice caught as my fear rose again. "It flung Nygard away from him, fifteen feet or more across the ground."

"Wait!" Ferris interrupted. "How was he there?"

"I don't know," I answered. My voice cracked and almost turned to a whine. "All I can determine is that he's somehow connected to me. He knew I'd run into trouble and came to help me. His spirit— his *huge* spirit—appeared there. After I finished off the shades, I ran over to him. He wasn't moving and it frightened me. When I woke up in the chapel, I knew I had to get home to him. I found him in my bedroom, barely alive." My tears burst through and I could only shake my head and blow my nose, trying not to break down in sobs.

"I can't lose him, Ferry. I can't bear the thought he might die because he protected me."

He twisted in his chair and pulled me into an awkward hug. I buried my face against his shoulder as the long-denied tears started to flow. I grabbed another tissue from the box on the end table and wiped my face as I cried.

"Shh, honey. Don't mourn him yet. He's a tough little guy, you know. Remember when he tumbled down the stairs as a kitten? He got right up and charged back up them again."

I sniffled and dragged my emotions under control again. "What's taking so long?"

I darted a glance at the check-in desk where the assistant chatted with a man who'd brought in his dog. No sign of Dr. Bindhi or any indication that anything was less than normal. Of course not. The crisis was only in my life with my cat.

He squeezed my shoulders and spoke quietly, "It's a good sign. It means he's still alive and they're still working on him."

"You think?" I asked, daring to hope he was right. As I gazed at him, I saw deep concern in his eyes and wondered at his real thoughts. "Do really believe it?"

"About Nygard? Absolutely. But I am worried about you." His voice carried a rough edge of strain as he spoke.

"Me?"

He pushed me back a little from him, so he could watch my face as he spoke. "If one of these creatures did that to him in spirit form, what could it do to you? What chances are you taking? Can it hurt you physically?"

I felt a chill scuttle up my spine. Hadn't I asked the same question? As I licked my lips and tried to frame an answer, I knew I didn't have one. I shook my head slowly. "I don't know... I..." I paused for a deep breath. "No one I've talked to knows for sure, but Gavin thinks they can. I guess this proves him right. Can they kill me? If Nygard dies, I guess we have the answer."

He frowned and I could see his eyes flicker as thoughts raced through his mind. "Earlier you said, 'when I woke up in the chapel.' Why were you asleep? You've never mentioned that before."

"Oh, I'm usually not..." My voice drifted off as I saw the petite form of Dr. Bindhi coming into the waiting area. I disengaged myself from Ferris and got to my feet in anticipation.

Her face looked concerned, not grim, and I hoped that indicated a positive sign. She got right to the point. "He's alive and I think he will be okay. We have him on an IV to replace fluids. He was very dehydrated. Was he shocked? Did he accidentally hit an electrical line?"

"Not that I know about," I answered, the weight lifting from my shoulders with the news. I couldn't tell her the truth on this. She wouldn't believe me anyway.

Although her dark eyes reflected her puzzlement, she went on, "When you brought him in, he seemed to be in shock, but I can't find any physical problem with him now. His heart is fine, lungs are good. No injuries or anything physical. I want to keep him until we close tonight so we can keep him on the IV and watch him a little longer."

"Of course," I agreed. "Can I take him home tonight?"

"Yes. We close at five-thirty, but I'll be here a little longer." She gave me a brief smile. "Do you want to see him for a few minutes?"

"Of course." I shifted my gaze to Ferris and saw the relief on his face, partly for Nygard, more for me. If anyone understood how much I loved my fur ball, it was Ferris.

The vet led me into one of the examination rooms and told me to wait and she would bring Nygard in. I waited nervously, still not believing he had survived the attack. A few minutes later, she came back with him hooked up to a kitty-size IV bag, a tube snaking to it from his left front arm.

Still a little limp, Nygard spread flat on the table and seemed content to not have to move. I leaned down to him, running my fingers through the hair around his ears. "Hey, kit, how's my guy doing?" I said in a subdued voice.

An ear flicked in answer, followed by an eye opening. A hint of his blue iris showed although the pupil nearly obliterated it. He looked like he'd been on an all-night catnip bender.

I slid my fingers under his chin, scratching and rubbing and he ducked his head into my touch. There was my boy. As I rubbed, I noticed the thin golden line between us again, an iridescent glow that connected us. Was he drawing energy from me now? Surely, not the other way around. I kept my fingers moving in a circle, hoping it was helping. After a few moments, I felt, more than heard, the rumble of a purr. More than anything else, that gave me comfort in the certainty he would be fine.

After a few more minutes, Dr. Bindhi came to take him back in the treatment area and reminded me that I could pick him up at the end of the day. Reassured, I watched her carry him off before turning to Ferris.

"I'm glad you were here. Thanks."

"Anytime you need me, babe," he said and pulled me into his arms again. "Look, we've got a few hours before you can take him home. Let's get a late lunch and talk for a bit, okay?"

I nodded, knowing he wanted to go back to his question. Food did sound good, though, and I needed his company.

"So, back to the remark about waking up," Ferris said after we'd eaten our food and had a pair of cold beers sitting in front of us. "What did you mean? I didn't think you slept while you were doing your singing." We sat side by side in a cozy booth at a small coffee shop.

I fortified myself with a couple of sips of the beer before I told him the truth. "I don't. When I was kneeling over Nygard in the cemetery, something touched me and pain shot through my soul. I recall that I screamed, but I didn't see what it was. It wasn't like the other shades. At that point, I blacked out and when I came out of it, I had slumped over the piano, passed out, and several people had gathered around me. It felt weird. I wasn't hurt, although I felt a little off-balance. But it passed in a minute or so."

I saw the worry form on Ferris' face and his eyes had grown larger while I talked. Now, his face resembled a thunderstorm, dark and ready to burst.

"I don't like this one bit, Gillian. This whole otherworld cemetery is dangerous. You could get hurt or killed. You need to stop it *now*."

"Do you think I don't know that?" I leaned toward him so I could speak lower. "I can't stop. I've been visited by spirits on the other side, who tell me I've been chosen for this task and I need to do it. If I stop helping souls that need closure, they haunt me."

"That's crazy," he responded and leaned closer until our foreheads almost touched. "Are you saying God or some similar deity has assigned this task to you?"

I shrugged my shoulders. "It seems that way. Yes, it scares me, and I don't know why I was chosen. What I do know is that the shades are bleeding over into our world and they are not here for peaceful purposes. They're soul thieves, Ferry. I can't stand back if I'm capable of fighting them."

His eyes took on a watery sheen and his voice caught as spoke. "Are you? It sounds like you're ill-prepared to take on these creatures and what if there's more than a couple? Can you fight a whole army of them? What if Nygard comes to help you again? Will you get him killed next time?"

Feeling a lump of fear in my throat, I swallowed hard. "I don't know. That's why I'm asking Gavin for help. He's been fighting them on our plane. If there are more of us, we need to unite. Don't desert me, Ferris. I need you, and Dig and Janna, to stand by me now. I need your support if I'm going to do this."

"I won't bail, honey. I'm just scared for you. I don't want to lose you." His eyes softened into pale puddles. "And I feel like there's nothing I can do to help."

On an impulse, I reached for his hand and squeezed it. "Just being here helps." I felt a tingle up my arm as if a thread of electricity shot up it. I shifted my gaze to where I touched him. Little golden sparkles glittered at the connection, something similar to the strands

I had with Nygard. Could I be gaining energy from Ferris?

He didn't seem to notice anything as his expression remained concerned, his mouth in a sad-looking downturn.

"You are helping," I said, lifting my hand from his and watching the thin thread that formed between us. "Your support helps me." *And maybe something else*, I added silently.

I reached for my purse, "We should go. It's almost time."

He nodded and grabbed the bill. I walked on ahead, stopping by the ladies' room while he paid. As I washed my hands, I thought about Nygard and all that had happened. How could I protect him?

I figured Ferris was right about one thing. Until I knew how to protect myself, and those I loved, I needed to stop singing at funerals.

Continued in "A Song of Redemption".

DEDICATION

For four short years, Milo Cat was my constant companion, much to the chagrin of three other cats in the house. He was a loving spirit and the most endearing animal to share my life. When I adopted him as a senior cat, the shelter estimated his age at eight years. My vet and I both believed he was older. Certainly, spiritually, he was a wise, mild-mannered cat with a passion for spicy food. He provided the inspiration, breed, and voice for Gillian's cat, Nygard. If there is a Rainbow Bridge, I know he was welcomed by my other beloved felines. I hope that transmigration is a possibility, as he was ready to become something more in his next life.

About the Author

A sometimes musician, sporadic artist, occasional poet, and obsessed writer, Lillian Wolfe has spent most of her life writing. From fan fiction to short stories, novels, training manuals, newsletters, and other documentation, she has constantly been putting words on paper or a computer screen. She is, in fact, extremely grateful for the invention of the computer because using a manual typewriter is tedious. While she loves all types of fiction, her favorites are fantasy and mystery novels.

Lillian shares her home in northern Nevada with her best friend for the past thirty-odd years, two feisty felines, and one charming Bichpoo dog. She is a member of the High Sierra Writers Group and the Fiction Writers Group.

You can contact Lillian through her web site:
http://www.lillianwolfe.me/loft/
or at her Facebook Page:
https://www.facebook.com/LilliansLoft

From the Author:

*T*hank you so much for reading my book. I have always loved writing stories, but it is much more gratifying to know that people read and enjoy what I write. So, if you've enjoyed this novel, please consider leaving an honest review at Amazon and/or Goodreads or any other book site that accepts reviews.

If you would like to know what I'm working on and what's coming up next, please consider signing up for my mailing list at my web home:

http://www.lillianwolfe.me/loft/

or connect with me at my Facebook Page:

https://www.facebook.com/LilliansLoft

I do Tweet now and then, but I'm not a frequent Tweeter, just so you know. However, if you want to follow my Twitter bits: @LI_Wolfe56

Look for *A Song of Redemption*, the fourth novel in my "Funeral Singer" series, which is planned for release in spring of 2018.

Enjoy these other novels from **Pynhavyn Press.**

Funeral Singer: A Song for Marielle - Book One
by Lillian I Wolfe (Paranormal Suspense)

As a musician-for-hire, Gillian Foster accepts many different jobs, some with her band and some solo, but she's taken aback when she's asked to sing at a funeral. She's even more startled to learn that a recent head injury has given her a paranormal gift as she finds herself face-to-face with the deceased in an ethereal cemetery.

But that's only the beginning. As more offers pop up, she's drawn into one in particular. A young girl, the victim of a brutal murder, demands Gillian's help in finding her killer. Can she turn sleuth and use her gift to bring the man to justice without revealing her unusual talent?

Funeral Singer: A Song for Menafee - Book Two
by Lillian I Wolfe (Paranormal Suspense)

Helping one soul to move on brings Gillian into contact with another lingering ghost, who needs more than just a guide to the next life and she is his only hope. Her band mates are pressing her to set up the overdue recording session. Complicating matters, she is trying to cope with the aftermath of a near fatal encounter of her own with a child killer while keeping the sordid details secret from her friends. With a trial looming in the future, a promise made to a ghost, and an album to record, is she pushing herself too hard?

O'Ceagan's Legacy: Book 1 (O'Ceagan Saga)
by Lillian I Wolfe (Sci-Fi Fantasy Adventure)

Trained by her grandfather to command, Grania O'Ceagan expects to one day inherit the family's space freighter, but first she must prove herself worthy to be captain. Her ambitious brother Liam is nipping at her heels and wants the ship as well. While she adores Vilnius, the dashing assistant stationmaster at Earth's space station, their lives are worlds apart.

On the return trip to their home world, they take on two unplanned passengers and find themselves facing a disaster that could destroy everything. Grania must muster her crew and apply all she's learned to save her ship and crew from imminent destruction. Can she prove herself the leader she expects to be?

For Eleven Million Reasons

by M.L. Weatherington - Police Mystery

If you think that winning the lottery is a dream come true, you need to read the possible dark side of publicized sudden wealth. In *For Eleven Million Reasons*, mystery author M. L. Weatherington takes you on a suspenseful ride of murder and intrigue as Lt. Arthur Franklin pursues a killer. Don't miss this thrill ride of a first novel.

idewiped!

by M.L. Weatherington - Police Mystery

Picking up from the first book, Lt. Arthur Franklin of the Lodi Police Department finds himself suffering from doubt and uncertainty as he recuperates from the injury suffered in his last case—the one that nearly cost him his daughter's life. Melissa has retreated more than Art, who has been seeing a psychiatrist, Amanda Burton, a stunning woman and Art is undeniably attracted.

Meanwhile, a new murder has hit the streets of Lodi. Even though Art is on leave, his partner, Walt, wants to get his input on the case and calls Art to the crime scene. With few clues to help them, it's a real puzzler. As things begin to escalate, Art is pulled into more than one mystery.

Can Art help Walt solve the murder and how does it tie in with a mysterious stalker at his house?

Bitter Vintage

by Riona Kelly - Suspense Romance

When the heir to the Claremont Vineyards in Northern California is killed in an accident, his sister Martinique returns home for the funeral. She finds her father reclusive and odd, her estranged half-sister in residence, and a mysterious person skulking around the property. As she learns more about her brother's death, she is convinced there is more to the story and is determined to learn the truth. But can she prove it?

Bitter Vintage brings the suspense of treachery, greed, and ambition along with romance and betrayal as the story unfolds against the California vineyards of the Napa-Sonoma region and the migrant workers' struggle for fair wages in 1964.

Alpha's Song (Les Loups-Garous)

by Angelina Fasano- YA Urban Fantasy

In quiet little Kennington, Massachusetts, dark secrets abound and some are buried deeper than others. Mysterious club owner Daniel Hawthorne keeps them close to his heart.

Following the devastating death of her mother, Christa Ellsworth never expected to return to the town where she grew up, but five years later, she finds herself dragged back to the scene of her family's tragedy. Christa's plan to finish high school unnoticed comes to a halt following a chance encounter with the devastatingly handsome club owner she can't get out of her head. She begins to uncover the extraordinary truth about the town she grew up in and an unusual birthright that is now hers. Can she handle it?